A Daughter's Promise

ALSO BY JUDY SUMMERS

The Forgotten Sister
A Winter's Wish

Judy Summers

A Daughter's Promise

WELBECK

First published in 2023 by Welbeck Fiction Limited,
an imprint of Welbeck Publishing Group
Offices in: London – 20 Mortimer Street, London W1T 3JW &
Sydney – Level 17, 207 Kent St, Sydney NSW 2000 Australia
www.welbeckpublishing.com

A CIP catalogue record for this book is available from the British Library

Paperback ISBN: 978-1-80279-661-2
Ebook ISBN: 978-1-80279-662-9

Printed and bound by CPI Group (UK) Ltd., Croydon, CR0 4YY

FSC
www.fsc.org
MIX
Paper | Supporting responsible forestry
FSC® C171272

10 9 8 7 6 5 4 3 2 1

Chapter One

Liverpool, May 1860

'You're not my *mother*!'

Annie regretted the words as soon as they'd left her mouth, but it was too late.

It was true, of course, that Delilah was her eldest sister rather than her mother; but Ma had died when Annie was just two years old and it had been Delilah who had brought her up, along with all the other siblings in between them. Annie knew, deep down, that she owed her sister love and gratitude rather than bad temper and arguments, but sometimes she was so infuriated that she just couldn't help it.

Delilah didn't shout back, which was a sure sign that she was really upset this time. She blinked away a tear before it could fall, but Annie saw it glisten as the candlelight caught it. Her temper receding as quickly as it had arisen, she opened her mouth to apologise, but once again it was too late.

'You're right, I'm not,' said Delilah, her voice quiet and with a hint of a shake. 'And you don't know how often I wish she was still here.' She left the room.

Annie wanted to run after her, to tell her how sorry she was and that she hadn't meant it, but a movement from the other side of the room caught her eye.

It was Jem, the next youngest after herself and the only other sibling still living here at the flower shop. He'd been sitting silently all the while, and now he moved forward so his hands could be seen clearly in the pool of light cast by the candle. *Best leave her alone for now*, he signed. Then he hesitated before adding, *But that wasn't kind.*

Annie kept her face in the shadows. *I know*, she signed back. *And I'm sorry.*

He nodded, gave a sad smile and hugged her before standing back. *Don't worry, she'll forgive you.* Then he went out as well, leaving Annie alone in the warm, cosy back room that served as both kitchen and parlour.

Well, not quite alone, of course, but the two little boys slumbering in their bed over in the corner had miraculously not woken during the row. Annie tiptoed over to her nephews – Billy curled up in a tight ball while Joe sprawled everywhere, just the same as usual – and straightened their disarranged blanket. She kissed her finger and touched it to the tops of their heads.

Annie sighed as she returned to sit at the table and stare into the bright flame. Guilt still sat heavily on her shoulders, but there was also a stirring of resentment. She loved all her nephews and nieces, just as she loved her sisters and brothers, and the husbands and wife of her three eldest siblings. But there was family everywhere she looked, and sometimes it just felt so suffocating that she could hardly breathe.

She poked moodily at a puddle of spilt and congealing wax, smearing it around the table as she sank into her own thoughts. The problem was being the odd one out. All her life she'd been the youngest in the family, and the youngest by a long way. Even Jem was nearly seven years older than she was, and all the others older still; Delilah would be *thirty* on her next birthday. And besides, Delilah wasn't even a Shaw any more but a Malling, which – however illogically – seemed to put more distance between her and Annie.

Delilah and her husband, Frank, had four children of their own, and part of Annie's current irritability – and the reason for tonight's argument – was that Delilah tended to treat her as one of the children even though she was fourteen. Almost an adult! And certainly old enough to go out and get a proper job, earning money of her own, rather than just helping around the place here. But Delilah was determined to keep her safe. That was the word she always used: *safe*. And with a panicky, worried expression on her face while she said it.

Annie was aware that the family hadn't always lived here in this nice place, with its sweet-smelling flower shop at the front, family room at the back, two bedrooms and an attic upstairs, and a yard of their own outside. They'd moved here when she was about six, and she still had vivid memories of the cold, damp single room they'd all been crammed into before that, with its cracked window in a rotten frame and an old straw mattress on the floor for everyone to share. Occasionally one of the others would mention that time, shuddering as they recalled how awful it was, but Annie would remain silent. What she remembered about it was leading an outdoor life, playing in the court all day with lots of other children, and she now looked back fondly on those days as a time of freedom: she and an older girl called Clara had skipped about and run wild and laughed and shrieked as much as they liked.

But then her family had moved here. There had been some talk that Clara might come with them, which would have made everything better, but that had come to nothing. Annie had been sent to school, spending her days trapped at a desk learning reading, writing, arithmetic and all sorts of other things she would never need to know, and her evenings and weekends trapped at home helping with domestic chores and in the shop. There was always an older brother or sister keeping a close eye on her, and even when her siblings had moved out, their place had been taken by the arrival of babies and children who also needed her attention. She'd left school and was now here all the time – always surrounded by family, never alone, never allowed to do what she wanted, never free. She missed Clara, with whom she had kept in contact for a number of years until Clara's visits had become more and more sporadic and then stopped entirely. Life revolved around home, and only home. Delilah might call it safe, but Annie had another word for it: *boring*.

The candle was guttering now. She ought to go to bed, really; it would be an early start in the morning with the delivery from the wholesaler, and it was her task to get up and light the fire in the little range so that Frank and Jem could have a hot cup of tea before they went out to work at the railway station. But a quiet evening, accompanied by the sound of peaceful breathing from the sleeping boys, was the only solitary time she ever had.

Delilah would forgive her. That was what Jem had said, and Annie knew it to be true. Delilah would always forgive her, because family was the single most important thing in her life. And that meant family in its widest sense: there were all sorts of unrelated friends who had been drawn into the nest over the years, and Delilah loved and cared for them all just as she did for her own children and siblings.

Annie sighed. She would apologise in the morning, and promise both her sister and herself that she would do better in the future.

The candle went out. It didn't matter; Annie could find her way up the familiar stairs in the dark, careful not to wake her nieces Daisy and Eliza as she slipped into bed in the room that they shared. She thought that she would probably lie awake fretting, but the moon was shining in through a gap at the edge of the curtain, and the patterns it made on the ceiling were the same ones that had been lulling her to sleep since she was a little girl. It wasn't long before her eyes closed.

Friday and Saturday passed without any recurrence of the argument, mainly because Delilah was very busy and Annie spent all her time walking on eggshells whenever she was near her sister. She also made a fuss of the children, helping Daisy with her writing and Joe with learning his letters.

'You're good at that,' noted Frank, when he arrived home on Saturday evening. He winked at them all, took off his uniform cap and tossed it expertly so that it landed on the hook on the wall on the other side of the room, and was immediately surrounded by children clamouring for his attention. As ever, he was glad to bestow it, throwing the boys in the air and tickling little Eliza under the chin before turning to the serious Daisy. 'And how's my princess this evening?'

Daisy put her pencil down with care before she replied. 'I'm not a princess, Daddy, you know that.' She always called Frank 'Daddy'; neither he nor Delilah could stand the word 'Pa', which was what most other children called their fathers.

He came to look over her shoulder. 'Well, you're a clever girl to do all that writing, whatever it says, and you'll always be a princess to me.' He dropped a kiss on to her hair.

Daisy kept her head down over her work, but Annie saw her pleased smile.

'Ah, I can see your face through the back of your head, my darling,' continued Frank. 'I know you love me to heaven and back. Now, what's for tea?' He carried Eliza over to the bubbling pot and made her shriek and laugh in pretend-fear by play-acting that he was going to drop her into it.

Jem wasn't far behind Frank. As usual he was filthy and covered in coal dust, so he attracted Annie's attention from outside the back door. *I'll wash before I come in*, he signed, and then turned to the pump in the yard.

Annie envied him. Or, at least, she envied his freedom and his wages. Jem had been deaf all his life; when he was younger, nobody had ever thought he'd be able to get a job, for who would employ him? He'd gone to a special school for deaf children – for there was such a thing in Liverpool – where he'd learned the sign language that he'd taught to them all, but nobody except his family imagined that he'd be able to do anything but the most menial tasks when he grew up. But then the railway had come. Jem had loved to visit the trains since he was a boy – and Frank, who was a porter and then a senior porter at Lime Street station, took him as often as he could – and eventually an opportunity arose. The trains ran on steam, and they needed men to work as stokers, shovelling coal into the engines as fast as they could to make the locomotives speed along. It was so loud that none of the men could hear each other anyway, so they communicated by gestures. Jem had been given a trial and he'd never looked back. He lived in the attic of the shop, paying rent to Delilah and Frank, and was otherwise his own man with his own freedoms, coming and going as he pleased. And, of course, because he was actually on the trains as they puffed their way up and down the kingdom, he travelled: he visited Manchester and Leeds regularly, and he'd even been to London a few times.

Annie contemplated this as she laid the table for tea. *Travel.* To see somewhere different, not this same shop and these same few streets, day after day, week after week. How lucky Jem was! It made Annie's frustration all the greater, and to top it all it wouldn't be long before she lost even the chance to learn about his journeys at second hand. Jem was engaged to a girl he'd met at deaf school, and once they were married they'd set up a home of their own, leaving Annie here with Delilah, Frank and their children. How long would this imprisonment last, she wondered? Would she still be here when she was thirty herself?

* * *

Annie awoke on Sunday morning knowing that the day was going to be a trial. It was everyone's day off, as the shop was shut and no trains ran. Most weeks they used the time to catch up with jobs around the house or went for a walk in the park, but once a month the whole extended family went to see Annie's second sister, Meg, for a meal. In terms of food, of course, it was certainly the highlight of the month: baked meat, potatoes, vegetables, gravy and always a wondrous cake or pudding to follow, much better than the sausages or stews that Annie or Delilah managed to throw in a pan in the midst of their daily chores the rest of the time. But a Sunday out was always an ordeal nonetheless, because it brought home to Annie how closely entwined all the older members of the family were, and how they had all shared many experiences that she was far too young to remember. Being among them all just made her feel more left out than ever.

William and Meg were the two siblings that Annie knew least well. William, the next oldest after Delilah, had lived in the flower shop attic for a while when they'd first moved in, but after a couple of years he'd left to get married. He hadn't actually moved far: he and his family lived in School Lane, just on the other side of St Peter's, in a house crammed with books. He was the only man Annie knew who didn't work in a manual labouring job – he had a very good position working for a printer and bookbinder called Mr Hughes, and he wore a starched white collar and a tie. Delilah was immensely proud of William, as well she might be; Annie was, she admitted, a little bit intimidated by his intelligence, but he was quiet and had a kind face.

William's wife, Bridget, was truly lovely in both looks and character. They had two little girls, Rosie and Maggie, who looked like they might turn out tall like William but who were both otherwise the spit of their mother, all creamy skin and flaming red hair. It was the bright heads of the girls Annie spotted first, ahead of them up the road as they walked towards Meg's place in Williamson Square, and soon five of the six children were squealing and skipping around excitedly as though they hadn't seen each other for years, while Daisy told them all to behave themselves.

Meg and Tommy were waiting by the open door, under the sign that said HOPKINS GROCER AND TEA ROOM, EST 1854. Meg had left home before a time Annie could even remember, sent first temporarily to the workhouse when times were hard after Ma died, and then moving straight from there into domestic service. She'd had to leave her position when she got married, and she and Tommy ran a modest but very popular concern between them. He managed the grocer's shop on one side while she cooked and baked and welcomed the customers who flocked from all over Liverpool to eat her delicious pies, puddings and confections.

They had no children. It wasn't Annie's business to enquire, but she didn't think this was by choice, as she'd seen the sad and wistful way Meg often looked at all her nephews and nieces. She remained cheerful and practical, however, and threw her heart and soul into her cooking. She and Tommy lived over the shop, and not quite alone: an old friend of Meg's called Sally lived with them and worked for them. The household was completed by a dog called Higgins, who guarded the premises and ate all the scraps he could find.

It was a fine family gathering, with two more to add to the mix today: Amy, Jem's fiancée, and an old family friend called Abraham, who had known Annie's Ma and Pa since before they were married, and who often came to the shop to see how Delilah was getting on and to help out with any odd jobs around the place. He was a familiar presence in Annie's life, quite an old man these days with a head of white hair contrasting with his black skin. What a life he'd led: he'd been born a slave in America before escaping from captivity and crossing the ocean to make a new home in this great city. Annie admired him very much, but thinking of all he'd experienced also reminded her that she'd never left Liverpool, and was never likely to. She sighed as she stepped over the threshold with the others.

Meg, as ever, was undaunted by cooking a Sunday dinner for seventeen people, and it was delicious. But Annie only pushed her food around in discontent, and then watched everyone break into their accustomed little groups, leaving her out. The children all played together, of course. Jem and Amy were off to one side of the tea room area, making puppy eyes at each other and signing so fast that she couldn't have made out what they were saying even if she'd wanted to. The older siblings were in their usual tight little knot, bound together by all sorts of ties that she couldn't even begin to understand. Bridget, William's wife, had been Delilah's best friend for many years before her marriage, and she also happened to be Frank's sister, which just made it all so much worse from Annie's point of view. She was too young for their group, too old to join the children, and too single to sit with Jem and Amy. She didn't belong anywhere.

In order to have something to do, Annie began to stack the empty plates and carry them into the kitchen and scullery at the back. Sally was already there, filling up the sinks, and it wasn't long before Meg came in, rolling up her sleeves. To Annie's surprise – for cooking and clearing up were always women's work – Meg was followed by Abraham with another pile of dishes. 'I told Delilah and Bridget to stay where they were,' he explained, placing them carefully on the side. 'They don't get much time to talk to each other these days.' He disappeared to fetch the rest.

To Annie the pile of washing-up looked enormous, but Meg and Sally were used to it and set to work without a qualm. 'Don't put your hands in that water,' cautioned Meg, as Annie reached out to help. 'It's too hot for you.' Her own arms were submerged up to the elbows. 'You have to get used to it from when you're young.' Annie watched her as she scrubbed vigorously, wondering how someone so tiny could be so tough. It was funny, she thought, how three sisters could look so different: Delilah was tall and willowy, Meg was so petite that Annie had overtaken her in height by the time she was ten, and Annie herself was of average height but sturdier and stronger than either of them. Funnily enough, the boys fell into similar groupings.

'Why don't you pass us the things,' suggested Sally, brightly, from the rinsing sink on Meg's other side, 'while we wash and stack.'

Annie realised she'd been standing with the same cake plate in her hand for some while. She passed it to Meg and they were all soon into a rhythm. Sally, who could find joy in anything, even began to sing.

'You haven't said much today,' remarked Meg after a while. 'You've had another argument with Delilah, haven't you?'

Annie mumbled something. There was no point in talking about it, was there? Meg would only side with Delilah.

'I can understand your position,' continued Meg. She sounded sympathetic, but Annie knew there was going to be a 'but' any moment now.

And there it was. '— but I don't think you understand how lucky you are to have your home with Delilah and Frank.'

'Of course I am,' said Annie, non-committally, picking a last bit of potato out of a serving dish before handing it over.

Meg's voice turned unexpectedly sharp. 'You've got a roof over your head, food on the table and family around you. Not everyone is so fortunate.'

'Yes.' Annie knew that her deliberate flat tone was guaranteed to irritate, but she really didn't need another lecture just now.

'And we can't always have what we want in life.'

Annie felt her temper fraying again. 'Well, you have.' She gestured at the kitchen and the door to the tea room.

'Yes, and I had to work hard for it!' Meg looked as though she might bang the serving dish down – which is probably what Annie would have done – but she passed it safely to Sally, who had by now stopped singing and whose face was beginning to crease into a worried frown.

'But don't you see?' cried Annie, the frustration breaking through. 'That's all I want – the chance to work for it! Tell me, what were you doing when you were fourteen? What was Delilah doing at my age?'

There was an unexpected silence.

Annie risked looking at Meg, hoping that she wasn't about to either cry or shout, but her sister's face was thoughtful.

The washing-up was finished in silence, and as soon as the final greasy cooking pans were gleaming and left on the rack to dry, they all returned to the tea room.

Tommy was sweeping the floor, the children assisting him, although Frank certainly wasn't helping by encouraging them all to race around with their brooms as fast as they could. But Tommy didn't seem to mind, and Annie wondered again how such contrasting characters as him and Frank could possibly be such good friends.

She sat down on her own once more, observing her family almost from the outside, as though she wasn't part of it, and finally allowed her mind to turn to the person who was missing. The one she tried not to think of, because she missed him with all her heart.

Sam was the brother who was most like her. The brothers in her family, as she had thought to herself earlier, were all different and more or less formed pairs with the sisters: Delilah and William, tall, grown-up and responsible; Meg and Jem, compact, quiet and determined; and herself and Sam. On a good day she'd say they were strong, reliable and protective, though she also had to admit to wild temper and an untamed nature.

Sam, who was a year older than Jem, had been the undisputed king of the younger half of the family. There had been four of them once, and Annie had shadowy recollections of a sister who came between Jem and herself. She couldn't remember her face or even her name, but sometimes, especially when she was slipping into sleep, she could feel a warm hand clasped in her own or arms about her neck, and a whispered, 'What shall we play?' A rocking and a gentle lullaby in her ear. And, for some reason she couldn't place, the sound of a baby crying. But that couldn't be right, could it? Because she herself was the youngest, so she hadn't known any of the others when they were babies.

Annie wanted to hold on to these memories, wanted to know more about them, but they were elusive, sliding away with the morning light. She'd once asked out loud, but both Delilah and Meg had started crying so she'd never dared to do it again. Her missing family was evidently to remain a secret, one that emphasised again that she was left out.

If only Sam were here, everything would be better. He was the leader, the hero who had looked after her and Jem when they were little. To start with the two boys had been inseparable – it was a family joke that when Annie was tiny she used to say 'Samanjem' as though it was one word – but when Jem went to his school they had grown apart a little, and Sam had lavished his attention on Annie. It was he who loved her and protected her, who stood up for her in arguments and fights, and he'd even taught her how to throw a decent punch in case she ever needed to defend herself when he wasn't around. Not, she thought ruefully now, that she was ever allowed out on her own to get into any danger of that kind.

But Sam had been more wild than was good for him. Always in fights, always in trouble, never holding down a job because he was continually being sacked. From what Annie could gather from occasional eavesdropping on Delilah, William and Meg, there had been a time when Sam was in serious danger of being drawn into Liverpool's vicious and violent underworld. He'd pulled himself back from that, apparently, but he needed to find an outlet for his aggression, and as soon as he'd turned sixteen he'd joined the army.

And that was it: he'd gone. Not only had he left home, leaving Annie bereft, but within half a year he'd been sent across the sea to somewhere called the Crimea. Annie had only the haziest idea of where this was, but she knew that it was a very long way away and that it was dangerous. She had cried herself to sleep for months.

To everyone's joy and relief, Sam survived it all; he'd returned after an absence of two years with a scar on his face, a medal that he never showed anyone, and a determination never to speak of what he'd seen or done. They still didn't know, even now. He'd thought about leaving the army, and Annie had hoped that he'd stay at home, but to no avail. He'd tried to hold down a job, but within months he was off once more, this time to enlist in the Liverpool Rifles, and he was gone again. At least this time he'd only signed up for home service, so he wouldn't be sent abroad again, and every time Annie heard the shop door or the yard gate she hoped against hope that it would be him. One day he would walk in, the same old Sam, and he would sweep her into a giant hug, a bull of a man who could still spin her off her feet even though she was full grown.

Annie felt her eyes pricking, and she came back to herself. Everyone was starting to say their farewells and set off, going home to their separate lives. There were hugs and kisses being bestowed everywhere.

They were such a happy family, so why did Annie not feel part of it?

All the way home, and all through the evening as she helped to put the children to bed, the black mood hung over her. There seemed to be no way she was ever going to get away from this life, to make her way in the world as her sisters and brothers had done.

And now here she was again, alone in the back room with only the full-bellied and contentedly sleeping boys for company while Delilah was upstairs putting the girls to bed. Frank and Jem had gone out for a night-time walk – another of the privileges of being male, she thought, morosely – and the gate of the back yard was still unlocked, ready for their return.

Annie was staring into the candle flame when there came a knock at the back door.

Was it Sam? Her heart leapt, just as it usually did, before she was brought back to earth by the realisation that Sam wouldn't knock. And neither, of course, would Frank or Jem.

It was probably nothing more exciting than a neighbour wanting Delilah. Still, Annie did as Sam had taught her when she went to answer the door at night: she kept her foot wedged behind it and a chair within reach in case she needed to slam and barricade it.

It wasn't a neighbour. And nor was it Sam. Of course it wasn't. But, to Annie's great surprise, it was the next best thing.

She kicked the chair back and opened the door wider to allow the visitor to enter. 'I haven't seen you for a long time! Come in.'

Clara stepped inside, pushing the shawl back from her head. 'Hello, Annie. Have you missed me?'

Chapter Two

Delilah had heard the knock and now bustled into the room. Her surprise was evident, but so was her pleasure. 'Clara! It's been so long. Come in and sit by the range.'

She started to fuss about, putting in some more coals and asking Clara how her mother was, but she was cut short by Daisy's voice from upstairs. 'Mummy! Eliza's crying again – I think it's her teeth.'

'Well, I'll leave you girls to talk,' said Delilah, on her way out.

Clara stared after her. 'She had another baby, then, since I last saw you?'

'How many did she have last time?'

'Two, a girl and a boy.'

Goodness, it really was a long time since Annie had last seen Clara. 'She's had another two since then, a boy and then another girl.'

'Four, already? She'll be taking after my Ma if she's not careful.' Clara shook her head. 'God rest her.'

'Oh, I didn't know! I'm so sorry.'

Clara shrugged. 'It was bound to happen one day. She was getting on a bit.'

'But still . . .'

'She never had all that much time for me, anyway.'

'Well, you had a very big family, I remember that. And you're the youngest, aren't you?' That was one of the things they had in common.

Clara made a face. 'Twenty-two babies, my Ma had, if you include the two sets of twins and the other ones who died. She told me that once. I don't think I've ever even met some of my oldest brothers, the ones from her first husband.' She shifted in her chair. 'Brought myself up, I did. Anyway, it don't matter.'

Annie thought it better to change the subject. 'So, what are you doing now? Are you living with one of your brothers or sisters?'

Clara broke into a wide smile. 'Ah, that's what I come to tell you about. I'm doing well for myself, and I thought you might like to hear about it.'

Annie listened with great and increasing interest to her friend's story. Clara was working in a cotton mill outside the city. Annie knew of such places, of course – you couldn't live in Liverpool without seeing the huge bales of raw cotton being unloaded at the docks and then transported through the streets and out to the mills, where it was spun into thread and then woven into cloth – but she'd never actually seen one. She wondered at Clara's tale of how big and busy it was and how many people worked there, suspecting her of exaggerating for effect, but the more she heard, the better it sounded. Clara was independent: she earned her own money, lived in a room in a house near the mill with no family members nearby, and outside of work hours she did whatever she liked.

An idea was already forming in Annie's mind when Clara came right out with it. 'So, I wondered if you wanted to come back with me and work there too?' She paused. 'I should say, I'm here 'cos they're offering a bonus to any of us who bring in more good workers, 'cos they're always looking for more hands, but I did think of you anyway, and what fun we used to have together when we were little. It could be just like old times!'

Annie's mind was in a whirl, but just then she heard Delilah coming downstairs again. 'I'll have to think. But listen, not a word about it in front of my sister, do you hear? Not until I've spoken to her myself.'

Clara nodded and cleared her throat just as Delilah was coming in. 'So, like I said, I come to tell you about my poor Ma, 'cos I thought you'd like to know . . .'

Delilah heard that, and was immediately all sympathy. Of course, back when they'd lived in the court she'd had more to do with Clara's mother than Clara herself, being so much older than the girls, so she wanted to know everything she could about what had happened, and to express her concern.

When Clara had said that her mother's death was 'bound to happen someday' because she was 'getting on a bit', Annie had assumed that it was due to natural causes. It was with horror, therefore, that she learned how she'd been knocked about by her latest husband, and that she'd succumbed to a fever after being sent flying so hard that she'd broken several bones.

Clara was speaking about it so unemotionally that Annie could barely believe what she was hearing, but it was even worse to see Delilah's reaction: she took it all calmly in her stride, saying she'd seen such things happen all those years ago, and lots of men were like that.

Annie vaguely remembered her own Pa, who had died a few months after they'd moved into the shop. That is to say, she didn't remember *him*, exactly, but rather a looming, terrifying presence that produced harsh, slurred words and stank of alcohol. Oddly, for reasons she couldn't fathom, she felt a pain in her arm every time she thought of him. Delilah and the others never spoke of him, which Annie had just put down to their normal reluctance to talk of the past, but surely he couldn't have been as bad as what she was hearing about Clara's father? Such horrible things could never have happened in her own family.

Clara was getting up to go. 'I've got lodgings with some of the other girls what've come into town at the same time to look for new hands.' She cast a glance from Annie to Delilah and back. 'Very respectable, we are, nothing to worry about.' Then she looked about her in a hopeful manner. 'Don't suppose Sam's about, is he?'

Annie couldn't bring herself to answer that, but Delilah obviously didn't feel the same way. 'No, he's still in the army, so we don't see him very often.'

'Oh, shame. I'd have liked to see him again.'

'We all would, but he'll be home as soon as he gets the chance, I'm sure.'

Clara smiled. 'I remember when I was about eight or nine, Johnny Best tried to shove my head down one of the privies in the court, just a joke, he said. I screamed like anything and Sam came over and didn't half give him a pasting!'

Delilah's voice took on a fond tone. 'That's our Sam.'

Annie swallowed down the lump that had come into her throat, accompanying Clara to the door to see her out. 'How long are you here for?' she asked, out loud, adding, 'I'll have to talk to you again before you go back,' under her breath.

'Oh, a couple more days yet.'

'Well, do come and see us again before you leave,' said Delilah. 'You're always welcome in our family, you know that.'

'That's kind, thank you,' said Clara, from out in the yard. 'I will.'

Just enough light spilled out from the door for Annie to see her wink before she left.

* * *

That night Annie really did lie awake. Clara's offer seemed almost too good to be true. A job, wages, independence . . . everything that Annie had been wanting. And although it wasn't that far away, just a few miles outside Liverpool, it would still be further than Annie had ever travelled before.

But how was she going to get Delilah to agree?

As the night wore on, Annie tried out different scenarios in her head, but they all ended in failure. Delilah, with her constant worry about Annie being 'safe', would never let her go off to a strange job in a strange town, and especially not to live there.

The only way to proceed was to go in stages. First, Annie needed to get Delilah used to the idea of her having a job, any job, outside the home. 'I'm old enough to be earning wages and contributing to the household' . . . that sort of thing. Maybe she would even have to get such a position, just for a while, so everyone became accustomed to it and she could make the next step. But no, that wouldn't work, would it? Clara was only going to be in town for a couple of days. Annie needed to go back with her if she was going to find her way to wherever the mill was and then be taken on there. She would need the recommendation, surely – they wouldn't employ just anyone.

She fretted until the sun came up.

Monday morning dawned bright and clear, just the sort of day to put everyone in a good mood, but Annie had no chance to talk to Delilah. The shop was always busy early on a Monday, with queues of uniformed servants arriving to pick up the fresh flowers that would adorn some of Liverpool's largest houses. Unfortunately the wholesale delivery had been slightly late, so the displays weren't quite arranged to Delilah's satisfaction before the first customers arrived, and she then spent the rest of the morning in a whirl of trying to catch up, fulfilling both the regular orders and the one-offs.

Annie was also rushed off her feet, helping to serve in the shop when she could while also seeing Daisy and Joe out the door to school and making sure that the younger two were fed and kept out from underfoot – easier said than done now that Billy was four and wouldn't sit still for two minutes. At least Eliza was more manageable, but as she spooned porridge into the little mouth, trying to avoid the red swollen gums at the back, it struck Annie that Eliza was now one and a half, and on previous evidence it probably wouldn't be all that long before Delilah was expecting another baby. Which would make it all the more difficult for Annie to get away. She had no desire to spend the best years of her life being Delilah's nursemaid, and shuddered at the recollection of what Clara had said about her own mother's childbearing.

Once the back room was tidy again, Annie went out to lock the gate and told the children they could play in the yard. Then she returned to the bustle of the shop, serving the housemaids and footmen without really thinking about it, because her mind was occupied with the difficult conversation she was determined to have before the day was out.

The chance came in the middle of the day. The shop was shut for an hour to allow Delilah and Annie to have a cup of tea and a small bite of something, and to feed Billy and Eliza bread and jam and then put them down for a nap. Billy was beginning to protest against such baby treatment, but Annie hoped she could keep persuading him for a few more weeks at least. Daisy and Joe wouldn't be home until later, and Frank and Jem never came back for dinner in the middle of the day, so it was effectively just the two of them.

Annie put her cup down untasted. 'I need to talk to you.'

The tone of her voice made Delilah pause in mid-sip. 'What about?'

There was no point in beating around the bush. 'I want to get a job.'

'But you already have a job.' Delilah made a gesture that encompassed the room and the shop. 'Don't we keep you busy enough?'

'Of course I'm busy, you know I am. But you also know that's not what I mean. I mean going out, somewhere else, to work for wages.'

Delilah was already shaking her head. 'We've had this conversation before.'

Annie felt her temper rising already, and tried to keep it in check. 'Yes, we have. And you weren't listening to me then, and you're not listening to me now.'

'I *am* listening. It's just that you don't know what you're asking. You're much better off here, where it's safe—'

There was that word again. 'What if I don't *want* to be safe?' Annie banged her hand down on the table, making her cup rattle and spill tea into the saucer.

'How can you say that?! Not want to be—'

'All right, all right!' Annie was getting flustered, she knew she was. And if she was going to win this argument she needed to be calm and rational. 'I didn't mean that. I know you want to look after me. But there's safe and then there's trapped, don't you understand? I can't spend my life in this house and this shop – I need to get out and do something, like the rest of you have.'

This was veering on dangerous territory, she knew. Reminding Delilah of the past would bring out all her memories and her protective instincts.

'You don't understand,' Delilah began.

'No, no, I don't,' retorted Annie. 'Because you never take the trouble to help me to understand, and none of you will even talk to me about anything!' She had to stand up, unable to sit still now the words were flowing. 'You all talk and you leave me out, all the time. I don't even know how many brothers and sisters I ever had, never mind what happened to them!

All I know is that I have to live my own life, and it's *you* who needs to understand that.'

Delilah put her now empty cup and saucer carefully on the table. Her hands were shaking.

'I promised Ma that I'd keep you all safe,' she said, quietly. 'At her *deathbed*, I swore it. They were the last words she ever heard from me, a daughter's promise to keep going, to keep the family together, no matter what happened, and I failed her.'

Annie didn't – couldn't – make a reply to that.

'I lost all my sisters, one after the other,' continued Delilah, in that terrifying soft tone. 'First Jemima when she was a baby, then Meg and Rosie to the workhouse. You were the only one left. I thought I would never see any of the others again, and I was terrified for you. Every day I had to leave you in that court and go off to work, first in the laundry and then on my rounds selling flowers. I didn't want to leave you, but I had no choice, because I needed to earn the money for rent and food. And every day – *every single day* – I lived in terror of coming back to find that I'd lost you too. That you might have wandered off somewhere and I'd never see you again.' She met Annie's eyes. 'Can you possibly understand or imagine what that was like?'

Annie found herself overcome by the unexpected mention of the names of her sisters. *Rosie*, that was it! She was the older sister whose shadowy presence Annie could still sometimes feel. And, of course, that explained why William and Bridget had given the name to their eldest daughter – Annie had thought it was just because they liked the sound of it, or maybe it was from Bridget's side of the family. But they'd called her Rosie in remembrance of the sister that William must have known for all of her short life. Annie had never heard of Jemima before, but that wasn't surprising: if she'd died as a baby then that would have been before she herself was born.

She wanted to know more about both of these sisters, about who they were and how they'd come to be lost, but that would have to wait: right now she had to stick to her purpose. 'You got Meg back,' she pointed out. 'And she's always worked.'

She was worried that Delilah might start crying, but she found herself taken aback by a wave of barely suppressed fury. 'Yes, we found Meg again, but that was nothing short of a miracle! And we could hardly hope to be so lucky twice if anything happened to you.'

'Oh, nothing is going to happen to me!'

'You can't know that!'

'Stop being so—'

'How can you say—'

This was going nowhere. 'Well, I certainly know that nothing will happen to me so long as I stay here!' shouted Annie. 'It will just be boredom and slavery until the day I die.'

She'd done it again. Overstepped herself. She hadn't intended to use *that word*, the one that meant so much to friends and family and had given them so much pain, and she definitely hadn't meant to sound so bitter as she said it.

Delilah looked as though she'd been slapped. Instead of retorting, though, she just stood up and said in a dignified tone that it was time to wake the children and reopen the shop.

Annie watched her sister's back, tense and ramrod straight, as she left the room.

Oh, *why* couldn't she stay calm enough during these conversations to get her point across in a way that would be accepted? What was it about family, and Delilah in particular, that made her feel so frustrated?

Well, whatever the reason, she was quite clearly never going to be able to persuade Delilah to let her go. If she reacted like that to the mere suggestion that Annie should work elsewhere, before she'd even brought up the idea of her actually *living* away from home as well, then there was no hope. So that left Annie with only two choices: accept life as it was and stay here, forgetting any dreams of getting away; or strike out on her own, Delilah or no Delilah.

As the afternoon wore on, the argument played over and over in Annie's mind, and eventually she began to see it in a different light. She hadn't failed to persuade Delilah because she wasn't eloquent enough; it was because her sister didn't listen, didn't want to listen, and was just being unreasonable. It was, in fact, all Delilah's fault.

The more she thought about this, the closer she came to making her decision.

* * *

Clara arrived in the evening, just as she'd promised. This time, though, everyone was at home so the room was crowded and Annie had no opportunity to speak to her privately. She knew now what she was going to do, so it was just a case of making Clara aware and then putting her plan into action. Delilah would be upset, but she would just have to cope. It was Annie's own life and she was entitled to live it in her own way.

She tried whenever possible to give Clara significant glances and make her understand that she had something to communicate. To start with, Clara was too busy to notice, chatting, talking to the children as well as the adults and making them laugh. She also wanted to catch up with Jem, whom she'd known when they were children, but she needed one of the others to interpret for her and therefore had little attention to spare.

Finally, though, Annie's constant eye-rolls and nudges got through and Clara, inspired, asked if she could visit the privy while she was here.

'I'll show you where it is,' said Annie, immediately, hustling her towards the back door before anyone could point out that Clara didn't need to be shown, for where else would the privy be but in the yard?

Outside there was enough moonlight for them to be able to see each other as they talked.

'I'm coming with you,' whispered Annie, glancing back to make sure that nobody was close enough to hear. 'But Delilah mustn't know. If she did, she'd try to stop me.'

Clara broke into a wide smile. 'Hark at you! I never thought I'd hear you say such a thing. Have you ever done anything in your life that she didn't give you permission for?'

Annie wasn't sure how that made her feel, but there was no time to think about it now. 'Can you be outside the back gate here later tonight, say midnight?'

Clara nodded. 'You're really going to run away, then?'

'I have to. There's no other choice. I'll leave her a note saying I've gone with you, but not exactly where that is, so don't mention your mill when we go back inside, in case she can find it. All right?'

'Yes.'

'I'll come out and meet you, and then can we go back to your lodgings for the rest of the night? Don't say where that is, either – even Delilah wouldn't be able to trace us in a place as big as Liverpool, not without some kind of clue.'

'That's fine. There's other girls there, so the landlady won't notice one more. And there's a wagon going back to the mill tomorrow morning.'

Annie's excitement rose. By this time tomorrow she'd have a job and her own independence. She'd write to Delilah again once she was settled, to tell her not to worry. It would be fine; she and the others would get used to the idea once it had actually happened.

She went back inside and tried to compose herself so that the others wouldn't notice anything amiss. Frank was busy amusing the older children, and Delilah would soon be putting the younger ones to bed, so they'd both be distracted, but Jem had a way of noticing things, and if he found out what she meant to do then he'd side with Delilah for sure.

Annie had a little qualm about the thought of upsetting Jem, who was certainly less to blame than Delilah, but it soon passed. He was all right, wasn't he? With his fiancée and his beloved trains, his work, his travelling and his wages. Why shouldn't she have the same sort of opportunity? It wasn't her fault she was the youngest and the others wanted to keep her a child forever.

As luck would have it, Delilah was upstairs with the girls when Clara stood up to go. Frank was doing his best to make the boys laugh, getting them too silly and excited to settle down, so while he was occupied over there, Annie took advantage of Jem turning away from them to whisper in Clara's ear. 'Tonight. Midnight. Don't forget.'

'I won't.' Clara squeezed her hand. 'I'm excited!' she whispered back. 'It's going to be just like old times. You and me.'

Then she was gone, and Annie was left to plan her movements between now and midnight.

It wasn't long before everyone was in bed except her, but that wasn't unusual, so nobody remarked on it. She waited until she was sure all was silent throughout the house, and then it was time.

There was paper in the shop, used for when Delilah had to write out bills, a labour she hated and found difficult. Annie took a piece and brought it, together with a pen and the inkpot, into the back room. Then she stared blankly at the sheet for quite some time while she tried to think what to write. At least in this she would be able to express herself properly – who could have foretold that her schooling would come in useful in this sort of situation? She almost laughed at the thought. Delilah couldn't read all that well, and Frank not at all, but Daisy was quite fluent now and if all else failed they could always get William to read it to them.

Keep it simple, she decided.

Dear Delilah,

I have left home to go and get a job. I will be working with Clara so don't worry about me. I will write again once I am settled to let you know that I am all right.

She paused with the pen in the air, unsure how to finish.

I'm sorry it happened this way. But it's my life and I have to live it myself.

With love to you all,

Annie

She folded the paper in half, wrote 'Delilah' on the outside, and left it in the middle of the table where it couldn't be missed.

The next thing was to fetch her clothes. She didn't own that many, but she did have a spare dress and some extra cotton underclothing upstairs, as well as the shawl that hung by the door down here. How would she do her laundry in her new place, she wondered? Would there be a yard and a tub? These were the sorts of things she would need to find out, but she was excited rather than daunted by the idea. Oh, to be doing something different!

She crept up into the room she shared with Daisy and Eliza. They were both asleep in their bed, so she drew out the box from under her own as quietly as she could. There were her clothes, and also a few sixpences and pennies wrapped in a screw of paper; she'd saved them from when the occasional customer left her a tip, or when Delilah had given her money for a treat from the baker and she hadn't spent it.

How to carry everything was the next problem, for she had no bag; in the end she laid the dress out flat on the bed, put everything else on to it save one handkerchief, then rolled it up tightly and used the sleeves to tie it all up and form a handle. That would have to do. Maybe when she was earning her own money, she would buy a travel bag.

It was just as she was leaving the room again that a sleepy voice sounded. 'Where you going, Annie? Is it time to get up?'

It was Daisy. Fortunately the room was dark enough that Annie could put the bundle down without it being seen, and she tiptoed over to the bed. 'Don't worry,' she said, smoothing Daisy's hair and kissing her. 'I left the candle lit downstairs, so I'm going down to blow it out. I'll be back in a while, so you can go back to sleep.'

Reassured, Daisy nodded and closed her eyes.

Annie breathed again, kissed the sleeping Eliza as well, and slipped out of the room.

She made it to the back room with no further alarm, and surveyed the kitchen. She would not take any pans, plates or food with her, because that would be stealing – her saved money was her own, but the rest of all this belonged to the household. And she no longer belonged to this household.

The clock on the mantel said that it was five minutes to midnight.

Annie shivered. It was too late to back out now, and besides, she didn't want to. She would make sure to leave everything tidy and safe, though.

She blew out the candle, making sure there were no remaining sparks. Then she made her way over to the bed and the sleeping boys, kissing them both. *I'll see you soon*, she thought, not daring to speak out loud even though they were such sound sleepers. *But not until I've made my own way.*

The key to the outside gate was hanging in its usual position by the back door, so she took it and made her way out into the cool yard. The moon was on the wane now, but the sky was clear and she could see where she was going. Happily both the bolt and the lock on the gate were always kept in good condition, so she was able to unfasten them both in silence and slip through.

Leaving the yard open to possible intruders had been her main fear as she'd formulated her plan earlier in the day, but she'd managed to find a solution that would be at least partly effective. She couldn't shoot the bolt back into place from this side, of course, but she could turn the key in the lock. Then she wrapped it in the handkerchief so it wouldn't bounce or make too much of a noise when it landed, and threw it back over the wall. If she'd aimed correctly then it would fall in the open space near the pump so it would be obvious when they saw it in the morning.

That was it. She was locked out now, and there was no way back in.

She didn't want to go back.

Annie picked up her bundle and turned to face the outside world.

Chapter Three

Clara was waiting, making Annie jump as she stepped out of the shadows. 'Wasn't sure you'd go through with it.'

'Well, I'm here now,' replied Annie, finding that her voice wasn't quite as steady as she expected. 'Where do we go?'

'Back to lodgings. It's this way, not too far.'

They made their way to the end of the back alley and were soon out into the wider space of Dale Street. Annie checked herself just as she was about to touch the front door of the flower shop as they passed it. This was no time to get emotional about leaving.

The streets of Liverpool looked and felt very different in the middle of the night. Dale Street itself was a respectable place with gas lamps, but even that felt a little ominous, with the mouths of dark alleys yawning at her, and by the time they had reached the end and turned into Byrom Street, she felt herself shrinking a little. Then it was along Scotland Road, with its entrances to narrower lanes and courts leading off it and groups of men hanging about on corners, and Annie began to feel really quite intimidated. 'Where are you taking us?' she hissed under her breath.

Clara was unabashed, seemingly appreciating the catcalls that Annie was trying to ignore. 'Don't worry, I lived round here all my life until a couple of years ago. I know where we're going.'

After a few hundred yards, Clara stopped and turned. To Annie's relief, it wasn't to go up a very dark and ominous-looking alley, but rather to enter a house that fronted on to Scotland Road itself. 'Lodgings,' explained Clara, briefly.

Once inside, they went up a flight of stairs and Clara pushed on a door on the landing. As it opened, Annie could see several sleeping forms, a couple of them on a bed and the rest on mattresses on the floor. 'Cheaper to share,' whispered Clara. 'And respectable, like I said – all girls in here and the men are in another room.'

Annie stepped through. 'So, we'll stay here until the morning, and then set off for the mill?'

'Yes. Get some sleep if you can.' Clara pointed to a spare mattress in the corner, then poked one of the girls in the bed and told her to move up.

Annie lay down. There was far too much going on in her mind to allow her to sleep, but she supposed she should get some rest while she could. The enormity of what she'd done now began to dawn on her. How would Delilah react when she saw that Annie was gone and read the note? What would the others say when she told them?

Don't think of all that, she told herself. *Think about what's ahead, not what's behind*. She was on her way to a new life, one in which she would meet different people, work hard in her job and earn her own money. When she did eventually return to the shop to visit her family, it would be in triumph and as a proper adult just like all the others.

She dozed lightly without ever really falling asleep, and soon it was time to get up. Some of the other girls looked at her strangely, as well they might, until one of them recalled that Clara had said she was going out late at night to fetch someone.

Clara herself was the latest to wake, but the first thing she did after sitting up was to look at Annie and grin widely. 'Ready to go?'

'Ready,' said Annie, and she was.

Some of the workers from the mill were leaving that day with the volunteers they'd recruited, while others who hadn't yet found anyone would remain for a day or two longer. After a trip to a really noxious privy that gave Annie her first touch of homesickness, they had a bite of bread and a cup of tea and then Annie, Clara and some of the others left the house to walk to Scotland Place. There they were met by a few other individuals and a couple of families while they waited for the arrival of the wagons that would take them out of town.

One small family caught Annie's eye: a father with two children, a girl who looked about Daisy's age and a younger boy. The father wasn't paying them much attention, and it was the girl who was trying to keep the boy under control and stop him skipping into the road and into danger from the passing early morning traffic. Annie caught her eye and smiled.

It wasn't long until several large wagons were seen coming up the road, and they stopped near the waiting group. To Annie's surprise, the first two were already half full and all the passengers were children.

One of the mill men standing near her noticed her bemusement. 'From the workhouse,' he said, nodding towards them. 'Gives 'em a job and a trade, and takes the cost of 'em off the city.'

The word 'workhouse' was an ominous one in Annie's family, encompassing as it did those years when Meg had been apart from them. But Meg had survived it, and had met Sally there, who had turned out to be a lifelong friend, so perhaps it wasn't that bad? And it was a good idea, surely, for orphaned and abandoned children to learn a useful trade. Though some of these ones did look very young.

'In you get, then,' said the driver, once the horses were still. Annie was one of the first to clamber up, holding on to her bundle. The wagons had long benches running down each side, and she found herself next to one of the workhouse girls, with Clara on her other side and the family she'd noticed earlier sitting opposite her. The little boy was still very excited, fidgeting and leaning over the edge of the vehicle, and his sister was holding firmly on to his jacket so he didn't fall out. Her own bare feet were swinging, her legs not long enough to reach the floor of the wagon.

Soon the horses were in motion again, and Annie had the unusual sensation and the pleasure of watching Scotland Road pass her by while she sat at leisure.

The workhouse girl next to her was wide-eyed, the experience presumably being a novelty to her too. 'Hello,' said Annie, cheerfully. 'Have you never been on a ride like this before?'

The only reply she received was one terrified glance before the girl stared firmly at her feet. She was wearing a pair of the scruffiest boots Annie had ever seen, scuffed leather with broken and knotted laces, and a flapping sole on one foot. She was also clenching fistfuls of her apron in tightly balled hands.

Maybe she'd been a bit too vigorous. 'Sorry,' continued Annie, in a gentler tone. 'I didn't mean to scare you, and you're probably not supposed to talk to strangers. But we'll be working together soon enough, I suppose, so it's no harm.'

Still no response.

'My name's Annie. What's yours?'

The girl looked up. 'Hannah,' she whispered.

'That's a nice name.' Annie cast about for ways to keep the conversation going. 'And how old are you?'

Hannah shrugged. 'Nine, I think.'

She didn't seem inclined to speak any further, but Annie detected a very slight relaxation of the clenched fists.

'My name's Charlie,' piped up a voice from opposite. 'And this is my sister, Alice.'

This one was less shy, and no mistake, reminding Annie of Joe back ho— back at the shop.

'Hello, Charlie. And how old are you?'

'Six.'

Without warning, the boy's father, who had appeared to be in conversation with the mill man on his other side, reached out and gave Charlie a hefty clip on the ear that nearly knocked him off his seat. Annie exclaimed, but nobody else batted an eyelid.

'I mean,' said Charlie, rubbing his ear, 'eight.'

Annie couldn't believe that for a moment. He certainly wasn't more than about six – that was Joe's age, and Charlie looked to be even smaller. She wondered why he should lie, or why his father should apparently want him to.

A damper had been put on the conversation, and everyone fell silent. Annie contented herself with looking at the scenery. They were already further out of Liverpool than she had ever been, and the crowded streets were giving way to fields and trees. There was so much greenery that Annie could hardly believe it, and neither could Hannah, from the looks of things – her eyes were almost falling out of her head as they passed an enormous vegetable garden, the crops and seedlings sowed in neat rows.

The view was spoiled after a while by the appearance of two large and forbidding buildings away to their left. 'Do you know what those are?' Annie asked Clara, but her friend only shrugged.

'Kirkdale Gaol,' said the mill man, breaking off his conversation with Alice and Charlie's father and nodding at the nearer building. Then he pointed at the second. 'And the Liverpool industrial school.' He laughed and gestured at the workhouse children filling the front half of the wagon. 'These little beggars should be grateful they're coming to the mill, and not there!'

The journey continued. The day was warm and sunny, with their movement creating just enough of a breeze to be pleasant; Annie hadn't had much sleep and she soon found herself being lulled into a doze by the swaying of the cart. Hannah's head was also drooping, her thin little figure leaning, and without really thinking about it, Annie put her arm around the child, just as she would have done to one of her nieces.

It must have been about noon when Annie was roused by an elbow to the ribs. 'Wake up!' she heard Clara say. 'We're here.'

Annie opened her eyes. Gone were the pleasant countryside views, the green fields and the trees; in their place were the narrow streets of a village, dominated by one of the largest buildings Annie had ever seen, towering at the top of the hill they were currently ascending. It was of red brick, and the main part was three or four floors high, and must have been hundreds of yards wide; it had more windows than

Annie could count. Attached to this was another part, almost as wide again but only of a single storey, with an odd-looking roof shaped like the teeth of a saw. There was also a slender tower containing a large clock, which confirmed her estimate of the time.

The wagon jolted as it passed over the cobbles of the street, and Hannah woke up. She seemed absolutely horrified that she'd been leaning on Annie in her sleep, and stammered out her apologies while looking at her feet and flinching away.

'It's all right, it really is,' said Annie. 'Now, look, this must be the mill. Is your mo—' She stopped herself just in time from asking a foolish question, and managed to reword it. 'Are any of these other children your brothers and sisters? Older than you?'

Hannah shook her head.

'Well, maybe you can stick with me and Clara, and we can look out for you.'

Annie found a pair of huge eyes gazing up at her, and Hannah's lips began to form what she thought was the word 'Why', but there was no more time for talk as they were all told to get down from the wagon.

Annie's legs were wobbly after the journey. She stamped her feet and took a few moments to steady herself, then turned to make a joke of it to Hannah, but all the workhouse children were already being led off by some mill workers. Annie tried to spot Hannah, but as she was looking at their backs and all the girls were dressed the same, she couldn't make her out. None of the children looked back; they just went meekly where they were told and kept their heads down.

'Now,' a man was calling out, 'the rest of you, listen up.'

Annie hoped she could find out later where the workhouse children had gone, and check that Hannah was all right, but for now she'd better concentrate. She needed to get off to a good start. What if they didn't want to take her on because she wasn't paying attention?

'All existing mill hands who've brought new workers, you stay with them while they register and you'll get your fee.' He pointed to two tables at one side of the yard. 'Then you're to get straight back to work. New hands – once we've got your names, families with children under twelve will report over there.' He pointed to a desk set outside a separate smaller building off to his left that Annie hadn't noticed before. Perhaps it was a school house? It would be nice if the little children like Alice and Charlie could go there while parents and older siblings were at work; much better than leaving them at home or playing in the streets all day. She wondered if the workhouse children might be able to attend as well, outside of their apprenticeship hours.

The man was continuing. 'Everyone else to those next four desks, separate lines for men and women, and those under or over sixteen.'

That seemed clear enough. The queues for the registration desks were about equal, so Annie and Clara joined one while the little family kept pace with them in the other. As they inched forward, Annie tried to ask Clara what the work would be like, but Clara said she couldn't say because it depended on which part of the mill she was put in: it was a long process to turn raw cotton into finished fabric, and the jobs were all different. Mixing, blowing, carding, spinning, beaming, warping, weaving . . . Annie was starting to feel very bemused indeed.

'But don't worry,' concluded Clara, squeezing Annie's hand, 'they'll show you how to do it properly, and you'll start off with one of the easier things to do.'

Annie certainly hoped so. Weaving was a difficult business, surely, and although she was keen to learn, she wouldn't want to be given something outside of her capabilities too early, or she might make a mess of it. If she started a job here and then lost it, there would be no alternative but to go back to Delilah and admit she'd failed.

She looked around at the queues of people. They would all soon be her workmates; would any of them turn into friends as well?

Her eye was caught by the opening of one of the mill doors. Three well-dressed men stepped out and stood to survey the goings-on in the yard. One was middle-aged and portly, while the other two were younger and bore just enough resemblance to each other for Annie to suspect they were related.

Annie nudged Clara. 'Who are they?'

Clara followed her gaze. 'Oh, that's Mr Carrington, the mill owner, and his sons. Mr Theodore is the taller one, and Mr Frederick the other. You won't see much of him – he's hardly here, and even when he is he mainly stays in his office. He wouldn't ever talk to any of us. His sons are learning the business, though, so you do see them about the place.' Unconsciously, she touched her hair.

Annie watched the men for a few moments as they surveyed their little kingdom. She couldn't imagine what it must be like to *own* something as huge as this mill, or to have the responsibility for so many workers. They stayed where they were for a few minutes, Mr Carrington occasionally pointing and making a remark to his sons, and then he consulted his pocket watch and they all disappeared back inside.

The family in the other queue reached the front of it, together with the man who had been talking to them on the wagon. He pocketed the fee paid out by a bored-looking official sitting behind a table and then walked off without another word.

The man at the table had in front of him a ledger book and a pen, as well as a box of coins. He turned to the family. 'Name?'

'Paul Jackson.'

'Any mill experience?'

'None.'

Paul seemed to Annie to be extraordinarily anxious, shaking and sweating as he gave his replies. How odd. But perhaps he was just concerned about providing for his family, and desperate for the work.

'Hmm.' The man made a note in his book, then looked up again. 'Children?'

'Two,' said Paul, indicating them. 'Alice and Charlie.'

The officer gave them a stern look. 'Minimum age for working in the mill is eight.' He addressed Alice directly. 'How old are you?'

Annie was so taken aback that she hardly heard Alice's reply of, 'Nearly ten, sir.' *Eight*? What sort of a place was this? When she'd heard the earlier mention of under-twelves, she'd thought—

'Nine – years – of – age,' wrote the man, carefully. He turned to Charlie. 'And you, boy?'

Paul gave Charlie a hard prod between the shoulder blades.

'Eight, sir.'

The man paused with his pen in the air. 'You don't really expect me to believe that?'

Paul leaned forward to murmur some words to him that Annie didn't catch, then fumbled in his pocket and passed over a couple of coins.

'Yes,' said the officer, as the money expertly vanished. 'Eight years of age. Both to be employed on children's hours and rates. You can find lodgings for all your family, or the children can stay in the dormitory here, though the fee for that and their food will be deducted from their wages.'

'I'll find somewhere for us.'

'Very well.' The clerk wrote something on a slip of paper and held it out. 'Take this and hand it over to the men allocating work.'

Paul took it and began to shepherd the children away. He assumed a hearty tone that, to Annie, sounded entirely false. 'Come on now, you two, let's go and see what they can find for you to do. You'll like it.'

Annie watched them head off in the direction of the smaller building, which was, she now guessed, not a school house.

She reached the front of her own queue. She was grateful at least that Clara stayed by her side after she'd been paid her fee, giving her confidence as she faced an elderly clerk wearing spectacles.

'Name?'

'Annie Shaw, sir.'

For some reason he looked at her intently for a moment, and then smiled. 'Age?'

'Fourteen.'

He nodded. 'That makes you a "young person" – that's in between a child and an adult – so you'll have those hours and wages. They'll tell you more when you're allocated to a position.' He passed her a slip of paper and indicated the desks at the other side of the yard.

'Yes, sir, thank you.'

'Now, you're too old for the dormitory here, so—'

'She'll come in with me,' broke in Clara. 'We've decided that already.'

The man raised his eyebrows at Annie and she hastened to agree.

'Very well. Go over there now, and they'll allocate you and tell you where and when to report tomorrow morning.' He paused. 'And welcome. I hope you get on well here.'

Well, that was nice. And how easy it had been! If it wasn't for all the shocks she'd just received, Annie could almost have skipped across the yard. *At last.* At last she had a job of her own, something she'd got without needing Delilah to give it to her.

'I have to get back to work now,' said Clara. 'See that gate? Wait for me there at nine o'clock tonight and I'll show you where we live.'

Annie almost tripped. 'Nine o'clock?'

'That's when I finish, 'cos I'm eighteen, don't forget. You'll have shorter hours.' She paused. 'All right? You've gone a bit pale.'

'I'm fine.' Embarrassingly, the realisation now began to dawn on Annie that her life so far had been what anyone else might consider mollycoddled. But this was the real world of work and she'd have to get used to it. 'I'll register and then have a look around the village. It will still be light until about eight, and I'll make sure I'm back here before it gets dark so I don't get lost.'

Clara smiled. 'You can't get lost around here – you just look up, and there's the mill. I'll see you later!'

Then she was gone. Annie, in no particular hurry now, made her way across the yard to the other desks and placed herself in the correct queue.

When she got to the front she handed over her paper. The man gave both it and her no more than a quick glance. 'You can start as a doffer in the spinning rooms. Eight shillings a week, hours six until six Monday to Friday, with breaks for breakfast and dinner, and six until noon on Saturdays.'

Annie had no idea what that first part meant. 'What's a—'

'Show me your shoes.'

'Pardon?'

'Your shoes, girl. Show me the soles.'

Annie moved to the side of the desk and turned her feet up. She was wearing proper sturdy boots; they were a little bit tight these days but still in good condition. Before she came away she'd been on the verge of asking Delilah for a bigger pair and putting these ones away ready for Daisy when she was older. She was baffled as to why she should—

'You can't wear those in the mill.' The man pointed to the nails that fastened the sole to the upper. 'Metal can cause sparks, and that's a fire hazard with all the cotton flying round. You can either get yourself a pair of wooden clogs, or leave these outside each day and work barefoot.'

Annie hesitated.

'That's all,' said the man, already looking past her to the next girl in the queue. 'Report to the spinning rooms on the top floor at six o'clock tomorrow morning.'

Before she knew it, Annie was walking towards the mill's outer gate. Oh well, looking for clogs would give her something to do for the rest of the day, and it was a good thing she'd brought her saved-up pennies with her.

It was a long afternoon, but Annie enjoyed it, savouring the freedom of walking round at her own pace. It was not difficult to find a shop selling clogs, for most of the village's population was employed at the mill, and it was barely mid-afternoon when she emerged with a pair tucked into her bundle. That gave her plenty of time to wander up and down the streets and have a look round – something she wouldn't get much chance to do once she started work, except on a Sunday. Most of it was rows of houses, of course, though on closer examination she found they were different from what she was used to. Instead of each having a yard behind it, leading on to an alley, the houses were built in a sort of back-to-back way so that each only had one door and you couldn't walk all the way through and out the other side. Annie wondered where everyone hung out their washing.

There were several public houses, some already half-full with men who must presumably be out of work. Oddly, she thought she spotted Paul just inside the door of one of them, but she must be mistaken – he would be busy finding lodgings for himself and the children now that they were secure of work.

It struck her again how young some of the mill employees were, but this was clearly the done thing here, and she didn't want to make herself look like a fool for expressing any surprise. She would just take everything in her stride as it came – and besides, the children would be on light duties, she was sure.

The village also boasted several shops, and Annie noted to herself where she would be able to buy food. In fact . . .

She stopped in a doorway and counted out how much money she had left. It was late afternoon by now – she might almost call it early evening – and she'd had nothing to eat since that piece of bread first thing this morning. If she had to wait for her tea until well after nine o'clock tonight she'd be starving, so maybe she could get something now? But wait. It was only Tuesday (was it really only the day before yesterday she'd been at Meg's with all the family?), and she wouldn't get paid until Saturday. She couldn't expect Clara to feed her for nearly a whole week, and she didn't want to have to start borrowing against her wages before she'd even got them.

Feeling virtuous, Annie passed the shop by. Budgeting was what adults did, wasn't it?

By the time dusk fell she was tired and very hungry. Mindful of the need not to get lost, she turned to make her way up the hill towards the mill. As Clara had said, there was no way she could miss it: light shone out from all the many windows. She reached the gate, set down her bundle and sat on it while she waited out the last hour, pulling her shawl around her against the mild chill of the evening. She didn't mind the wait: the view from here was a real novelty after the endless streets and buildings of Liverpool, and she gazed out past and over the little village to the hills and countryside beyond until it was too dark to make them out.

A loud whistle sounded, making her jump, and people began to flood out of the mill almost immediately afterwards. Men were pulling their jackets about them as though it was freezing, and women lifting their shawls over their heads. Most of them wore the same sort of wooden clogs that Annie had bought that afternoon, though a few were barefoot and made their way over to a heap of boots and shoes in a covered area of the yard.

Clara was among the first out, and she spotted Annie straight away. 'Right! Let's get you home so you can see the place, and then we'll see what we want to do with the rest of the evening.'

Annie was rather hoping that what they were going to do was eat, though she didn't say so.

Clara led her back into the village and down one of the identical-looking streets, stopping outside a house about halfway down. It was one of those built back to back, with just one door, and she pushed it open and went in. 'I'll tell Mrs Otway you're here, so she knows who you are.'

There was only one room on the ground floor, the sort of kitchen-and-parlour that Annie was used to, although it was smaller and not as clean and comfortable as the one back ho— back in Liverpool. It was very odd not to be able to see a back door, though; the only thing in the far corner of the room was a steep staircase.

There was no range, but a small fire was burning in the grate, over which a pot was being stirred by an elderly woman. She stood up as they came in. Or, rather, she got to her feet; she was so stooped that she was virtually bent double and could hardly be said to be standing upright.

'This is Annie,' said Clara.

Annie bobbed a slight curtsey. 'I'm pleased to meet you, ma'am.'

Mrs Otway's face creased into an almost-toothless grin. 'My, what manners! Oh, you'll do, girl, you'll do.'

It wasn't long before two other young women entered, and soon Annie was crowded around a small table with a dish of stew in front of her.

This was even better than she had expected: food would be provided with the lodgings, so she wouldn't even have to cook when she came home each day. Mrs Otway was a widow who was retired from working in the mill; she had no surviving children to support her, so she rented this house from a landlord and let out the two upstairs rooms in order to make enough money to buy food as well as cover the rent. The two other young women, both also mill employees, shared the room on the first floor while Clara, Annie and a third girl would sleep in the attic.

'It's seven and six between you for the room,' explained Mrs Otway, in between slurps of her stew. 'And you can divide that how you like. Then another two shillings each for food, and for that you get bread and jam in the morning, and your tea when you get home. You have to buy your own dinner at the mill in the middle of the day.'

Annie's schooling in arithmetic now came in useful. Seven and six divided by three – assuming they split the cost of the room equally – was two and six. Add another two shillings and that made four and six, leaving her three and six out of her eight-shilling wage. Even after she'd bought dinner every day that would certainly leave some spare, so she'd be able to put some aside. She hugged herself at the thought.

Each week's rent and food money was supposed to be paid in advance; Annie hadn't thought of that, and even if she had she wasn't in possession of that amount anyway. She admitted as much, but luckily, given that she was now a mill employee with a steady income, Mrs Otway agreed that she would wait until payday on Saturday, and then take payment for these four days as well as next week's. So Annie wouldn't be able to save much straight away, but still.

After tea, Clara showed her upstairs. The first flight led to a tiny landing with a door, and then the second flight came up directly inside the attic room, where there was one large and one small bed. 'Maisie has that one,' said Clara, pointing. 'You won't see her much, 'cos she works at the pub, so she don't get back until late and then she's still asleep when we get up in the morning. You can come in with me.'

Annie looked around for somewhere to put her clothes, but the room wasn't big enough for much more than the two bedframes and a tiny washstand, so she just pushed her bundle under the bed. She would use some of her first spare money to buy a new box.

An urgent question had to be answered before she could think of anything else. 'Where's the privy?'

'Ah, I'll show you. Bit late to be going out to it now – there's a pot under there if you need it at night – but I may as well show you so you know for next time.'

They went back downstairs, where Mrs Otway was just settling herself in a little box bed in the corner. 'She can't manage the stairs,' whispered Clara, 'so she couldn't have one of the bedrooms even if nobody was in it.'

Then they were out on the street, and Annie was still perplexed. But Clara led her a few doors down and indicated a sort of tunnel that led between the ground floor of two houses. It was by now pitch dark, but Clara led the way confidently, so Annie followed. They emerged into what she could feel was a wider space, though she still couldn't see much.

'The front houses look out on to the street,' explained Clara, 'and the back ones face into here. Then there's the houses from the next street along that do the same, and this is the court in the middle. There's a wash house for sharing, and a row of privies.'

The word 'court' had never been a positive one in the Shaw household, and Annie felt a first tinge of misgiving at the sense of going backwards. But there was nothing to be done now, so she visited one of the privies and then followed Clara back to the street, into the house and up the stairs.

'I s'pose it's a bit late to be going out now,' said Clara.

'I should certainly think so, if work starts at six o'clock in the morning!' It must be well after ten by now, Annie guessed, though there was no clock in here to check. 'Wait – how do we know when to get up in the morning?'

'Ah, you'll see. All right then, let's get in bed and we can talk a bit instead of going out. It is Tuesday, I suppose.'

The bedstead creaked, and the mattress wasn't exactly comfortable, but Annie didn't care.

It seemed as though she was still halfway through a conversation with Clara when a sharp noise sounded, making her jump awake. What—?

'All right, all right!' came Clara's voice. 'Annie, go and tweak the curtains, and then he'll know we're up.'

Annie did so, looking out of the window to see an old man in the street carrying a very long stick. He waved when he saw her, and then went to bang on the windows next door.

'The knocker-upper,' explained Clara, with a yawn. 'He gets paid to wake everyone up who works at the mill.'

It didn't take long to wash and dress. Annie tried to do so as quietly as possible, so as not to wake Maisie, but the other girl was soundly asleep and didn't stir even when Clara was much less careful. Then it was downstairs for some bread and jam, and off out into the street, workers pouring out of every house to make their way up the hill. Annie's new clogs sounded on the cobbles along with everyone else's.

'First day,' said Clara. 'You ready?'

Annie looked up at the huge building as they approached it. 'Yes. Yes, I am.'

Chapter Four

The spinning rooms on the top floor, Annie had been told. That shouldn't be too difficult to find, and Clara pointed her in the right direction before vanishing into the single-storey building with the saw-tooth roof.

As Annie went up the stairs she found that she was not the only new employee heading in the same direction. Of course she wasn't; many new hands had been taken on yesterday. But it was reassuring to know that she wouldn't be the only complete beginner in the room.

As they clattered their way up, the temperature rose and Annie started to feel quite warm. Then they reached the top, the door opened and she was hit by a blast of hot, wet air. She stopped on the threshold in surprise.

'Get used to it,' said an older man, taking off his jacket and rolling up his shirt sleeves as he pushed past her. 'The finer the thread we're spinning, the hotter and more humid it needs to be, or the thread breaks. And once the machines start it'll be noisy, too, and the fly in the air.'

Annie had no chance to ask him how flies might get in the air up here, with all the windows shut, as he strode over to one of the many frames that filled the cavernous space, idle at the moment but each with hundreds of bobbins standing ready. He began to check it over. It all looked very complicated; not just the threads all over the place but also a maze of belts and pulleys and shafts that ran overhead. Annie had a sudden thought that Jem would like to see the machinery, and then bit her lip. She'd explain to him, and to all of them, soon.

'New hands, over here,' called another man, and Annie and a few others made their way along the end wall, careful not to touch anything, to a corner where he stood with two women next to a table on which were placed some reels of thread, scissors, bobbins and a few other items. She looked at her companions. They were mainly girls of about her own age, with a sprinkling of men and women in their older teens and twenties, but no children.

'Right,' said the man. 'This floor is the two spinning rooms. By the time the cotton gets here it's already been through the card room to prepare the fibres, and then we spin it into the thread that's used for weaving. Warp thread in one room and weft thread in the other – same process, but different types of bobbin.' He paused and looked at their blank faces. 'My, we are all wet behind the ears, aren't we? The warp is the thread that runs lengthways down the cloth, set up on the loom before the weaving starts, and the weft is the thread that's woven side to side.'

Annie repeated the words carefully to herself.

There was a sudden loud noise as all the machines started up at once, making all the new hands jump.

The man raised his voice. 'Now, watch the machines for a few moments so you can see how they work.'

Annie did. It was like magic: somehow all the belts turning overhead made the machines function, and different pieces moved in unison. The end result was that the hundreds of spinning bobbins that started off empty were filled with thread. The operators walked up and down, checking everything, feeding their machines and making various adjustments that Annie couldn't fathom. When the spinners saw that a bobbin was full, they raised a hand and shouted, and someone ran in from the side of the room, took the full one off and replaced it with an empty one, and *all while the machine was still running*.

'That's called doffing,' shouted the man instructing them. 'And that's what you'll be doing to start with. Watch carefully.'

He nodded to his two female companions, who picked up full and empty bobbins from the table and demonstrated slowly the movements needed to swap them over. Then they all had to take a turn, practising until they could do it fast enough to satisfy the eagle-eyed women.

The man had been watching, and now he nodded and pointed to Annie and a couple of the younger girls who had managed the best. 'You three can get to work straight away.' He turned to his assistants. 'See that they're properly wrapped up – we don't want any accidents.'

No, we don't, thought Annie, looking at the heavy, fast-moving machines. One of the women mimed to her and the other two girls to throw their shawls on a pile in the corner of the room – which Annie was glad to do, given how hot and sweaty she was already – and then picked up a discarded offcut of cotton fabric. She wrapped it tightly round Annie's waist so that the hem of her dress was trapped inside it. 'It's all right for the men,' she shouted in Annie's ear, 'but we have to make sure our skirts don't get in the way.' Then she cut a smaller piece and tied it round Annie's head. 'Always, *always* keep your hair away from the threads.'

Annie nodded, gulping now as she was directed to a place at the side of the room, clutching an empty bobbin. Her hands were shaking – that wouldn't be any good, would it? What if she messed everything up and they had to stop the machines and it was all her fault? Oh, why had she come? Maybe she would have been better off after all staying in the sho—

The nearest machine operator shouted and raised a hand. He was looking directly at her.

There was nothing else for it.

Holding her breath, Annie ran across, flipped the bobbin off exactly as she'd practised, replaced it with the empty one and ran back. It was all over so quickly that she'd barely had time to think about it, but here she was with a full bobbin her hand; the machine was still running and nobody was shouting. She allowed herself a relieved smile while she waited for her heartbeat to return to normal.

'First one's always the hardest,' came a voice from nearby. It was a girl of about twelve or thirteen, one of those who'd been at work all this time, so not a new hand like herself. 'I'll show you where to – oh, hang on, wait!'

Annie watched as the girl darted forward, swapped a bobbin of her own and returned. 'The full ones go over here,' she shouted, pointing to two very large baskets. Annie followed her, stacked her bobbin in one container and picked a new empty one out of the other.

After that she didn't have much time to think. With so many machines spinning so many bobbins, she barely had more than a minute or two between each exchange. Once she got the hang of it, it was quite easy, but she made sure that she was concentrating hard each time – she didn't want to get too offhand and risk making a mistake. She got safely through her first hour error-free. Some of her fellow new recruits, she noticed, weren't so lucky, and they were berated by the overlooker and the machine operators alike.

But it really was hot in here, and by now there were cotton fibres flying around in the air – ah, was that what the man had meant by 'fly'? – and the noise was beginning to give her a headache.

Before she knew it a whistle was sounding and the machines were slowing to a halt. 'Breakfast break,' explained her younger and more experienced companion. 'Come on.'

Annie followed the crowd out the room, down the stairs and into the fresh air of the mill yard. She immediately wished she'd brought her shawl with her – it was a fresh spring morning, but it felt freezing after the heat and humidity of the spinning room. All around her people were alternately taking in gulps of air and coughing, some of them quite badly.

'So, we get a break in the mornings?' Annie asked the girl.

'Half an hour for breakfast, and half an hour for dinner in the middle of the day.'

'That's good – I was worried we'd be in there all day without a break. Oh, I'm Annie, by the way. Annie Shaw.'

'Grace,' said the girl.

'Have you been working here long?'

'I went up from kiddies' jobs to a young person last year, when I turned twelve. Shouldn't really still be a doffer, but my Ma and Pa both work in the spinning room so they were happy for me to stay there for a while even though it's less money than some other jobs.' She indicated a couple who were standing in a queue that snaked towards the small building Annie had noticed yesterday.

'Butty shop,' said Grace. 'You can buy bread and treacle in the mornings and bread and dripping during the dinner break.' She made a face. 'It costs, and it's not very nice, but you're not allowed to bring your own food, and there isn't time to get home and back.'

Annie was glad that Mrs Otway had provided breakfast before she went out, even though it meant getting up even earlier, so that she didn't have to buy two meals a day here. She'd end up giving half her wages straight back to the mill, which she supposed was the point. She watched as the couple entered, then came out with several slices of bread. Grace and an older boy and girl ran over to them, and soon they were all munching.

Grace beckoned to Annie to join them. 'This is Annie,' she said to her mother, licking treacle off her fingers. 'She's new today.'

The woman nodded. 'Yes, I saw you. And doing well so far, from what I could see.' She paused. 'Did you forget your breakfast money? You'll be hungry by dinnertime.' She started to hold out the half-eaten bread in her hand, but Annie, touched at such kindness to a stranger, hastened to explain that she'd already eaten.

'Oh, Jane Otway?' the woman's face creased into a smile. 'You couldn't do better. She looked after me years ago when I first started here.' She ate the rest of her bread.

Annie began to feel more cheerful. Earlier, that had just been a moment of weakness brought on by nerves and everything being new. She was doing all right so far, and she'd already met some nice new people. Everything was going to be fine.

'Not long till the whistle again,' said Grace's father, who had until then been silent. He looked at the large mill clock, which stood at just before half past eight. 'Best get ready.' He watched his elder daughter and son as they crossed the yard, then coughed heavily into a handkerchief. Annie couldn't help but notice that his left hand only had three fingers.

'How long does it take to get used to the noise?' she asked, to stop herself from staring, as the whistle shrieked and everyone started to make their way back in again. 'In the spinning room, I mean.'

'Oh, that's nothing,' said Grace's mother. 'At least in there you can still just about be heard over it. In the weaving shed it's even worse. We have to use signs to each other.'

Annie laughed. *That's not a problem*, she signed.

Grace and her parents all looked bemused. 'What's that, then?'

'I thought you said you used sign language.'

'Well, yes, but not like that. It's called mee-maw, and there's only certain things you need to be able to say. Like, if you needed to go out for a moment while your looms were running, you'd say keep your eye—' she touched her eye '– on my –' she touched her chest

'– frame –' she mimed touching a machine '—while I go out.' She pointed outside.

'Oh, I see.'

'There's other things, too,' said Grace. 'What do you think this means?' She stroked her cheek and pointed to Annie's feet.

'Er . . .'

'It means,' said Grace, delightedly, 'I like—' she stroked her cheek again '—your clogs.'

'Oh, I see.' Annie really was learning a lot of new things today.

The machines were still at rest when they entered the spinning room, and a couple of men were poking at the one nearest the window, a bag of tools at their feet.

'What's the problem?' The overlooker hurried over to them. 'I need to get all these started again.'

There followed some kind of technical explanation that Annie didn't understand, though she gathered that there was a danger of some of the spindles flying off the machine if it were put in motion.

'Never mind that,' said the overlooker. 'All this row of machines run off the same belt, and I can't keep them all idle. If spindles are going to fly, everyone will just have to look out for themselves.'

The older of the two mechanics nodded and began to pack away his tools, but the younger man – Annie put him at about eighteen or nineteen – shook his head. 'Someone will get hurt.'

'Someone *might* get hurt. If they do, that's their own lookout, just like it is for everyone else in the mill. And it's better than having to explain to Mr Carrington why eight spinning frames were out of action.' He flapped his hands to try to shoo them both away.

The young man folded his arms and stood his ground. 'It's not right. If—'

The overlooker started to lose his temper, probably not helped by the audience of interested machine operators and doffers that now surrounded them. 'Don't you talk back to me, Jack Howard! You get out of the way right now, and that's an order.'

The mechanic looked as though he was going to argue, but with an effort he stopped himself. 'All right. But I'll wait in here for a while to see how it goes.'

'That's your own lookout,' replied the overlooker. 'As long as I can get these frames moving again. He turned to the spectators. 'Back to work. Now!'

Everyone started to move, but not before Annie had heard Grace's father mumble under his breath about someone being a 'troublemaker'.

As she moved back to her place by the wall, her attention was caught by a group of children who were standing in the same corner where she'd been given her instructions earlier.

'Sweepers and piecers,' said Grace. She raised her voice as the machines started up. 'They start at six normally, same as us, but they got a lie-in today so they didn't have all the new hands starting at once. If there's too many people in the room who don't know what they're doing, the work would slow down.'

While being careful to keep her eye out for machine operators needing her service, Annie cast regular glances over at the children. Alice and Charlie were both among the group, though she couldn't see Hannah anywhere. Come to think of it, from what she could make out, these were all children who had arrived with families, and none from the workhouse.

Charlie, who was by far the smallest of the children, was given a hand brush, as were the next shortest boy and a diminutive girl. All three were then pointed in the direction of the frames, where, to Annie's horror, they were set to crawling in the confined space underneath, sweeping up dust and fluff while the machinery continued crashing and banging only inches above them. The more she looked, the more children she could see already performing the same duty, and she tried not to think about Grace's father's missing finger.

Alice and the slightly older children were having some kind of lesson with bobbins over in the corner. The overlooker took up the scissors from the table and deliberately cut a piece of thread from a bobbin, and then – from what Annie could see in between darting backwards and forwards to keep up with her own work – he was showing them how to tie the ends together. Annie looked at the spinning frames with their whirling bobbins and hoped that tying broken threads was not another job that had to be done while the machines were still running. Judging by the attitude of the overlooker, however, and his insistence on not stopping, it seemed likely that it would be. Alice and the others would have to be light on their feet and have very quick fingers – which was presumably why children were wanted for the job in the first place. At least Annie was able to see the girl being wrapped up in a cotton apron like her own, and one of the older women covering and tying her hair up for her.

It was about an hour after the end of the breakfast break that there was a sudden snapping noise, followed by a series of pings and cracks, shrieks and a clattering.

'Stop! Stop the first row of machines!' That was the overlooker, and Annie saw the young mechanic, Jack, leap forward to pull on some levers. With a hiss, the machines ground to a halt and then they could all see the damage – bobbins and spindles everywhere and tangled threads.

Charlie emerged from under the machine, his face white. 'It wasn't me,' he began.

'Don't worry, lad, we know it wasn't you,' said Jack, hauling him out and setting him on his feet. 'It was obvious what was going to happen.' He glared at the overlooker. 'I told you—'

'And I told you we needed to get the machines going!' The overlooker was irritated, though Annie got the impression it was more with the inconvenience of the stoppage than the possible danger. 'We got an hour's extra spinning in, and this will soon clear up.' He waved an arm at the spinners now standing idle. 'Get this all untangled so we can start up as soon as possible.'

'Yes, we'll soon clear it up,' retorted Jack, 'and I'll adjust the frame. But it was sheer luck nobody was hurt.'

Annie looked around, relieved to see that nobody appeared to be injured. However, there were several cracks in the window panes where the flying bobbins had hit them at speed, and she winced at the thought that someone's face could have been similarly struck.

The overlooker stalked off without saying anything else, leaving Jack to examine the frame and a group of adults and children to start on the mess of threads. Annie wondered if she should offer to help, but the machines in the rest of the room were still running and she thought she'd better stick to the job she was supposed to be doing.

She took her position back by the wall, next to Grace. 'He's trouble, my Pa says,' said Grace, nodding at Jack.

'Trouble? It wasn't his fault the frame broke – why, he'd even warned against it.'

Grace shook her head. 'No, I don't mean that. I mean he's always talking back, when it's better to keep your head down and get on with it, Pa says.' She ran off to change a bobbin, leaving Annie to cast surreptitious glances at the young mechanic, now totally absorbed in his work.

The dinner break eventually arrived, and this time Annie remembered to fetch her shawl before she went outside. She queued up with everyone else and emerged from the butty shop with a piece of bread and dripping, which she took over to a quieter corner of the yard.

She spotted Alice and Charlie, standing on their own. 'Where's your Pa?'

Alice shrugged. 'He isn't working with us. He wasn't going to be quick enough, the man said, so he was to go to the warehouse and carry things. I don't know where that is.'

'But he's left you some money to buy your dinner?'

Alice shook her head.

'I wish he had,' piped up Charlie. 'I'm hungry.'

Annie did a quick mental check of how many pennies she had left to last the week until her first payday. It was just about going to be enough to buy one piece each day, and no more, so she couldn't afford to buy their dinner as well as her own. But . . .

She tore the bread and dripping in two and gave them half each.

Charlie immediately began wolfing his down, but Alice hesitated. 'But what will you eat?'

'Don't worry about me, I had a good breakfast earlier.'

'Well, if you're sure . . .' Alice was staring at the food. 'We didn't have breakfast either, because there wasn't time. Pa had to be here early, so we had to come too, in case we overslept after he'd gone.'

'So you've been here since six o'clock even though you didn't start until eight?'

Alice nodded, her mouth too full to speak.

Annie watched them eat. It wasn't all that unusual, in Liverpool, to eat a meal only once a day, but it wasn't pleasant and certainly not for growing children who had to work all day on empty bellies.

It wasn't long before the whistle sounded again, and they all trooped back in.

Everything was running smoothly again now, but it was a long, long afternoon. The novelty of being in a new place with a new job soon wore off, and as the hours passed Annie found herself exhausted, sweaty, covered in fluff and worn down by the noise. She couldn't see a clock in here, but surely it must be nearly six?

Even Grace, who was used to the work, was drooping, and the newer and younger children could hardly stay on their feet. Charlie had treated it all as a great lark during the morning, crawling and rolling nimbly under the machines as though he was playing in the street, but now he was markedly slower and Annie began to worry for him.

She looked around to see if she could spot Alice, and saw her tying a broken end of thread on a machine not far away. Once she'd done it she stepped back and wiped her hand across her face. She looked absolutely done in, and the cloth tied round her hair was starting to come loose, letting a few locks escape.

The words spoken to Annie that morning came into her head. 'Always, *always* keep your hair away from the threads.' She saw Alice leaning over another machine, having to stand on tiptoe to reach the part she needed.

Annie tried to shout, but Alice didn't hear, her loose hair dangling ever more precariously close to the whirring threads.

A spinner was shouting for Annie, but she ignored him as she started to hurry over to Alice to warn her of the danger.

But it was too late. Before Annie had gone three steps Alice's hair was caught up, and she screamed in terror as she was dragged into the machine.

Chapter Five

Annie stood frozen in horror, and there were shrieks from all around her. Someone was still alert enough to act, though, and a figure shot past her to grab hold of Alice, picking her bodily off the ground and trying to pull her away from the machine.

It was Jack, the young mechanic. He held Alice in one arm and tried at the same time to disentangle her hair from the threads, but he couldn't. Alice's shrieks grew louder as her hair started to tear away from her head.

A picture flashed into Annie's mind. Yes!

She ran to the table in the teaching corner and picked up the scissors, then darted back to the spinning machine. In one swift movement she cut Alice's hair where it was being pulled taut, causing Jack to fall backwards. He crashed to the floor but kept Alice safe, cradled in his arms.

The severed locks of hair were swiftly pulled into the machine, causing it to make a very strange noise and for some threads to break. Annie tried to duck and close her eyes in case any bobbins were going to come flying out, but just at that moment the machine, and those around it, rattled to a halt as someone pulled the lever.

There was a moment of silence, broken only by Alice's weeping.

Slowly, Jack began to get up, but before he could say anything the overlooker was upon them, shouting in incoherent fury. Jack ignored him, setting Alice gently on her feet and asking if she was all right. Alice looked around her at the faces of all the strangers, and then threw herself at Annie, sobbing and burying her face in her apron.

The overlooker, seemingly even more riled by Jack's calmness in ignoring him, was raging about having to endure a second loss of time and work in the same day. To start with, his ire was directed at everyone involved, but he eventually exonerated the spinner who had stopped the machine, on the basis that he had prevented worse damage that would have resulted in an even longer shut-down, and the man gratefully melted back into the crowd.

The overlooker had no qualms about bellowing in red-faced ferocity at the still sobbing Alice, and Annie felt her own shock and fear dissolving into anger at him as he went on and on. 'Stupid little idiot, what did you think you were doing? I'll have you put with the workhouse brats if you're not careful, and then you'll know about it!'

Annie tried to shield Alice, and was about to interject on her behalf when her own turn came. 'And as for you—'

'She had nothing to do with it,' said Jack, swiftly.

'Oh, really?' sneered the overlooker, pointing to the scissors that were still in Annie's hand. 'They got there by magic, did they?'

'What I meant was—'

It didn't really matter what Jack was about to say next; the point was that he'd managed to direct the man's anger away from Alice and Annie and towards himself. As he endured the tirade, Annie was able to slip backwards a little until she was surrounded by other women, who helped to dry Alice's tears and comfort her.

The overlooker was still going when the whistle sounded for six o'clock. That meant it was time for anyone under sixteen to leave, though Annie was loath to. None of this had been Jack's fault, and she wanted to remain for a while in case she could stand up for him. He'd saved a terrified little girl's life – or, at least, saved her from horrific injury – and it just wasn't fair that he should be punished for it. Perhaps if she could just explain . . .

But the altercation seemed to be drawing to a close. 'I'm reporting this,' said the overlooker, wagging his finger in Jack's face. 'You'll be in to see Mr Carrington tomorrow morning.' He whipped round and pointed at Annie, still observing. 'And that goes for you, too.'

Annie was stunned. Was she about to lose her job after one day? She felt sick. But then again, she felt even more sick at the thought of what might have happened to Alice if they hadn't intervened, and she wasn't sorry.

Fortunately Alice had now disappeared, so the overlooker was left to flap his hand and finish rather lamely with, 'And that stupid child will have her wages docked, too.'

It was time to go; Annie made her solitary way out to the stairs, the other children and young people having already gone.

By the time she reached her lodgings, the anger and defiance had ebbed away once more, and she had to work hard not to cry as she opened the door.

Mrs Otway was just starting on preparations for tea; the fire was so small that the pot would take all of the next three hours to simmer the potatoes and soften the cheap cuts of meat. She looked up as Annie entered, but the words of welcome died on her lips, and 'Bad first day?' was all she came out with.

Annie sat down heavily and told her all about it. 'So, anyway, I might not even have a job by noon tomorrow, and then how will I pay you what I already owe you for two nights? Have you got any chores I could do instead? Or—'

'Don't you worry about that just now,' said Mrs Otway. She pursed her lips. 'Now, if I know anything about that mill, it's that you won't see Mr Carrington himself tomorrow, but one or other of his sons. They might be more sympathetic about a child getting hurt, but best not rely on it. So what you need to do is to persuade them that cutting the girl's hair was the best thing for *them* – that the damage and the loss would have been worse if you hadn't.'

'But won't that then put all the blame back on Alice, for getting her hair caught in the first place?'

Mrs Otway hesitated. 'Well, yes, but . . .'

Annie shook her head. 'It's not fair on her. She's only little.'

Mrs Otway sighed. 'Let's think on, and maybe we'll come up with something.'

Annie thought that she'd better stay busy, so as not to think too much about it all. Besides, she and her landlady would have these three hours to themselves every day, because all of the other girls in the house were over sixteen, so she might as well make herself useful while she could.

By the time nine o'clock came round the whole house had been swept and dusted, and the floor of the kitchen-parlour scrubbed. Annie went out and round into the back yard to empty the bucket of dirty water, and familiarised herself with the location of the pump and the wash house. Laundry was heavy work, and if she could take some of the load off Mrs Otway's frail, bent shoulders when wash day came around, so much the better.

If she was still here next wash day, of course.

* * *

Annie was surprised to find that she needed waking by the knocker-upper the next morning; she must have been so tired that even the worry couldn't keep her awake.

It was with a very heavy tread that she made her way up the hill with the others. Clara squeezed her hand as they parted, and then Annie went in, surprised to be allowed to take up her position by the wall and start work. This was soon explained, however, and it was obvious when she thought about it – of course the mill owner and his sons wouldn't be here at six o'clock in the morning! She was informed that she was to attend their offices at half past ten, and that the overlooker, who had a watch, would tell her when the appointed time arrived.

There was nothing for it, then, but to work. She made it through the first two hours of the shift, survived the breakfast break despite the looks and pats of sympathy from other women that nearly made her break down, and then felt the minutes tick by very slowly when work started up again.

A more cheerful point was that Alice didn't seem to be too much affected by what had happened. She arrived with her hair looking lopsided where it had been chopped, but once one of the older women had tied a cloth around it – very securely indeed, and checked twice – she didn't look any different. She went about her work quietly and efficiently and didn't seem to be too scared of approaching the machines. She did have a bruise coming up on her face, which was odd as Annie didn't recall her actually hitting her head on the frame, but then again Annie had initially been so shocked herself that she probably hadn't been paying attention properly.

She felt a tap on her shoulder. 'It's time.'

Her legs were shaking as she went out into the mill yard and approached the door where she'd seen the Carringtons the other day.

She hesitated. Was she supposed to knock? But this was just an outside door, surely. She pushed it open and peered through, rewarded by the sight of an outer office where various clerks sat at desks. There was a further door on the far side which presumably led through to an inner sanctum where the Carringtons themselves could be found.

Jack was already there. She attempted to give him a smile of solidarity, but he didn't acknowledge it and merely stared at the wall over the top of her head. Hurt, she shrank back a little.

'Shaw, is it? Annie Shaw?' The chief clerk was looking at her over a sheaf of papers.

'Yes, sir.'

He consulted his pocket watch. 'Half past ten exactly. I'll go and tell Mr Theodore that you're both here.'

The clerk knocked deferentially on the far door. A voice called from within and he opened it hardly more than a crack, into which he inserted himself in such an obsequious manner that Annie would have found it amusing, had her own situation not been so serious. There were a few murmured words.

Annie thought she heard Jack make a sound of exasperation at the cringing clerk's back, and she looked at him again, wondering if he was thinking the same as she was. He still wouldn't meet her eye, so she had the leisure to examine him more closely than she otherwise would have done. Her first impression of his age had been about right, she thought; eighteen or nineteen, a year or two younger than Jem. He was taller than Jem and shorter than William, though of a more muscular build than either of them. He'd obviously shaved only that morning, ahead of this meeting – his chin was smooth and there was a small nick on his jawbone. Actually his jaw looked clenched, and Annie wondered if he was as nervous as she was.

As the clerk returned to tell them to enter, she reminded herself that a child's life had been at stake, and that all else paled into insignificance. She held her head high as she stepped over the threshold.

Mr Theodore, the elder of the two sons, was sitting behind an imposing desk, his hands folded on the blotter in front of him and his expression stern. His brother was also there, but he was lounging informally against one of the side walls. The clerk hovered, still bowing and scraping, and was told to remain for a few moments.

Annie should have been thinking about her situation, she knew, but she was struck by the thought that she had never in her life been so close to such gilded beings as these two brothers. Oh, you saw rich people from a distance sometimes in Liverpool, in their carriages as they bowled up and down the streets, or sometimes going into the very fanciest shops, but she'd never seen one at close quarters, and her gaze was curious.

They looked so different from normal people. It wasn't just the very expensive clothes, the clean hands or the waft of cologne – it was the way they just *oozed* health, wealth and self-confidence. Men like this ran the world, and they knew it. Even if they'd tried to disguise themselves as ordinary people they couldn't possibly be mistaken for anything else but what they were.

Annie's examination was cut off by Jack taking a solid stance directly in front of her, so she was mostly looking at his back.

'Howard,' said Mr Theodore, in a tone that Annie didn't much like. 'Here we are again, I see.'

'I didn't ask for it, sir.' Jack's tone was confident – bullish, even – and Annie was astounded. Was he trying to get them in more trouble?

'But with a new companion this time, I see. Friend of yours?'

'Never seen her before yesterday, sir, and I didn't even notice her in the room until the incident happened.'

Annie was both crushed and annoyed. Not noticed her? And to speak in such a dismissive tone – who did he think he was?

Over to the side of the room, the chief clerk was whispering in Mr Frederick's ear. The latter gave a nod, and the clerk was dismissed.

'Well?' Mr Theodore was addressing his brother.

'Robinson says they gave no signs of knowing each other at all while they were waiting outside just now.'

'Very well, I'll take that on credit. Now, Howard, explain to me what your part in all this was.'

Annie listened to a wooden narration of events that was very much to do with the technical specifications of the machine, and hardly mentioned Alice at all.

'And you, girl? How did this all involve you?'

Annie took a step sideways so she could see him properly, and opened her mouth. However, she was forestalled by Jack, again in that infuriating dismissive tone. 'She won't be able to tell you anything, sir. Just a foolish girl like all the rest, and not understanding how these fine machines work.'

What? How dare he!

But Jack was continuing, in what Annie considered was an increasingly patronising tone. 'I can't remember exactly, but I think she had the scissors in her hand already. She probably thought she was doing you and the mill a favour, sir.'

'Is she a good worker?' Mr Theodore was now also talking about Annie as though she wasn't even there, and she felt her temper rise.

'No idea, sir – like I said, I never noticed her before.'

'Hmm.' There was a pause while Mr Theodore considered. He still looked stern.

Annie cast a surreptitious glance over at Mr Frederick, wondering if he might be more sympathetic.

He didn't appear to notice her gaze, but he broke in anyway. 'It all sounds like a storm in a teacup, Theo,' he said, in an easy tone. 'These accidents will happen, especially with children, and no harm has been done other than stopping the machine for ten minutes, which might have happened for a number of other reasons anyway.' Now he looked directly at Annie, with the barest hint of a smile. 'Indeed, quick thinking might even, as this fellow says, have done us a favour. Perhaps the overlooker was a little too alert in sending them both here for such a minor infraction, when we've plenty of other calls on our time.'

Mr Theodore came to a decision. 'Very well. Count yourselves lucky this time, the both of you.'

Relief washed over Annie, and she wondered if that was actually a dismissal when Mr Theodore looked at her properly for the first time. 'Still, it wouldn't do this girl any harm for us to have a little chat about proper behaviour in the mill.' He tapped his fingers on the desk. 'You head off to prepare for the meeting, Fred, if you wish, and I'll follow in due course.'

Annie saw Jack shift uncomfortably.

'You can go, Howard,' snapped Mr Theodore. 'And don't let me see you in here again this side of Christmas, or I won't take such a lenient view next time.'

Jack didn't move. 'Sorry, sir, but I'm under orders to make sure she goes straight back to the spinning room, as they're short-handed in there.'

Was he an idiot? They'd just both been let off, and now he was deliberately antagonising the man who held their jobs and livelihoods in his hand? Annie's temper went up another notch.

Mr Theodore was almost spluttering in his anger at such presumption. 'Under orders? By God, man, who do you think owns this—'

Once again it was Mr Frederick who had some calming words to say, and a reference to his pocket watch, and his brother gave up. 'Oh, all right! Get out of my sight, the both of you.'

Jack nodded, strode to the door and opened it, holding it wide for Annie to pass through first. She did so, still seething at his behaviour. He'd ignored her, patronised her, talked over her, and seemingly brought down even more trouble than there was to start with.

She paused as they left the Carringtons' office, wanting to remonstrate with him about it, but he simply marched past her, and the watching clerks, to exit into the mill yard.

His pace meant that he was well ahead of her by the time she came out, and she ran to catch up. He shook her off, however, and only paused when they were both inside the mill building at the bottom of the staircase leading up to the spinning rooms.

'What did you think you were doing in there?' she hissed, controlling her anger just enough to avoid a public shouting match, though with the noise of the mill it was unlikely that anyone else would be able to hear them anyway.

'I would have thought that was obvious,' came the short reply, enraging her even more.

'What – talking over me like I was a child? Not letting me speak for myself?'

'Yes, all of that.'

He was so infuriating! It almost made her want to scream. 'Next time, just keep your mouth shut and let me speak for myself, whether you've "noticed" my presence or not.'

'Fine.' He made as if to move off.

'Is that it?'

He paused. 'Is that what?'

'No apology, no explanation?'

They were interrupted by several mechanics clattering down the stairs, and he waited until they'd gone. 'No, none.' He took several steps up, but then paused. 'One word of advice, though.'

'Advice? From you? As if I need such a thing.'

He shrugged. 'It's up to you whether you choose to take it. And I've no right to give it to you, really – I'm not your brother or any kind of relative. But just . . . don't end up alone with Mr Theodore if you can help it. Especially not in a confined space. He's got a reputation.'

His face reddened and he turned swiftly away, taking the stairs two at a time.

Well, of all the nerve! Who did he think he was? Telling her what to do. She'd had enough of that at home from all her real brothers and sisters.

Annie began to ascend the stairs, taking them slowly so there was no danger of catching him up even if he paused. He didn't, and was soon out of sight.

Amid the fuming of her temper, a sudden and rather unwelcome thought pierced Annie's mind. It taunted her as she thought of how angry she was with Jack and how annoying he'd been – and as she remembered the expression on his face as he'd looked at her, that chiselled jaw outlined against the light in the stairwell.

No, you're definitely not my brother.

Chapter Six

From that time onwards, Annie tried her hardest to avoid Jack Howard, though whether this was because she was still annoyed with him, or whether it was because she wasn't sure what her own feelings would be if they were to meet again, she couldn't say.

The problem was that as a mechanic he could be called to any part of the mill, rather than staying in one place like everybody else. If you worked in the spinning room you didn't see the weavers, and if you worked in the warehouse you didn't see the spinners, and so on. But a mechanic might appear unexpectedly anywhere at any time, and Annie was continually on the watch for Jack in her determination *not* to see him.

Fortunately there were no more serious incidents in the spinning room, so Annie was able to concentrate on her work. She grew quicker and nimbler every day, much to her own satisfaction and the appreciation of the spinners. She was paid her first week's wages, and then her second, allowing her to hand over what she owed to Mrs Otway and begin her savings. She did have one set of purchases to make urgently, though: she went to the post office counter at the grocer's shop in the village and bought paper and a pencil, and then returned later with a letter to Delilah in which she gave vague details about being in a mill north of Liverpool, not far from the market town of Ormskirk, and saying that everything was fine and nobody needed to worry. She was happy, she was getting on well and she would hope to visit soon.

That last bit was a little white lie, because Annie didn't want to go back to the shop too soon, in case Delilah managed to keep her there and prevent her from returning to the mill. But she'd put it in, agonising over the wording, so that they knew she hadn't forgotten them and didn't want to cut herself off from them forever. Still, she didn't include a return address. And the rest was certainly true: it was all very hard work, and she was tired in the evenings, but she was enjoying her freedom and independence.

Taking the completed letter back to the post office, buying a penny black stamp and affixing it, and then posting the letter in the town's bright-red pillar box was exciting, and Annie felt that she was a real person out in the real world.

To top it all, she hadn't been at the mill much more than three weeks when she was moved to a new and more interesting position. A new group of recruits arrived in the spinning room to be given work as doffers, meaning that many of the others were moved on. Some, like Annie, who were dexterous and efficient, were moved up to jobs requiring greater concentration, while her less nimble-fingered peers were shunted out to even more menial work. Grace was overjoyed to be given charge of her own spinning frame, just like her mother and father, while Annie was moved into the room on the middle floor of the mill to start as a beamer.

This was, she learned, the next stage of the textile production process after spinning. It involved setting up the warp threads, those which ran vertically, on a beam that would then be taken and put on a loom in the weaving shed, ready for a weaver to start work. That sounded quite straightforward until you remembered that there might be as many as five hundred warp threads to set on each beam, and that a single mistake could result in an instant tangle – or, worse, an error that wouldn't be discovered until the weaver had already invested several hours of time on the piece and it had to be cut down and discarded. So Annie was obliged to concentrate hard, and she enjoyed it very much, not least because it involved less running around. The new job didn't mean an immediate pay rise, but there was a promise that if she did well she would be considered for a move to weaving: a significant promotion in terms of both wages and status. She would be sure to tell Delilah all about this in her next letter.

Life wasn't all joy, of course. The new work was interesting, and, after some initial nervousness about the possibility of causing a catastrophe, Annie soon became adept, but there were a few things troubling her, at least two of which had nothing to do with Jack Howard.

The first was Clara. When she'd invited Annie to come away with her to the mill, Annie had imagined that they'd be working together, that they could laugh and joke all day as they went about their tasks. But Clara worked in the weaving shed – the single-storey building with the saw-tooth roof into which she disappeared every morning – and Annie hardly saw her. They spent a little while together first thing, between half past five and six o'clock in the morning (when, it had to be admitted, neither of them was at their best), and then they were apart until nine at night. They had their tea together at their lodgings, but then as like as not Clara wanted to go out, while Annie didn't see the necessity or even want to do so, not every night.

The village was lively on a Saturday afternoon and evening, of course, with all the mill workers finishing early and being paid. On both of her Saturdays so far, Annie had accompanied Clara to the nearest public house, something she thought very daring and which she hadn't even realised was a possibility for women. Back in Liverpool, Frank and Jem, sometimes with Tommy or William, went out for a quiet half-pint, but none of the females in the family would think of joining them. Here, though, half of the customers seemed to be women, and the landlord certainly wasn't going to turn down their money. So Annie sat with a ginger beer and enjoyed the camaraderie, laughing with Clara, but sometimes it got a bit raucous for her taste and she certainly didn't like to see fights breaking out.

The problem was that Clara wanted to do this every night of the week. She was constantly short of money, despite being paid a very generous twelve shillings a week, and she had permanent smudges under her eyes from the endless late nights and early mornings. But, as she said, 'I'm here to live and I'm living, aren't I?' and she never failed to get up for work.

Annie had tried to keep up with her for the first few days, but she wasn't all that keen on some of Clara's drinking companions, especially the ones who stank of gin, which reminded her viscerally of her Pa; and besides, she was determined to save a good portion of her money. She wasn't going to live like a hermit, or in the sheltered way she'd been obliged to at the shop – that wasn't the point of being here – but moderation in everything was the key. So during the week she stayed in with Mrs Otway, went to bed within an hour of finishing tea, and put up with being woken when Clara and Maisie got back late from the pub.

The other thing that was really starting to bother Annie was the question of the workhouse children. Since Hannah had been taken away along with all the others on the day they arrived, Annie hadn't seen her at all. Where was she? And why wasn't she, or any of the others, working alongside the other children?

It might have been easiest just to ask, of course, but there wasn't much leisure for chat while everyone was concentrating on threading their beam correctly. Besides, she didn't know any of the workers in this new room well enough to broach the subject, and it never seemed to be the right time to mention it to Grace's parents during a break, given that they spent little enough time with their own children as it was. So perhaps she should just try to find out herself.

Logically, Annie thought to herself one stifling afternoon, as she tried not to let the sweat on her hands stop her from tying knots properly, they must all work in a part of the mill that she'd never been to herself, otherwise she would have seen them. That cut out the top floor and the middle floor. And they would probably not be in the weaving shed, which was for skilled adults and young people, or the warehouse, which was staffed by strong men. And they certainly wouldn't be in the offices with the clerks.

That still left lots of other locations, for the mill enclosure was huge, but the obvious place to start would be the ground floor of the main building. This, she knew, was where the raw cotton was brought in and prepared before it could be spun, though it was difficult to imagine what small children would be able to do in there – it would be hard physical labour.

At six o'clock that evening, when the whistle sounded, all those in the beaming room who were under sixteen stopped what they were doing and filed out. All of them, that is, except Annie. A couple of the others asked her if she was so deaf already that she hadn't heard it, and teased her when she said she only had half a dozen threads to go on this beam and she'd prefer to finish it now. 'It'll still be there in the morning!', and other such comments, came her way, but they were good-natured and none of them were bothered enough to stop and remonstrate with her. Most of the hands in this room were adult workers, anyway, so it was still three-quarters full once the young people had left and none of them gave Annie a second glance, concentrating as they were on their own beams.

Annie was, as it happened, at the end of the room nearest the door to the stairwell, so she gave it a few minutes until she could hear that everyone from upstairs had passed by. Then she said 'There!' in a tone of satisfaction as she tied her last thread, nodded at her finished work and made her way to the door. She had no need to try to conceal herself as she made her way down the stairs, for she was leaving just as she ought to be. But when she reached the ground floor she did look about her surreptitiously before approaching the heavy door to the carding room and hauling it back, just a tiny bit, so she could apply her eye to the crack.

The scene inside could have come straight from hell.

First there was the incredible, overpowering noise. Then there was the cotton flying around in the air, so much of it that she could barely see, and she started to feel choked by it even from the doorway. The machines in here were *huge* – no wonder they were on the ground floor, they must weigh several tons each – with enormous rollers and spikes, churning and pounding and crushing great wads of cotton. They were being fed by many tiny hands, exhausted little workhouse children having to put their fingers terrifyingly close to the heavy, fast-spinning metal in order to push the cotton through. Annie recalled Alice being slowly drawn into the spinning machine upstairs, and how horrifyingly close she had come to serious injury; well, thank goodness at least that she *had* been up there, for there would be no chance of escape at all from these monsters if anyone lost their concentration for a single moment. She felt sick just thinking about it.

At the far end of the room, from what she could make out through the flying, choking debris, was an even earlier stage in the process. Slightly older children and a few young people of perhaps her own age were lugging huge bales of raw cotton, doubled over with the weight, unpacking them and manually picking through it all to pull out – what? Seeds or dirt, she supposed. And yet others among them were piling the stuff up in layers to bring over to the rolling and crushing machines.

Every single child in the room looked dead on its feet, staggering round almost blind with exhaustion. They were all painfully thin, and most of them were coughing. Why hadn't they finished work for the day? It was well after six o'clock. But there was no sign of a halt. There were some grown men walking about the place, carrying straps of some description, and Annie wondered that they didn't have watches even if it was too loud in here to hear the mill whistle.

Then, as she continued observing the activity, a small girl – not Hannah, whom she couldn't see despite her best efforts – dropped the heavy wad of raw cotton that she was about to push into a rolling machine. Her knees folded under her and she collapsed to the floor. Annie cried out in alarm, but thank heavens the child had fallen backwards, away from the danger. One of the men moved swiftly over to her, and Annie waited for him to pick her up and move her to safety until she recovered.

The man lifted his strap and brought it down on the prone little girl, hard.

Everything in front of Annie suddenly turned red. She yanked the door open further, and was already halfway through it when a hand grabbed her arm and pulled her back. 'I wouldn't do that,' came a voice she recognised.

It was Jack.

'Let go of me!' She struggled to free herself, but he was much stronger and she was drawn away from the door, which slammed shut behind her.

'You can't help, not like that.'

'You didn't see what happened! She was – and then he—'

'I've been in there often enough. But if you go in there, you'll lose your job on the spot and she'll still get beaten – probably even worse than she would have done, for being the cause of a disturbance. How will that help?'

Annie was still furious and upset, but the logic of that did – however unwillingly – get through to her, and she stopped struggling and stood still. 'All right! I won't go in.'

'Good.'

After a few moments of silence she looked at his hand. 'You can let go of my arm now.'

He dropped it like a red-hot poker. 'Sorry.'

'What on earth is going on with those children? How can this be happening?'

He looked around, but they were the only people in the stairwell. 'What is happening,' he said in a savage tone that barely contained his fury, 'is that those children have been *bought* by the mill owners, and the workhouse was glad to sell them so it doesn't have to feed and clothe them any more. They call it an apprenticeship, so the poor little mites don't even get paid – just food and board, if you can even call it that.'

Annie was so horrified that she couldn't speak. A fleeting vision of Abraham passed through her mind. Why, what the workhouse children were going through sounded no better than . . .

But Jack hadn't even finished the litany of horror. 'They work from six until nine, like the adults, with only one break in the middle of the day. They don't get to come out into the mill yard with everyone else – there's a separate one for them out the back, fenced like a cage. Most of them just lie down for the half hour because they're so tired.'

Annie recovered some of her voice. 'But how can this be? And how long do they have to stay?'

'They're supposed to be indentured until they're twenty-one, though almost none of them get that far. They're treated as disposable: they die, from accidents or sickness or choking on all the fly they breathe in, or they get too injured to work. Nobody cares: they just ship the next lot in. Some of them manage to escape and run away, but God knows what happens to them if they fall into even worse hands than they're in here.'

Annie felt tears running down her cheeks.

'But,' said Jack, 'this is going to change, one day. I'm going to make it change.'

The determination and confidence in his tone surprised her. 'How can you do that?'

'I can't, or at least not on my own. But if every worker in every mill would just come together and demand it, the mill owners would have to do something. They can't sack all of us, and they can't run their mills without us. That's what I keep telling everyone.'

'So, we all need to pull together? And ask for better working terms?'

'Not ask – demand. As is our right as fellow humans, not that some of the mill owners see us as such.' His eyes began to light up as he continued. 'Shorter hours, less physically demanding work for women and children, and better attention to safety for everyone. There's no need for people to be losing fingers and eyes, or worse. But the problem is that everyone is too frightened, too keen just to keep their heads down. I can understand that, when they've got families to feed, but they have to look past that, at the bigger picture.'

'Surely, if they knew more about what was going on . . .?'

He snorted. 'They do. Everyone knows. Maybe not every single little detail, but they know these children are here and that they're being badly treated. And they prefer to turn a blind eye.' He stopped, his voice catching as the emotion got to him. 'And someone has to take the bodies away and bury them.'

Annie choked on a sob and he looked at her again, his face softening just ever so slightly. 'Sorry. I didn't mean to—'

A sound came from further up the stairwell. 'Go!' he said, giving her a hard shove towards the outer door. 'Don't be seen with me.'

Annie was so surprised that she did as she was told. As she got to the door she looked back; he had gone a few steps up and turned, as though he was only just coming down, and then he crouched to fumble for something in his tool bag.

Once Annie got outside she tried to calm down. It was a balmy summer evening, just right for wandering with friends and feeling good about the world. But how could she? She was so shocked about what she'd seen that her hands were shaking and cold, and she set off briskly to try to walk some life back into herself.

She was also hurt by the very abrupt manner in which Jack had got rid of her, after spilling out all those words so forcefully. Was he ashamed of having shown so much feeling, or of being seen talking to her? But she refused to dwell on that. How could she possibly feel sorry for herself when all those children were suffering? Poor, poor Hannah. Annie should think of all of them, she knew, but she couldn't help dwelling on the one little girl who had sat next to her for those few hours, and who had fallen asleep in her embrace like a niece or a little sister.

Sister. Good God, what had Meg gone through during her time in the workhouse, if this was the way they treated children? And her friend Sally? Had there been a real danger that she could have ended up like this?

A wave of dizziness rolled over her, and she paused for a moment in the street in case she was going to vomit. She did not, however, and made it safely home. It was stifling in the house even with the door propped open and no fire burning – they were eating cold meals in all this heat just at the moment – but Annie paid that no mind. Giving Mrs Otway only the briefest of greetings, she headed straight upstairs to her sweltering room.

At least there she could be alone, and she gave way to the tears that she'd been holding in. She wept for Hannah and for the other workhouse children. She also cried tears of shame at the way she'd complained and been so ungrateful about her own upbringing: how could she possibly have been so *selfish*? Complaining about being looked after and cared for! Then she sobbed some more as she thought of her family and how she'd let them all down, and finally she shed tears of helplessness about how bleak and unalterable the situation was.

Eventually there were no more tears to fall, and Annie lay back on the bed in the stifling attic with her chest heaving.

After a while she sat up. *This is going to change, one day. I'm going to make it change.*

She got out of bed and reached under it, drawing out her as-yet meagre savings. She began to count the money, wondering how much it would cost to buy a child out of an apprenticeship.

* * *

It was during the breakfast break the next morning that Annie made her first small attempt to make a difference.

She was standing with Grace and her family as they all turned their faces up to the sun in the fresh morning air. Luke and Nora, as Annie had been invited to call Grace's parents ('Because we all work together, after all') were finishing off their bread and treacle.

'I was just thinking,' began Annie, casually, 'that it would be nice to see my little friend Hannah again. Do you know if the workhouse apprentices are allowed to have visitors?'

Nora made a sympathetic noise. 'Poor dears.'

'Now, don't be like that,' said Luke. 'It's difficult for them, I know, and we might wish matters were different, but they aren't and that's just the way things are.'

'They're not terribly well treated, from what I've heard,' continued Annie. 'Which is why I'd like to check up on her.'

Luke shook his head. 'Now, don't you be saying things like that, not out loud where anyone might hear you.'

'So you don't think they're not well treated?'

He looked nervous. 'That's not what I meant.' He gave a little cough. 'You just . . . what I mean is, you've got a good job here, and doing well, and you don't want to start making a name for yourself as a troublemaker with that kind of talk.'

This was not a good start. If even raising the subject was deemed to be 'troublemaking', how would she ever . . .

'You take that Jack Howard, now,' continued Luke, nodding at where Jack stood completely by himself on the other side of the yard. 'He's always on about that sort of thing, and forming Friendly Societies, or unions, or whatever you call them, and he's lucky to still be here.'

'Why is he still here, then? I mean, if he causes so much bother and people don't like it?'

'It's because he's a mechanic,' broke in Nora, laying a calming hand on her husband's arm. 'Looking after all the machines in a mill is skilled work, and there aren't many men who can do it. Any normal mill hand started talking like that, and especially a woman or a young girl like you or Grace – well, we're two a penny and we'd be out of here before we could even shut our mouths.'

'You have to be so careful,' added Luke. 'Now, I know you've no parents here at the mill with you, but if you did then I'm sure they'd tell you to just keep your head down and concentrate on your own work. Why, just being known as a *friend* of someone like that Howard boy is enough to lose you your job for the slightest thing. It's happened to some good workers. Why do you think nobody'll go near him?'

Annie looked over at the solitary figure, remembered the scene in the Carringtons' office, and realised that she owed Jack an apology and herself a large slice of humble pie.

The effort of so much talking had made Luke cough harder, and he was by now hawking and spitting into his handkerchief, so Annie didn't have the heart to pursue the subject further.

She wasn't put off, though, and when the dinner break came around she decided on bolder action. If the workhouse children had a separate yard, it would make sense that it was close to where they were working, so perhaps it was around at the back of the main mill building. Annie had never had cause to explore round there, because she didn't need to; she arrived through the front gate and followed everyone in through the main door.

At dinner, therefore, she drifted through the crowd until she was at the very edge of the building, and then slipped round the side. If anyone asked, she would say that she was new and was looking for the privies, a row of which stood at one end of the yard. Fortunately she heard no shouts, so she was able to make her way around to the back of the mill. And there it was: an area surrounded by a high wooden fence that encompassed, by her calculations, the place where the far door of the carding room would be.

She crept closer. The fence wasn't terribly well made and there were plenty of gaps to which she could apply an eye. She was now past the point where she could come up with any kind of plausible excuse for what she was doing, so she'd just have to trust to luck. *Here goes.*

Her heart wrenched when she looked through the fence, for it was just as Jack had said: exhausted, sick-looking children collapsed all over the place. A very few were sitting in little groups making desultory attempts to chat, but most were just lying down in the sun or the shade, many of them clearly asleep.

Annie moved a few yards in order to be nearer to a little knot of girls who were sitting with their backs against the fence. 'Psst!'

They jumped and squeaked in alarm.

'It's all right,' Annie said, in a low voice. 'I'm one of the mill workers. I'm looking for a girl called Hannah, who came here from the workhouse last month. About nine years old. Do you know her?'

They whispered to each other, then one of them pointed. 'Over there.'

Annie saw a small figure curled up on her side. Hannah was about ten yards away, but Annie didn't want to risk shouting. 'Can you fetch her? Please?'

Another whispered consultation. 'Will we get in trouble?'

Annie wanted to reassure the girls, but having already seen some of the injustices prevalent in the mill, she couldn't in all honesty do so. Fortunately, at least, the men with straps did not appear to be patrolling out here – presumably they left the children to their own devices while they went for dinner. 'Just wander over as though you're going to talk to her normally, and then get her to come back and join you here.'

Much to Annie's relief, this was successfully achieved.

Hannah came close to the fence, and Annie had a full view of her white face and dead eyes. 'Who are you?'

'It's me, Annie. Do you remember, on the day you came here, I was sitting next to you in the wagon?'

A spark of recognition. 'You said I could stay with you.'

'I know, and I'm sorry you couldn't. I didn't realise you'd all be taken away separately. Is it . . .' she tailed off, aware that there was no positive way to end that question. Of course it wasn't all right. 'Listen. I'm going to try to get you out of here, to free you from your apprenticeship, but it's going to take some time. In the meantime, is there anything I can do to help?'

That lifeless, empty little gaze met hers through the gap in the fence. 'Why do you care? Nobody's ever cared before.'

'Because . . .' There was no time for complicated explanations. 'I just wanted you to know that you had a friend.'

Hannah's eyes grew suddenly wide, and then her face crumpled into tears.

'I have to go now, but I'll come back whenever I can.' Annie turned away, her own eyes stinging. All the suffering the little girl had endured with such stoicism, and it was one tiny act of kindness that made her cry.

Somehow, and it must have been because the heavens were smiling on her for a good deed, Annie got back to the mill yard unobserved, and just before the whistle went to signal the resumption of work.

During that whole afternoon, it wasn't just her hands that were at work; her mind was busy too.

Chapter Seven

The summer wore on, and Annie grew frustrated at her lack of progress. She saved every penny that she could, of course, but she still didn't have any firm idea of the process by which she might be able to release Hannah from her apprenticeship. The only mill worker she felt that she might approach to ask directly was Jack, but he seemed determined to avoid her. She now understood why, and she knew she wouldn't be able to do anything for Hannah if she lost her own job, but still his deliberate absence was unhelpful in the present circumstances.

It had struck her more than once that the other person who might know, or who would be able to find out, would be her brother William. He was so clever, and he read the newspapers and kept up to date with current affairs – he was bound to be able to find a way.

But if Annie were to write and ask him, it would mean giving a return address so that he could reply, and she still wasn't quite confident that Delilah wouldn't come storming north and drag her back to Dale Street and 'safety'. So she confined herself, in her now regular letters, to a sort of one-way communication about how everything was going well and she was enjoying life.

She had managed to slip round the back of the mill a few more times, though she tried not to do it too often as it would do neither her nor Hannah any good if she were to be caught. She almost was, once; a weeping mill girl ran past her from somewhere further round the back of the building, and Annie only just had time to duck into a corner before Mr Theodore followed. Thankfully he was walking quite quickly and didn't stop to look about him, for her hiding place was meagre – and if he'd spotted her she'd have been out of a job before the end of the day.

The most useful and practical thing Annie could do in the short term, she thought, was to try to smuggle extra food through the gaps in the fence, but this was extremely difficult to disguise. Sidling out the main yard and round the building was difficult enough without having to hide bulky pieces of bread. She had managed to address this partially by visiting the grocer in town and buying small items such as biscuits and sweets, which could be easily concealed and then shared by the children once she could get it to them. It wasn't exactly the proper food that such starving mites needed, but then again she could hardly be pushing a cooked hot stew through the fence, could she? The main thing was to try to keep Hannah's spirits up and give her some hope, and the kind words and occasional barley sugar seemed to help. Recently Annie had thought she could detect at least a glimmer of life in Hannah's expression.

In her attempt to learn more about the situation of the workhouse children, Annie had tried asking a few diffident questions around the place, always casually and always to different fellow workers, so that nobody would put two and two together. She had gleaned a few pieces of information about how the apprentice system worked and how the children lived, but the overwhelming response was one of apathy: it was a terrible shame that those poor little nippers were being treated like that, but it was just the way of things and nobody could do anything about it.

What she really needed to do was to talk to Jack. But how? He avoided her at work, not even meeting her gaze when she tried to catch his eye from a distance across the yard. He was never in the pub, not even on a Saturday night. She didn't know where he lived –

and, besides, she couldn't possibly visit the lodgings of a single man anyway. It would be all over the mill by the following day, and she'd get what the other women called 'a bad name for herself'.

In between all this, she continued to work hard and well. It was a boom time for cotton production, that's what everyone kept saying, and new hands were arriving at the mill every couple of weeks. They could hardly keep up with demand, and Annie was sure that the evening whistles sometimes went off late. The little clock on Mrs Otway's shelf was ancient, but it kept very good time; and by its hands Clara and the others often didn't return home, after their five-minute walk from the mill, until nearly half past nine.

The expanding capacity of the mill certainly worked in Annie's favour. The new workers all needed to start on the simpler jobs, meaning that anyone who had been employed for even a few months was considered an old hand and moved on – and it was one morning towards the end of September when she was told to stop work on her beam and report to the weaving shed.

She could hardly believe it. Weaving! A pay rise to ten shillings a week *and* the opportunity to work alongside Clara. Annie dropped what she was doing, to be replaced at her beam immediately by a former doffer, and hurried off.

Unfortunately she then ran out of the door so fast that she cannoned into Mr Frederick, who was just about to enter. She was profuse in her apologies, but her luck held; he laughed it off, said that no harm was done and asked her where she was going at that time of day.

'To the weaving shed, sir – I've been told I'm being moved there!'

He looked her up and down, with a serious expression. 'You're quite young to have that sort of responsibility.' For one moment she thought he might be about to countermand her precious promotion, and her heart was in her mouth, but then he nodded. 'Which means that you must be good at what you do, so well done.'

He disappeared into the room she'd just left, and she continued on her way, walking on air.

* * *

The weaving shed was, as she'd been warned, even louder than the spinning room.

Annie hovered in the doorway, trying to see if there was any particular person she should report to. Most of the weavers seemed to be women, but there were one or two men at frames and others walking about who were inspecting the cloth everyone produced. Of course, the overlookers would all be men.

One of them saw her and came over. Thankfully the noise was marginally less here by the door, so she could hear him speak. 'Yes? What do you want?'

'I was told to report here to start work. I've come from the beaming room.'

He looked her up and down, dismissively. 'Name?'

'Annie Shaw.'

'And you're under sixteen, are you? No untruths, now – I can easily check with the mill records.'

'I wouldn't think of lying! Yes, I'm fourteen.'

He grunted. 'And you've been, what? A doffer and a beamer? That's how girls usually get here.'

'Yes.' Annie's high spirits were waning already, and she tried to pull them back. 'I'm looking forward to starting in here,' she said, brightly.

He grunted again. 'Well, we'll see about that. Got any relatives in here? Mother, aunts?'

'No.'

'All right, we'll have to find you . . . yes, she'll do. Follow me.'

The weaving frames were very large, and there was minimal space in the alleys in between. As she followed the overlooker down the narrow gaps, Annie was glad of the lap apron that stopped her skirts spreading out too much. As with everywhere in the mill, there were small children crawling about under the machines, and Annie hoped that they too were skilled and experienced workers rather than new hands, so their chances of accident were less.

The overlooker stopped by an old woman who was hunched over as she scuttled between several looms. Annie was surprised to see someone of that age still working; she wasn't quite as elderly as Mrs Otway, but there can't have been much in it.

The overlooker bellowed in her ear. 'New girl for you to train!'

Annie was examined by a pair of very bright, lively eyes, and she received a nod. 'Just watch to start with!' the woman called out, matching her words with gestures as she pointed at Annie's eyes and then at the loom.

Annie did. To start with it all seemed hideously complicated, but as she observed closely things began to make more sense. The loom was powered, like other machines in the mill, by a series of belts and shafts that ran overhead. The warp threads were tied round a beam – she certainly knew what that was – and then they ran lengthways, with the weft being woven from side to side, the cotton thread wound round a shuttle. It was the shuttles all over the room that were making much of the noise, rattling and banging continuously from one side to another, shooting through the frame as different layers of warp thread were raised and lowered automatically.

One of the shuttles on the loom was running out of thread. The woman picked up a new full one and stood ready, and the next time the old one reached one side, she dexterously flipped it out of the way, the last tiny bit of thread trailing off, and set the new one running. She had done it all without interrupting the rhythm of the machine.

Annie suspected that her hands, young and nimble as they were, would take some while to match the ease with which her instructor's gnarled ones had achieved the feat.

The woman stood close and cupped her hands around Annie's ear. 'Always try to make sure you fit a new shuttle at the end of a run – don't let the thread run out halfway across. You can always tie up the loose end at the side, but if your join's in the middle the overlooker will count it as a flaw and your wages will be docked.'

Annie nodded to show that she'd understood. The woman moved to the neighbouring loom and, once more gesturing to Annie to watch, did the same again. Then she pushed a shuttle into Annie's hand and pointed to another, flying across the machine, which was running low.

Terrified lest she should make a mistake and lose money – or cause her companion to lose money – Annie took a deep breath. *You can do this*, she told herself. And, just she had done on her first day in the spinning room, she made it through this first test without error. The old woman smiled and nodded.

Annie spent the rest of the morning shadowing, watching a real expert at work. Had her instructor been a man she would probably be an overlooker by now, but instead the elderly woman used her well-honed skills to work on no fewer than six looms at once.

It was a huge relief to Annie's ears and head when the whistle sounded for the dinner break and the looms came to a halt. With the silence ringing in her ears almost louder than the machinery had done, she followed the others outside.

'Annie!' That was Clara's voice, and she ran over to hug her. 'Oh, I knew you'd make it into here one day – and how quickly you've done it!' Annie's cheerfulness returned, and she slid her arm through Clara's as they queued up at the butty shop.

Once she had her bread and dripping she looked around for Alice and Charlie, as she usually did. Paul had apparently not 'forgotten' to give them any dinner money on that first day months back, but rather expected them to work all day without food so as not to spend precious pennies. As the head of his family that was his decision to make, but Annie did think it was a little harsh, especially when the children were actually earning their own money. But perhaps he was renting somewhere that didn't leave much spare – after all, he worked as an unskilled labourer in the warehouse, and children's wages were low.

She spotted them, and was delighted to see that they were both already tucking into slices of bread – a gift from Nora, no doubt, who was just walking away from them and back to her own family, with Luke tutting and shaking his head at her.

Clara spent the break in high spirits, chatting away about what Annie could expect in the weaving shed. 'And which overlooker will you be under, over on that side of the room? Oh, Amos Potter, I suppose.' She made a face. 'Well, you'll just have to make the best of it. I'm sure you won't make too many mistakes once you get going.'

The afternoon's work began. Back when she'd been doffing, Annie had started to work on her own account after only a very minimal amount of training, but this was much more complicated and she was glad to be told only to shadow and assist again for the rest of the day. Changing the shuttles on a machine that was already set up wasn't too bad, but when a piece of the calico cloth was finished and cut down, and taken away for inspection, the loom had to be set up again – and that really *was* a complex operation.

'This grade of cotton is called Middle Orleans,' came the cracked voice in her ear. 'It's from America and it's the standard that we work on most. Sea Island, also from America, is the best, but we get that less often, and they wouldn't set a beginner to it anyway, as it's expensive.'

Annie watched her instructor's deft movements as the empty loom was made ready and then came to life again, the shuttle beginning its loud journey back and forth. 'With the lower grades you have to be extra careful, because the fibres are short and they break easily, which means you have knots in your piece.'

That idea caused Annie to look over to the bench at the side of the room, where Amos, the overlooker, was examining the work of a couple of young women. He berated the first, who looked about Annie's age or a year or two older, shouting something in her face as she flinched. He pointed at what were presumably defects in the weaving, before dismissing her back to her loom with an angry gesture. Annie saw her wipe away a tear as she passed.

The second girl was in her early twenties, Annie thought. A more experienced weaver than the other, no doubt, but her reception was no better: a red-faced tirade that made her face fall. She, too, was sent away, but, as she turned, Amos gave her a scornful push and then slapped her hard on the bottom. Annie saw her pained expression and the deep flush of red that came to her cheeks, but she didn't retort or even react at all – just walked away quietly back to her place. Annie was full of indignation on the girl's behalf, and a thought shot into her own mind: *He'd better not try that on me, job or no job, or we'll all find out just how well Sam taught me to throw a punch.*

* * *

The rest of the week passed in something of a blur. With her break times taken up by Clara and the other girls she introduced, Annie had no opportunity to slip around to the workhouse children's yard, and nor did she get much time to talk to Alice and Charlie, though she did make sure they were fed every day. Their bruises were getting more noticeable, and when she managed a few moments with them at the end of one dinner break, she joked that they should be getting less, not more, clumsy as they went on at the mill.

Charlie opened his mouth to say something, but Alice elbowed him in the ribs. 'That's right,' she said.

'We're clumsy, aren't we, Charlie? Though we have managed not to get caught in the machines again, like I did that first day.'

Annie was pleased to see that the cloth round her head was wound and secured tightly, and said so.

'Well, yes,' began Charlie, 'but that's because—' Another elbow, accompanied this time by a sharp look, brought him up short.

Annie was about to enquire further when the whistle blew, and they had to hurry off in their separate directions.

There wasn't a dinner break the next day because it was Saturday: when the whistle went at noon everyone queued up for their wages and then left. Annie was still in line when she saw Alice and Charlie hurrying off, their coins clutched in their hands. Off to have a proper dinner, she hoped; most mill hands ate better on Saturdays and Sundays than they did the rest of the week.

'So are you coming this afternoon, then, or not?' asked Clara.

'I'm still thinking about it.'

The event in question was a Michaelmas fair in the nearby town of Ormskirk. It was a big occasion, apparently, one that drew in visitors from all the smaller local towns and villages every year. There would be games and amusements, stalls selling wares, and tents of food and drink. Such was the interest from their little mill village that a carrier was putting on several wagons, with a penny fare to be transported there and back.

Annie had been tempted to go, because it would be nice to do something for an afternoon that wasn't all work – after all, that was why she'd wanted a job of her own, wasn't it? To have money and the freedom to spend it? But she was also aware that her savings were coming along quite nicely, and if she went out to the fair she would end up spending some of it. She supposed that she could go just for the experience, laying out the penny for the transport, and then look round without buying anything, but that would probably be even less fun than not going in the first place. She hadn't managed to talk to Jack yet, so she still didn't know how much she might need in order to buy Hannah out of her apprenticeship. The sensible thing to do would be to stay at home, help Mrs Otway out with a few chores and perhaps even put her feet up for a while. The trip did sound like fun, but she couldn't justify it to herself. Could she?

She prevaricated all the way home, Clara talking excitedly about the gingerbread she was going to buy, and how last year there was a tent where many different varieties of local beer were on offer.

They reached the house. Annie dutifully paid over what she owed for rent and food, and then went upstairs to stow the rest of her coins in the box under the bed.

'So, are you coming then, or not?' asked Clara, impatiently. She had the entirety of her wages, minus what she'd paid to Mrs Otway, wrapped up in a handkerchief and ready to go. 'The wagons will be picking up from the corner any minute now.'

Annie still wavered. Of course, she *had* just been paid those extra two shillings, thanks to her promotion to the weaving shed . . . but no, she owed it to Hannah to get her out of her torment as soon as possible. She might not know how that was to be done, but she did know that it would cost.

They were both drawn to the window by the sound of rumbling traffic. Three carts were making their way past, the first one already half full of those who lived further down the hill.

'Well, I'm off,' said Clara. 'Last chance?' She was already at the top of the stairs.

Annie looked down at the wagons and saw that one of the passengers in the first one was Jack Howard.

Quickly, she dropped her wages in her box, then picked out a penny and four sixpences and stuffed them in her apron pocket. 'Wait for me!'

Chapter Eight

The girls ran down and out into the street, joining the crowd that pressed around the wagons once they stopped.

Annie hung back a little, because she knew exactly where the last space would be once everyone had crammed in. And there it was. 'Well, if it's the only seat,' she called out loudly, 'it'll have to do.' She pushed her way up the middle of the vehicle, picking her way over everyone's feet and legs, until she reached the front, where Jack was sitting directly behind the driver's seat with a gap between him and the next person on the bench. Boldly, Annie sat in it.

Neither of them said anything until the wagon was in motion. Everyone else was chatting excitedly, so there was little danger of them being overheard.

'All right,' he said in a low voice. 'You can sit there while we're away from the mill, but just keep acting as though you've no wish to know me once we get there.'

She looked at him quizzically. 'I wouldn't have had you down as the sort of man to go out for enjoyment to a fair.'

He laughed. 'I'm not. There's some very interesting engineering work going on in Ormskirk, making agricultural machinery, and I'm off to look at it and then go to a talk later this evening. It'll be after you all set off home, and I'll walk back, so nobody will need to force themselves to sit by me.'

His tone was dry. He always seemed so self-sufficient, but now Annie wondered if it really did upset him to be shunned all the time.

She shook her head. Never mind that. She had a few brief miles now to make the most of the opportunity, so best not waste it.

How to begin? 'I need to ask you something,' she said, cautiously, keeping her voice low. Luckily, nobody was paying them the slightest bit of attention, so she continued. 'About the workhouse children.'

She felt him tense next to her on the bench. 'What about them?'

'Do you know how much it would cost to buy a child out of her apprenticeship, and how I would go about it?'

'Her? Do I take it you're thinking about one particular child?'

Annie began to outline her plan, but she'd hardly started when she saw he was shaking his head. 'What – you don't think it's possible?'

'Of course it's possible, but what good will it do to rescue one child? The others will still be there.'

'Well, yes, I know, but . . .'

'What we have to do is get everyone together in order to stop the whole system, to get them all out.'

'And how long will that take? And what if it isn't even possible?'

He turned to look at her, and she noticed what a nice shade of dark brown his eyes were. 'What time do you stop work at the mill, Monday to Friday?'

She was taken aback by the change of subject. 'Six o'clock. You know that.'

'And why do you think that is? Why do you not work until nine, like the adults?'

Was this some kind of trick question? 'Because I'm under sixteen.'

'Yes. And the Factory Act says that nobody under sixteen can work more than sixty hours a week, or twelve in a day.'

'The Factory Act?'

He nodded and continued, becoming more animated than she'd ever seen him. 'It was years ago, but it came about because a group of people got together and demanded better conditions, and their demands got all the way to parliament. The law was changed, and the mill owners have to abide by it. That's the sort of change we can bring about, if we try.'

'But that would take a long time.'

'Of course it will. But we can win in the end.'

'And what does Hannah do in the meantime?'

He paused. 'Well . . .' then he recovered himself. 'But like I say, getting one child out is neither here nor there. It has to be all of them.'

'So, because I can't help everyone, you think I shouldn't help anyone? Is that what you're saying? I should just give up and abandon her to her fate, when I could do something about it if I tried?'

He was silent. Annie wondered if she'd offended him, but she didn't care; the subject was too important. And yet she *did* want him to understand, to be on her side.

After some while, Jack spoke in a more conciliatory tone. 'Do you know, I've never thought of it exactly like that.' He gave her another direct look. '"Because I can't help everyone, I shouldn't help anyone" . . . You've made me think differently.'

'And . . . do you mind that?'

'Not at all. No, I've learned something from you, and we should all strive to learn, all the time.'

'So, you'll help me find out what to do?'

He sighed. 'All right.' He thought for a moment. 'I would guess that something that might make it easier is if you can say she's related to you.'

'She isn't, but I don't mind saying so if it helps her to get out of there.' Lying was wrong, but what was happening to Hannah and the others was a lot more wrong, in Annie's opinion.

'All right. So, let it be known that you think a cousin of yours has been put with the orphans – well, that she is an orphan but that she isn't completely without family. Do it gradually, and while you're sorting that out, I'll see if I can find out about money and paperwork.'

'Thank you. I mean it – I'm grateful. I do want to save them all, but if I can help just one in the meantime, then that's something.'

He looked away, out at the passing countryside, and it was some while before he said anything else. Indeed, they were approaching Ormskirk now; Annie could see some of the tents of the fair in a field.

When he did speak again, his tone was abrupt. Not unkind, mind, but sounding as though he found it difficult to get the words out. 'I knew there was something about you. That you were worth keeping in the mill. It was that very first day.'

She thought back. 'Because I helped you keep Alice out of the machine?'

He paused again. 'Partly that, yes. But it was even before that. I saw you out the window during the break, when I was looking at the cracks in the glass.'

She tried to recall what he might have seen.

'You took your own dinner and you gave it to those children. Because they had nothing to eat, you gave them all of it. That's when I knew.'

For a moment she was too taken aback to answer. By the time she regained her voice the wagon was coming to a halt and he was already on his feet, climbing over everyone to jump out the vehicle at the rear. He walked off without looking back.

* * *

The fair was just as exciting as Clara had promised. They walked arm in arm up and down its streets, looking at the brightly coloured swing-boats and watching the games, listening to the music and sniffing the air as they passed the food stalls. Then Clara and some of the other mill hands wanted to visit the tent selling beer, which didn't appeal to Annie, so she continued wandering round on her own. She couldn't get lost as long as she stayed within the confines of the field, and she knew where the wagons would be setting off from at dusk, so there was neither concern nor hurry. She could take a few hours to enjoy herself and have some leisure to think.

They hadn't had time for their dinner before they came away, so Annie bought a hot pie and ate it as she strolled. She didn't waste money on any games or competitions – although she did feel that she could probably knock a turnip off a pole by throwing a ball at it rather better than most of the other women who were trying – but her attention was caught by the several gingerbread stalls, all promising the best and most authentic version of the traditional local recipe. A piece big enough to share with Mrs Otway when she got home was soon tucked away, and Annie completed her purchases for the day at the sweet stall. A quarter of lemon drops, divided into two paper bags, went into her pocket: one for Alice and Charlie, and the other to pass through the fence to Hannah, for her to share out as best she could with some of the other workhouse children.

As Annie walked, her mind was at work. She thought about Jack's suggestion that she try to claim

Hannah as a relative, which gave her a new idea. Could she possibly . . .? Well, it was a bold resolution, but it was certainly worth a try. She would make the attempt tomorrow.

She almost laughed at herself when she thought of it. Here she was, the youngest of the family, always the one to be looked after and cossetted, moving away to find her own freedom – and immediately becoming the 'big sister' to three smaller children. But she'd had no choice, really, and she wouldn't want it any other way. One thing that life with Delilah had taught her was that family came in many different guises, and that a bit of love went a long way, especially to those who weren't used to it, like Sally and Abraham. What would Delilah or Meg say if they were here now, if they knew what hardship Hannah, Alice and Charlie were suffering? What would Sam do? The answer, she was confident, was that they would do exactly what she was doing, although possibly rather more efficiently. Still, she was making her way and trying her hardest, and she thought the rest of the family would approve.

The afternoon passed pleasantly, and it didn't seem long before the crowds thinned and the stall-holders began to pack up. The only part of the fair remaining crowded – and by now rather raucous – was the beer tent, and Annie gave it a wide berth as she made her way back to the point where the wagons were to pick them up. There would be no Jack to sit next to on the way back, of course, but she could think of him – *of what he had said*, she corrected herself – while she chatted to Clara and the other girls.

But where was Clara? The mill hands appeared in dribs and drabs until the wagons were nearly full, and still she didn't return. Annie asked some of the others who'd been in the beer tent, but all they said was that she'd left them about an hour ago in the company of a man, ignoring their efforts to tell her that she'd already had a bit too much to drink and that she should stay with them.

The wagon driver became impatient, saying that if she didn't turn up in the next few minutes then he was going to leave anyway, because he wanted to be back in the mill village by the time it was properly dark.

Annie scanned the now rapidly emptying field, worry beginning to gnaw at her. She was just wondering if she should jump down herself and go to look when relief flooded over her. 'There she is!'

Clara was bidding farewell to a man Annie didn't recognise, and now he was swaggering off while she began to weave her way back to the wagon, the only one of the three still remaining. 'Well, she's enjoyed herself a bit too much,' came a comment from the crowded benches. 'Had one too many of those local ales.' This was followed by some rather more ribald remarks that made Annie's ears burn.

Trying to ignore them, she clambered to the back of the wagon. Clara seemed incapable of getting in, and the driver had to come round and shove her up. She landed, inelegantly, on the floor of the vehicle. 'Keep her right at the back,' the driver instructed Annie. 'If she's going to be sick on the way, make sure she does it out on the road and not inside, otherwise she'll be cleaning it up herself when we get back.' He returned to his seat, and soon they were in motion.

Clara seemed perfectly happy, smiling at everyone and putting her arms round Annie while Annie tried to persuade her not to sing. She supposed she should be aggrieved at being deserted almost as soon as they'd got to the fair, but she wasn't – she was just upset that Clara would do this to herself and risk the public criticism. Still, it was her own choice, and Annie would look after her no matter what happened. Clara was her friend and honorary sister, and always would be.

As luck would have it, they were all the way home and safe in their bedroom before Clara vomited, and Annie had enough warning to be able to get the chamber pot in place in good time. She held Clara's head and stroked her hair until she was sure it was all over.

'Ah, you do look after me,' said Clara, in a maudlin tone.

'That's what friends are for,' replied Annie, gently, patting her shoulder.

She took the pot round to the privies in the yard, tipped out the contents, rinsed it under the pump, and found her way – familiar by now – back inside in the dark. Clara was already snoring, but Annie didn't mind. She didn't really want to share the details of what she planned to try out tomorrow, because there was plenty of potential for it all to go very wrong.

Chapter Nine

'You want to *what*?'

The man's voice was incredulous, so Annie repeated herself, keeping her tone firm and confident. 'I want to take my cousin out for the afternoon. It's Sunday, so I know she's not at work.'

Jack had advised that Annie should take her time about the business of letting it be known that Hannah was her cousin, but Annie had decided to take the bull by the horns. She had therefore made her way to the building that housed the children's dormitory, banged on the door and told the man who answered it that one of the apprentices was her cousin, and that she wished to take her out for a walk. The man's flabbergasted expression told her that this had probably never happened before. But, as Annie thought to herself, nothing ventured, nothing gained. The worst he could say was 'no', and she'd be no worse off.

He was hesitating now, clearly not sure how to respond to such an unusual request.

Annie had come prepared. 'Look, I work at the mill – my name's Annie Shaw and you can check that. And I'll also pay a deposit against her safe return, if you like.'

'A deposit?'

'Yes.' Annie took out the three shillings that she'd brought with her. 'Take these while we're out. You can be sure I'll bring her back, because I don't want to lose that, and I certainly don't want to lose my job and end up on the streets, which would also happen if she came out with me and didn't return.'

A gleam of interest showed in the man's eye. 'All right then. You can take her out for a few hours. Back before six, mind, as that's when they have their supper on Sundays, and I won't be held responsible for her being missing.'

'Agreed.' Annie handed over the money.

'You wait there, and I'll have her fetched.'

It wasn't long until a very bemused Hannah appeared. Her face began to light up with hope when she saw Annie, and Annie, kicking herself, had to rush to tell her that it was only for the afternoon. 'I will get you out of here permanently as soon as I can, but today you'll have to go back, I'm sorry.'

'It's all right.' Hannah was initially composed when she heard the bad news, but then she seemed overcome simply by the act of walking out of the mill gates, and her eyes were wide as they made their way down the hill and into the village. A few people out on the streets gave them strange looks, as the little girl was clearly dressed in a shapeless workhouse garment, but Annie either bade them good afternoon or simply stared them down, and they soon returned to their own concerns.

'I'm not sure there's much to show you,' said Annie. 'All the shops are shut on Sundays, of course, but we can walk up and down the streets as much as we like, and then I'll show you where I live.'

The further they got into the village, the more Hannah shrank against Annie's side. At first Annie was at a bit of a loss, but then it struck her that Hannah had probably never walked about freely like this, or at least not since she'd been sent to the workhouse in the first place. Perhaps she was intimidated. 'Would you like to hold my hand?' she offered. As Hannah took it, Annie added, 'And maybe you can tell me a little bit about yourself. How long have you been in the workhouse?'

This, again, seemed to overwhelm Hannah, and she spoke in fits and starts. Her story, once Annie had put the pieces together, was both short and tragic. She'd never set foot outside the workhouse until she was brought to the mill, and the outside world was strange and frightening. She'd been born in the forbidding institution on Brownlow Hill, to a mother who had arrived destitute and already in labour, and who had died shortly after her baby was born. Hannah didn't know much about her mother except that the staff had later said she was wicked: she'd been in domestic service but had 'got herself into trouble' and been sacked. She'd probably tried to find another place, but who would hire a woman in her condition? So she'd ended up in the workhouse as a last resort.

Hannah had no idea who her father was, and neither did anyone else, and nobody had ever come to look for her. Her surname was Smith, but that had only been given to her because nobody knew what it really should be, as her mother had died before she could be properly registered as an inmate.

In short, Hannah had nothing and nobody. Annie grasped her hand more tightly.

'Girls normally get sent out to work when they're fourteen,' Hannah continued, in a flat tone that contained an astonishing lack of self-pity, given what she'd just related. 'But they said they needed smaller children for the mill, so any of us who were orphans with no family at all were told we were going. They said it would be a grand life, that we'd learn a trade, get schooling as well, and then when we were older we'd be taken on and earn a wage.'

'But . . . it hasn't worked out like that, has it?'

Hannah shrugged. 'I didn't expect it to.'

There was such emptiness in her voice that Annie felt her heart begin to bleed again. Conscious that it wouldn't do either of them any good if she broke down in tears in the street, she cleared her throat and changed the subject. 'Look, here's the grocer's shop. If you look in at the window you can see the glass jars at the back – see them? That's where I get your barley sugar and biscuits from.'

It might have been coincidence, but Hannah's stomach gave a growl.

'Well, the afternoon's getting a bit chilly. Let's go back to my lodgings for our last hour, shall we?'

Hannah shrank again. 'They won't want me there.'

'It's all right. I told Mrs Otway what I was doing this afternoon and she said it would be fine. She said we could have a cup of tea together!'

The answering gasp of excitement spoke volumes.

They reached the house and Annie pushed open the door. Mrs Otway was on her own in the little kitchen-parlour, the other girls either out or upstairs in their bedrooms. She was just lighting the fire, pushing small pieces of kindling into it until she was satisfied they'd caught, then adding a few coals and turning to where the ingredients for a pan of scouse were set out on the table.

She saw them. 'Come in! Come in out the cold, and shut that door behind you.'

Hannah seemed frozen on the threshold. 'It's all right, you're allowed,' said Annie, softly, thinking her hesitation was due to shyness, but she was mistaken: Hannah's gaze was locked on the food.

'Look,' said Annie, 'I have to be honest and say that you won't be able to stay here long enough to have your tea with us – we'll both be in all kinds of trouble if I don't get you back by six o'clock, and this won't be ready until much later. But we each have a slice of bread with ours, and if Mrs Otway doesn't mind then you can have mine now.'

Mrs Otway cast a sympathetic look at the thin, pale child. 'Sit yourself down, girl, and eat this.' She took up one of the six slices of bread that were already cut, spread some jam on it and set it on a plate. 'And once the kettle's boiled there'll be tea.'

Hannah seemed hardly able to believe her luck, and was soon eating with relish, torn between the need to get it down as fast as possible and the desire not to look too rude. Annie thanked Mrs Otway and added under her breath that she'd put a little bit extra in the food kitty.

Mrs Otway shook her head. 'I can spare a scraping of jam and some tea leaves, thank the Lord.' She gazed at Hannah in pity. 'Do you know, that's one of the things that's actually got *worse* over the years since I was at the mill? Apprentices used to have shorter hours, half of them in school in the morning while the others were at work, and then the other way round in the afternoons. They learned their letters, and they got fed. But then everything got busier and busier, and they shipped so many of them in that the dormitory wouldn't hold them all. And then even that wasn't enough and they started to work longer and longer hours.' She addressed Hannah directly. 'Do you get any schooling at all, chick?'

Hannah finished her mouthful and paused. 'An hour on a Sunday morning.'

'And what will you have for your tea when you get back?'

'Porridge.'

Well, that didn't sound too bad, thought Annie, until Hannah added, 'Made with water, and it's so thin you don't even need a spoon, you just drink it.'

Mrs Otway tutted to herself and set the kettle over the fire, which was now crackling merrily.

By the time the water was boiled and the tea made, Hannah had finished her bread. She sipped and watched with interest – and a better-lined stomach – as Mrs Otway set about preparing the scouse. 'How do you cook it, then?'

Annie watched the old woman explaining her every move to the intensely concentrating child, smiling as she remembered what Nora had said about Mrs Otway being a good teacher to her when she'd first come to the mill.

'And then you just leave it to simmer, needs a good couple of hours, and a stir every now and then to make sure it doesn't stick to the bottom of the pot.' She held out the wooden spoon. 'Do you want to try?'

Hannah was both eager and hesitant – worried, Annie guessed, that she'd make a mistake and ruin everyone's meal. But she stirred the pot safely without spilling anything, and then sniffed appreciatively.

As they finished drinking their tea, Annie looked at the little clock. With a heavy heart, she put her cup down. 'I'm sorry, Hannah, but we need to get you back to the dormitory now. If we're going to be allowed to do this again, we have to stick to their rules.'

Instantly obedient, Hannah was on her feet. She bobbed a curtsey to Mrs Otway. 'Thank you, ma'am.'

'Well then,' came the reply, 'you're welcome here next time Annie can bring you out. Off you go now, and don't be late back.'

Annie felt her own steps slowing as they approached the mill in the gathering gloom. How cruel was it to have to force Hannah back into what she'd so briefly managed to escape? How upset was the child going to be when they had to say goodbye?

They reached the dormitory building.

Annie crouched so that they could look at each other more directly. She opened her mouth, but before she could say anything she was taken aback by Hannah flinging her arms about her neck. 'Thank you!' came the words into her ear. 'This has been the best day *ever*.'

Annie could say nothing, instead just hugging her tightly and then standing to knock on the door.

The same man opened it. 'Here we are,' said Annie. 'Exactly as promised.' She squeezed Hannah's fingers in farewell and then watched her go inside. Then she held out her hand.

'Ah yes,' said the man, smoothly. 'Here's your two shillings back.'

Annie looked at him, her hand still held out.

'And if you ever want to take your . . . cousin, was it? out on a Sunday again, under the same arrangement, we can sort that out.'

Annie was fuming, but too sensible to argue about it. She wouldn't be able to do it every Sunday, not at that price, but if it meant less fuss then she would just have to bear it.

She nodded, then turned on her heel and left.

It was only as she was out in the mill yard that she realised how odd it was that the main gates were open on a Sunday. Normally they were shut and chained out of hours, with only a small side entrance, near a porter's lodge, available. Not that any of the mill hands were in any way inclined to approach the place on their one full day of rest, but some workers or managers did need to slip in and out.

The mystery was explained by the lights glowing from the windows of the mill offices. Mr Carrington must be working, or – no, now she was thinking about it, she could hear numerous voices – holding some kind of meeting. Annie had heard words like *shareholders* and *board members* and *committee* bandied around during her months at the mill, which all basically meant rich men in suits; the main gates would certainly be opened for the likes of them.

Annie wasn't overly curious about what was going on, but she had turned to look at the lights and was now walking almost backwards. She stopped abruptly when she ran into a warm body.

'Well, well, what have we here?'

Annie knew that voice, and her blood ran cold as she realised that she was alone in the darkening yard with Mr Theodore.

She tried to remain calm. 'I beg your pardon, sir. I was just leaving, so I won't get in your way.'

He already had hold of her, his arms having encircled her reflexively when they bumped together. 'But what are you doing here – that's the question I have to ask. Have you been in a quiet corner with some lucky young man?' Fortunately she was well wrapped up in layers of clothing, but his hands were already insistent, groping about her waist and seeking to get inside her tied shawl. 'I'm a better prospect than any of those chaps, I can tell you. As you'll see.'

Annie was beginning to panic now. She couldn't let him continue, but to strike him or even to lay a hand on him to push him away would mean instant dismissal. Her job gone, all her ideas of helping others . . . but she had to get away. 'Please, sir, this isn't what I was—'

At that moment there was a burst of light and sound as the door to the offices opened and a number of men emerged. Mr Theodore was distracted for just long enough to loosen his grip, and Annie was able to wriggle free and escape.

She fled out of the main gate, hardly knowing what she was doing. Would it be better to run straight down to the village, or find somewhere to hide until they'd all gone, Mr Theodore included? She couldn't think straight.

In her hurry she slipped on the cobbles and felt a stab as she twisted her ankle. Not seriously, she thought, but enough that it was going to be painful for a couple of hours and stop her running if she needed to. She turned back towards the high wall of the mill and found one of the pillars that stood a little proud of it. It wasn't ideal, but it would have to do; she huddled in the recess on the far side from the gates. It was now almost full dark, which would help.

'Yes, the carriages are all ready to come up, Father,' she heard Mr Theodore say, the smoothness of his tone giving no hint of what had just passed.

Annie now heard horses' hooves, and watched as several very upmarket conveyances entered the yard.

'Well, there's little to be done, Carrington, except to hope that this ridiculous business in America blows over quickly.' A rich man's voice, for sure, but Annie didn't recognise it.

'Yes, we'll have to keep an eye on it.' That was Mr Carrington himself, she thought. 'Abolition of slavery, indeed! It was bad enough when they got rid of it here, but over there? Who's going to pick the cotton, might I ask?'

'Well, if there is to be a war then I trust our friends will put these abolitionists back in their place. That way trade won't be disrupted for more than a few weeks, and we've enough raw cotton in the warehouses to tide us over if that happens.'

A younger voice sounded. Mr Frederick's, definitely. 'Pardon me for interrupting, sir, but what if it's not over in a few weeks? What if the disruption continues?'

'It won't, I'll answer for it. The world still needs cotton, so they'll have to get it to us one way or another so we can spin and weave it.'

Men were now getting into carriages, from what Annie could hear. The horses of the first one emerged past the gate and she shrank further back into her niche, but fortunately nobody was looking in her direction.

She watched them all leave until there was only one carriage left. It pulled out of the gate and then stopped, leaving Annie terrified that she'd somehow been spotted, but it was only that Mr Frederick was following out on foot so he could fasten the chain around the gates. Then he got in alongside his father and brother, and they were gone.

Annie sagged in relief. She waited until long after the carriage was out of sight and she could be absolutely sure of there being no danger of it returning. Then she began to limp down the hill.

What an afternoon it had been. She'd succeeded in her bold plan and managed to get Hannah away from her hellish existence just for a few hours – and, moreover, Hannah had enjoyed it for what it was, instead of being upset that it wasn't more. This gave Annie a warm glow that pushed away thoughts of the pain in her ankle.

But then to have all that happiness destroyed in an instant like that! Of course, it could have been worse, much worse – Annie remembered the girl fleeing from the back of the mill building that day – but still. Her distress turned to anger again as she contemplated just what these rich men could get away with if they chose to. Mr Theodore, by virtue of his position, had basically a free licence to do whatever he wanted with – or *to* – the mill employees. Particularly the girls, who were, of course 'two a penny' and could simply be replaced if they kicked up a fuss. Annie fumed as she tried to think of any way in which things could be made better – and better for everyone, like Jack said, not just for a lucky chosen few. Being free from molestation was just as important as pay or working hours.

As she neared the house, Annie's mind turned to the snatches of conversation she'd overheard. Was this anything to worry about? Something about America and slavery? It was a shame she couldn't ask Abraham, for he always kept up to date with what was going on there through frequent contact with sailors at the docks. She certainly hoped that slavery would be abolished in America, as it had been here, though it seemed to be only a prospect, not a definite thing, from what she'd heard. More immediately, was there going to be a shortage of cotton? And what would that mean for the mill and its workers? Still, that other man had said, hadn't he, that they had plenty stored that would tide them over until any trouble was over. It would all be fine.

Chapter Ten

Christmas came – and with it, disaster.

There had been rumours all through November and December that the situation in America was serious. News travelled fast from there, Annie learned, even though it was so far away: modern ships could cross the ocean in as little as ten days, so the Liverpool merchants were kept well informed of developments. Everyone at the mill kept hoping that it was all going to blow over, but those who read the newspapers were not optimistic, and there was plenty of gloomy chat during break times.

It was on Christmas Day itself that the blow fell.

All the hands were given the day off, but this was usual and happened every year, so nobody thought much of it. Rather the opposite, in fact: although it meant forgoing a day's pay, it was a time of cheer and celebration, with the workers either spending the day with family or – in the case of the young and single – congregating in one of the village's public houses. It was such a treat to be away from work on a Tuesday that nobody begrudged the financial loss while times were good and wages decent.

Annie had been persuaded, late in the afternoon when Mrs Otway was having a rest, to join Clara and the others at the pub. She'd been in there about an hour now, glad that she'd come – the convivial atmosphere and the warm fug of the enclosed room were going some way towards helping her forget that this was the first Christmas she'd ever spent away from home. There, Christmas was the most important day of the year; everyone loved it, and Delilah often said it was a time of miracles. Right now everyone would be gathered together, enjoying Meg's cooking, and all the excited children would have been given a gift each.

Annie tried to stop herself from sighing. She reminded herself that she had friends here even if she didn't have family, and that was the next best thing. She sipped her ginger beer appreciatively.

It must have been sometime between five and six o'clock when the door opened. It remained open for longer than expected, causing a chilly blast to enter, and a few people called out to whoever was entering to get on with it.

Annie looked up and saw that it was Jack, brandishing a newspaper. His expression was – well, Annie hardly knew how to describe it. Different measures of upset, frustrated and absolutely livid.

He stepped in, kicked the door shut behind him, and then strode over to the bar and slapped the paper down.

'What's all this?' asked the publican.

'Today's *Liverpool Mercury*,' came the reply. 'Just arrived from town. And the news is very bad.'

There was a murmur, partly at what he said but also, Annie felt, some annoyance at Jack himself for interrupting their happy party.

'Go on, then,' called out a resigned voice. 'Read it out so we can all hear it.'

'May as well get it over with,' said another. 'And then we can get back to getting drunk.'

Jack picked up the paper. 'A steamship called the *Arabia* docked in Liverpool yesterday, over from America, carrying letters and news.'

The room fell silent, and he began to read.

> The news by the *Arabia* is confirmatory of all previously received. The political excitement had not died out, nor was there any prospect of its doing so. It was impossible to move produce or negotiate bills. The secession of the Southern

> States appeared to be inevitable. Less cotton would be planted; for, independent of the resolve of the Southerners to plant more grain to make themselves less dependent on the North for breadstuffs, labour - that is, slave labour - would be disorganised to some extent even under the most favourable circumstances. Altogether the news is most unwelcome to our cotton spinners, and how their mills can be kept at work during the coming year with a scant supply of cotton is a problem not easily solved.

Annie hadn't understood all those words, or the way in which some of the article was phrased, but she grasped enough to know that the news was bad.

'The last line is the most important,' said Jack, his gaze sweeping the room. He referred to the smudgy black type once again, which he read out.

> This state of affairs may promise a golden harvest to the importers of the staple, but it threatens to ruin the manufacturers and to throw thousands of hands out of employment.

With a sudden anger that made everyone jump and the tankards rattle, he banged the paper down again on the bar. '*Now* will you all believe me? *Now* will you realise that we should all have been standing together, forming unions? Now that it's far too late?'

'Surely it won't be that bad . . .' someone began, but then he tailed off.

'It will be,' said Jack, shortly. 'If any more than half of us have still got a job in the morning, I'll be very surprised.'

'Well, what's to be done?'

The room was full of people of different ages: mostly young men and women, but also a few older hands, men who would consider themselves important among the company. Every single one of them, Annie noted, was looking to Jack.

He threw up his hands in frustration. 'I just don't know. What we should have done is band together earlier. The only thing I can think of right now is that tomorrow, when we turn up for work to find half of us laid off, is that everyone, even those who still have a job, refuse to work.'

There were sounds of dissension at this. 'What, turn down work even if we've still got it? No fear,' Annie heard, and also, 'But that's no good anyway – they'd just take on hands from those who've been laid off from other mills.'

This exasperated Jack even more. 'Yes! Which is why *all* the hands from *all* the mills should be in unions – if every single skilled worker in Lancashire refused to work, they'd soon come round to better conditions.'

'Maybe we could nominate someone to talk to them?' called out another man. 'Jack?'

Jack laughed. 'As if I'm not going to be the first one turned away tomorrow morning. And none of you will be safe, for all you've been trying to avoid me so as not to be *tainted*.'

This last came out in a tone of bitterness, and Annie felt sorry for him again when she thought of how lonely his existence at the mill was, constantly surrounded by fellow workers who would hardly even look at him, never mind pass the time of day.

She also couldn't help noticing that all those who had spoken so far were men, despite nearly half of those in the room being women. They were going to be affected too, these women and girls – and their families – so why didn't they speak up? Did she, one of the youngest people present, dare to open her mouth?

Shouts and calls were now breaking out all over, and nobody was listening to what anyone else was saying.

Rather unexpectedly, it was the publican who took control, banging a tankard down on the bar until he could command attention. 'Stop! This is no good, all this shouting. We need to come up with some ideas as to what can be done.'

'What's it got to do with you?' came a call. 'You're not going to be laid off, are you?'

'This is going to affect every man, woman and child in this village,' replied the publican. 'Those who lose work won't have money. They won't have money to spend in my pub, or at the grocer's or the butcher's or the baker's. Those businesses will lose money and fall behind on their rent, same as everyone else.' He turned to Jack. 'Now, I don't know who this young man is, but he sounds like he's got a head on his shoulders. Let's listen to what he has to say.'

Jack nodded at him and addressed the room. 'It's no good me standing here saying what we ought to have done months ago – we didn't do it and that chance has gone. What we need to do is decide what can be done *now* to make this less bad than it could be. And if anyone has ideas, let's hear them.'

'Thing is,' said – inevitably – a man, 'we don't know yet who's going to be out of a job and who isn't.'

'But that's exactly it,' replied Jack. 'If we knew already, the lucky ones could just say "well, I'm all right and devil take the hindmost". But right now, at this exact moment, we're all sitting in the same boat.'

Yet another man was clearing his throat. Annie forestalled him, taking her courage in both hands and standing up.

There was a general ripple of the room being taken aback. But she'd started now, hadn't she. What would Delilah do? She'd keep going. 'One of the things we should do is to make sure everyone will still have enough to eat, whether they have a job or not.' She hoped that her voice didn't sound as unsteady to them as it did in her head.

One or two of the other women were nodding. 'How?' one of them asked.

'Well, maybe everyone who's still in work could pay a penny or two of their wages into a fund, and that could be shared out?'

'What?' A nearby man seemed quite irate at the idea. 'Hand over my hard-earned wages to some stranger, when I've got my own family to feed? Don't be daft, girl.'

Clara leaped to her feet. 'Don't you talk to Annie like that! She's only trying to help, and if you've got a better suggestion then let's hear it.'

Emboldened by her friend's public support, Annie continued. 'Or, you know – just take in a friend, or a friend's child. That way you're not giving money to "some stranger", but at least you're saving one person from starvation.'

Instinctively Annie looked across the room at Jack. Their eyes met, because his were already on her. 'She's right,' he declared. Despite the fraught situation, he gave her half a smile. 'Just because you can't help everyone, it doesn't mean you shouldn't help anyone.'

The meeting didn't last all that much longer. No more specific ideas were put forward, but there was a general agreement of goodwill, and that they should wait to see what the morning would bring and then do their best to get all the workers and their families through the crisis. And, perhaps it was just because it was Christmas Day, but there was also a general optimism that maybe it wouldn't be as bad as it sounded, maybe there wouldn't be mass layoffs in the morning, and even if there were, perhaps it would be of short duration.

People began to drift out. Annie and Clara stayed so they could walk home with Maisie, who had been behind the bar all this time. She was busy collecting up the dirty pots, while the publican was talking to Jack.

'Thanks for standing up for me,' said Annie to Clara, 'and especially in front of all those people. I wouldn't have been brave enough to keep going if it hadn't been for you.'

Clara hugged her. 'That's what friends are for, isn't it? But you were wonderful. I thought you were brave, taking them all on like that – you reminded me of Sam.'

It was a throwaway comment, and Annie wondered if Clara knew what a compliment she'd just paid. She felt herself glowing on the inside.

Jack had caught the name and now turned towards them. 'Sam?' he said, rather quickly. 'Friend of yours? Or of both of you?'

'Sam is Annie's brother,' said Clara, smiling slyly as she observed the relief that came into Jack's expression. 'And I've known him since we were nippers, too.'

'And a favourite with both of you, I can see,' he replied, more easily. 'I'd like to hear more about him sometime.' He sighed. 'You won't have to avoid me for fear of losing your job any more, because I'm as certain as I can possibly be that I won't be at the mill later than one minute past six tomorrow morning.'

'Will you . . . will you leave here completely? Go and find work somewhere else?' Annie was surprised by how bereft the idea made her.

He shook his head. 'I don't think so. Or, at least, not to begin with. I've got a bit saved up, and now I've started all this agitating about better conditions for all, I've got a responsibility to see it through.'

'You're a sound lad,' said the publican, who had just finished wiping the bar. 'But it's time to go now. Maisie, you all done there?'

'Yes, ready to go,' came the reply.

The four of them were shown out the door and wished good luck for the morning. Then it shut behind them and Annie heard it being locked and bolted.

Jack addressed the general area above all of their heads. 'Might be a few drunks around – can I walk you all home?'

Clara elbowed Maisie in the ribs. 'Of course. Or you can take Annie here, while Maisie and I follow along.'

'But we all live in the same place,' said Annie, puzzled. 'It makes much more sense for us all to walk together.'

Clara rolled her eyes. 'If you say so. And I s'pose it's more proper, and all that.'

Jack accompanied them to their door, then bade them all a very sober good night and disappeared. The girls went inside to bed, to await as best they could what the morning would bring.

* * *

It was a very subdued procession of people that made its way up the hill in the dark the following morning. Word had got around, of course, as those who were in the pub had gone home, and a few more copies of the newspaper had been circulating in the village.

The sky was low, and Annie wouldn't be surprised if there was snow before the end of the day. *Where will I be by then?*, she wondered. If she were to be laid off, she thought she would still remain in the village for a while longer. Partly so that she could help out – and certainly until she knew what was going to happen to Clara, Hannah, Alice, Charlie, Grace and all her other friends – but also, she had to admit, because she couldn't bear the idea of having to go back to Dale Street in defeat.

It was obvious that something was going on when they got near the mill. The gates were shut and chained, and outside them stood a row of clerks with pieces of paper and, rather more ominously, a gang of the tough-looking men who acted as guards and nightwatchmen.

All the workers gathered and stood in uneasy silence, the men with their collars turned up against the cold, the women with their shawls pulled up over their heads. There were worried, pinched faces everywhere that Annie looked, and even the many children were quiet.

Mr Carrington and his sons were standing among the clerks, and now he stepped forward. 'This is a sad day,' he announced. 'I'm sure you're all aware of the present trouble in America, and the consequent disruption to our supplies. With very little raw cotton arriving, there is not enough work to go around, so regrettably we have no choice but to let some of you go.'

There was an angry murmur, which seemed not to bother Mr Carrington in the slightest. 'Robinson will now tell you all how the process is to be managed.' He gestured to the chief clerk, whom Annie recognised from her visit to the mill offices after the incident with Alice and the spinning machine.

His address finished, Mr Carrington and his sons stepped through the small open gate by the porter's lodge, and disappeared. 'Too cowardly even to say it himself,' came a discontented voice from somewhere behind Annie. 'Aye, and off for a hearty breakfast while he sentences us to starve,' said another.

They were shushed into silence as the clerk began to speak, his voice not as penetrating in the cold air as Mr Carrington's had been. 'For each area of the mill, we will call out a list of names of those who will continue to be employed. As your name is called, you will step through—' he pointed at the small entrance '—and go to work as usual. The main gates will not be open today.'

'And what about everyone else?' came a cry.

'I'm coming to that,' snapped Robinson, waspishly. 'As a mark of Mr Carrington's generosity, you will all receive half a week's wages, even though you have only worked one day this week so far. This will be paid out here, in sections according to your area of work, in good order.'

'And then what?'

The clerk shrugged. 'And then, you are no longer an employee of the mill and may disperse and seek other employment as you wish.'

There really was a muttering at this. *Other employment*, thought Annie – what else was there around here? They'd all have to pack up and head for Liverpool, or even further afield, and what would their chances be there, when they didn't know anybody? Good jobs were hard to come by at the best of times, even with recommendations.

The very elderly clerk who had registered Annie on her first day now stepped forward and began to read out the list of warehousemen who were to be admitted. It did not include Paul, who was left in stupefaction as he stood with Alice and Charlie huddled next to him. Annie's heart sank.

What was even worse was the brevity of the list. By Annie's calculations and those of several people around her, only around one third of the men had kept their jobs – if this were to be replicated across the whole of the mill then the consequences would be brutal. The clerk seemed to be genuinely sorry as he finished reading out the names and stepped back, which was more than Annie could say about any of the Carringtons themselves.

Next came the engineers, boiler-room men and mechanics. Annie held her breath. This list was much longer; in fact, when it was completed she heard someone in the crowd say that they'd kept on every single man except one.

There was no need to guess the identity of that one.

Annie craned her neck, but she couldn't spot Jack anywhere. She knew he was in the crowd, though, because she could see a circle of other workers all turning round to stare in the same direction. There could be no question that this was a targeted attack and that Jack had been singled out.

The spinning room proved to have a list almost as brief as the warehouse one. Thankfully Alice and Charlie were called forward, as was Grace – but neither of her parents. She was crying as she left them and moved into the mill yard.

Now it was the turn of the weaving shed. The overlookers were called first, Amos Potter among them. Then the weavers themselves, and Annie went weak at the knees as the roll call started. It seemed to be in alphabetical order, so she was on tenterhooks while the clerk moved from A to R. But then 'Annie Shaw' was heard loud and clear, and she slipped through the crowd and into the yard.

She wanted to pause, because Clara's surname was Tate, but she was chivvied along by the porter and had no choice but to follow the short line of others into the weaving shed.

It looked very strange in there. Oh, the looms were all in the same place, of course, but the workers – all women now, except the overlookers – were directed to take up positions by only two rows of them. These machines rattled and steamed into life, but the rest of the room remained silent and still.

Clara wasn't here.

Annie tried to concentrate on her work, but it was difficult to see through her tears.

* * *

Annie used the day's two breaks to find out as much as she could about her other friends. During breakfast she edged towards the ground floor of the main mill building; the windows were too high for her to see through, but she could clearly hear the heavy machinery of the carding room, so the workhouse children must still be in there. But of course they were – they didn't get paid at all, so the Carringtons would get as much work out of them as possible in order to get their money's worth after having bought them.

She shared her dinnertime bread and dripping with Alice and Charlie, as usual, wondering how on earth their family was to manage on only two children's incomes. Perhaps she might manage to talk to Paul about it? She didn't know him well, but it was hardly possible that he wasn't aware of her friendship with his children.

Grace was standing with her brother in the unusually empty and subdued mill yard, her sister having evidently lost her job along with their parents. Annie tried to recall what the brother did; she never saw him except at break times, and had an idea that he worked in the main boiler room, where they created all the steam that ran the machinery. Something like what Jem did on the locomotives, maybe, except that the boilers were standing still? Anyway, whatever it was, she hoped it was well paid enough to tide them over.

Back in the weaving shed she was told that from now on she'd have to run two looms at once. She was now confident enough at her work to do so, but she couldn't help feeling it was a shame that they couldn't have kept on another hand to share the load. Amos Potter, she noted, was still there and still bullying women and children alike; the proportionately smaller workforce would each have to bear the brunt of more of his temper.

The whistle blew as usual at six o'clock, and Annie saw with bemusement that fully half of the weavers in the shed were leaving. It took her a few moments to work it out, but eventually she did: they'd kept on a greater proportion of younger workers because they were cheaper. Annie produced as much work during her allotted hours as an adult weaver, but was paid less, so she was presumably a better investment. Similarly, women were paid less than men even though they did the same job, so if the mill had enough spun thread to need some weaving work doing between six and nine in the evening, it would make more financial sense to keep the female hands.

Financial sense, maybe, at least for the Carringtons, but catastrophic for all those families who relied on having a male breadwinner.

As Annie left the weaving shed and shivered, her breath steaming as an early frost began to form, she saw the two Carrington brothers coming out of the door to the offices. She stopped, politely, to give them way, and they swept past without acknowledging or noticing her.

She didn't mean to eavesdrop, but they had such loud, confident voices that their conversation carried across the still air as they walked.

She heard Mr Theodore's drawl first. 'Well, that all went reasonably well, I thought. We've cleared out enough dead wood to make sure we'll still be in profit this quarter, regardless of the situation in America.'

'Hmm. I didn't like to say so earlier, so as not to be seen contradicting Father, but I think we might even have laid off a few too many.'

'Then those who remain will just have to work harder to compensate, won't they? And they should be glad to do so given that they're lucky enough to still have positions. They owe us their gratitude.'

'It's hard for them all, Theo.'

'Oh, stop being such a bleeding heart, Fred. It's difficult for all of us, you know.' Mr Theodore suddenly guffawed. 'Why, Mama will have to do without her new carriage now, and she will think that the *greatest* of hardships.'

'Keep your voice down, will you? We've already heard about the unrest in some of the places over towards Manchester, and we don't want any of that here. Try to be sympathetic, for God's sake, at least in public. We have to keep up appearances.'

'Oh, you do amuse me. Unrest? From these cowed little men, creeping about? We got rid of the only one with a bit of spark, and these others wouldn't say boo to a goose.'

'They might, if they think their families are going to starve.'

'They'll find something else,' said Mr Theodore, airily. 'Their sort always do. There's always some industry that needs its ants.' There was a pause. 'And, Fred, you're not thinking of the advantages.'

'I beg your pardon?'

'Well, there's going to be a lot of desperate girls about, and you know what that means.' He chuckled. 'Anything for a few coins, what?'

Annie didn't hear Mr Frederick's reply, because they'd crossed the yard by then and were heading away from her. She was so angry that for a moment she couldn't even move, and she had to wait until the red mist had dissipated a little. Up until now she'd been imagining that the Carringtons had been involved in desperate meetings, aware that their business might founder thanks to circumstances beyond their control, and frantically working out how they might best weather the storm and keep as many of their employees in work as possible. But now she saw what a fool she'd been. It was no more than a game to them.

Or to Mr Theodore, at least – she could feel a little more kindly towards Mr Frederick, she supposed. But it was abundantly clear that the mill owners had much more concern for their own profits than for the welfare of the people who toiled for them day in and day out. If the mill workers and their families were going to get through this, they were going to have to do it on their own.

More fallout from the day awaited Annie when she got back to her lodgings. Maisie was out at work – the publican having told her that he would make no decisions until he knew more about what the future might hold – but Annie was the only one of the four other girls in the house to have kept her job.

An anxious scene met her eye as she entered. By the light of a single candle she could see Clara striding up and down, swearing, and Mrs Otway wringing her hands in despair. The two girls who rented the room on the middle floor, it transpired, had both already left, having families in Liverpool they could go back to, and now the poor old lady was terrified that she wouldn't be able to pay the rent. 'And then what shall we do?' she cried.

Annie took a deep breath. Could her anger carry her through this? 'Right,' she said, in a confident tone that made them both stop what they were doing and look at her in surprise. 'What we do is we look at the situation calmly. It's no good crying about what's past – we can't change that. What we need is to sit down, accept what's happened and work out how we're going to deal with it.'

She set the kettle over the fire and laid out three cups and saucers on the table. 'Let's get to it.'

Chapter Eleven

It wasn't long before they had the beginnings of a plan.

Before she'd gone out to work, Maisie had already indicated to Clara that she would temporarily be able to help out with her rent, and Annie now said the same. The three of them would continue in the attic room while Clara looked for another job, and Mrs Otway would get her seven shillings and sixpence between them somehow. With regard to the middle room, they all agreed that a family currently renting a whole house might be glad to find somewhere cheaper, and that maybe a mother and children, or even a family with a father if he were a quiet family man, should be looked for. Mrs Otway had some old friends around the place she could talk to, and Annie and Clara promised to make enquiries wherever they could.

The question of what else Clara might do was a more difficult one. There was no hope that she might be able to join Maisie at the pub, as Maisie wasn't even sure of her own job and the publican certainly wouldn't want to take on any new employees. The same went for the village shops, which would presumably already have been inundated with requests. There wasn't really anything else in the immediate locality. Ormskirk was three miles away, which wasn't impossible in terms of walking there and back each day if there was work, but if Clara were to get a job in the town it would make more sense for her to find lodgings there as well, which would defeat the object of her staying here to contribute to keeping the roof over all their heads. Similarly, there were a few big houses and estates out in the countryside who might be looking for domestic servants, but they would be required to live in, and Clara would be lost to them anyway.

Annie didn't say it out loud, but she couldn't really see Clara settling into domestic service. She knew a little bit about it from Meg and Sally, and was aware that a servant had to give up her own existence almost entirely in order to fit into the household. Clara valued her independence too much, and she still had that wild streak after so many years running around the streets and courts of Liverpool with no restrictions on her behaviour.

'Well, I'll just have to get married, then,' was Clara's flippant response to the closing off of every possibility.

At first Annie thought she was joking. 'Married? But you're not even walking out with anyone!'

Clara looked at her in bemusement. 'What's that got to do with it? Being married is just a job like any other. You find a man with work and an income, get a roof over your head and hope he don't smack you around too much. You have to . . .' she looked at Annie and made a face. 'Well, anyway. You have his babies and cook his dinner, and that's that.'

The prospect was so bleak, and Clara's acceptance of it so matter-of-fact, that Annie was astonished. She thought of Delilah and Frank, Meg and Tommy, William and Bridget . . . had her family background spoiled her, raised her expectations too high? But there were other relationships like that around, surely. Poor Clara was no doubt influenced by what had happened in her own life and her mother's, and didn't see that things could be any different.

Mrs Otway was stirring a pot of stew. 'There's going to be too much in here now. The girls were paid up until the end of the week, so I'd bought it first thing, before I knew they were going to be off.' She sighed. 'It's a shame your little workhouse friend isn't here.'

Annie briefly wondered if she might be able to go and fetch Hannah, but she'd only ever done it on a

Sunday afternoon before, and couldn't see that she'd be allowed to take her out on a dark Wednesday night. Goodness, had Christmas only been yesterday? It felt like weeks ago. And so much for it being a time of family miracles.

Then she had an idea. *Family*. 'Mrs Otway, I'm sure Paul doesn't cook himself, and that he probably buys tea for himself and Alice and Charlie. What if I go to find him, and see if he'd pay the pennies to you instead, for them to come and share this?'

In the light from the fire Annie saw Mrs Otway nod, and she slipped out.

It was *bitterly* cold out here, enough to take her breath away. She didn't actually know where Paul and the children lived, but there was bound to be someone in the pub who could tell her, so she headed there. She expected it to be half empty, but in fact it looked even more crowded than usual as she pushed her way in. The atmosphere was different, though; the room was not full of convivial chat but rather of men who seemed intent on drinking themselves into oblivion. As it happens, one of them was Paul.

Well, that would save her a lot of effort. Annie made her way over to him and tapped him on the shoulder.

He turned around, and Annie was hit directly by the smell – he absolutely *reeked* of gin. Dizzily, she was transported back to the part of her childhood that she could barely remember, confused images of fists mingling with the sounds of shouting and that odd pain her arm.

'What?' He was staring at her, and she realised she'd been standing in silence. 'Oh, it's you. Whadyou want?'

Annie certainly wasn't about to invite him back to Mrs Otway's house in that condition. 'Where are Alice and Charlie?'

'At home, if they know what's good for 'em.'

'Yes, but where's that?'

He was confused, waving his arm all over the place and giving no idea at all of any particular direction. 'Home.'

Fortunately, one of his drinking companions was not quite so worse for wear, and he was able to give Annie better information.

She thanked him and made her way out again, then through the village streets to one that looked exactly the same as their own, a row of identical houses on each side. She found what she thought was the correct door, and knocked. 'Alice? Charlie? Are you in there?'

There was a sort of scampering sound. 'Who is it?'

'It's me, Annie. It's all right, I've just spoken to your father and he said I could come, so you can open the door.'

A crack appeared, though no light shone through it. 'Annie?'

'Can I come in?'

The door opened wider. There was no candle lit inside, but from the distant light of a street lamp Annie could make out a room exactly the same in layout as Mrs Otway's except that there was no table or chairs, and the floor was covered in mattresses. She could also see Charlie and Alice, the latter with her head shaved almost bald.

Annie stared. 'Alice, what . . .?'

The little girl shrieked and put her hands to her head. 'I forgot! No, you're not supposed to see me!'

Annie stepped inside. 'Now, calm down. I won't tell anyone if you don't want me to, but what happened?'

Alice was busy over in the shadows, putting something on her head, and it was Charlie who answered. 'Pa sold her hair.'

'He did *what*?'

'Charlie, stop it!'

Charlie rounded on his sister. 'No! I'm going to tell her, 'cos she's nice, and kind, and someone ought to know what he's like.' He turned back to Annie. 'When he saw her that first day with a little bit of it cut off – you know, in the machine – it gave him an idea. So he asked around, who might buy it, and he found someone. Then a few weeks ago he cut the whole lot off and got the money for it, and said we weren't to tell anyone. But I have, now, and I'm not sorry.' His high little voice rang with defiance.

Annie looked about her as best she could. 'How many people live here?'

Alice started to reply. 'It doesn't—'

Charlie cut her off. 'Fourteen. I know that 'cos I counted, and I remembered my numbers up to twenty from that time we used to have Sunday school, before we came here.'

'Fourt—' Annie could hardly believe it. 'And they're all out now?'

Alice came forward, a piece of rag now wrapped around her head, and nodded. 'They're all grown-ups except us, and they go to the pub.'

'Leaving you here alone?'

'Most nights, yes.'

'And . . .' the grate was stone cold; Annie could feel that from here. 'What do you eat?'

'Whatever we can find, mostly. Pa says we're not to starve as we couldn't work then, but he says nippers don't need much, so it's a bit of bread or a potato, normally.'

Annie was by now feeling thoroughly ashamed of herself for not noticing all this sooner. She knew of the sufferings of the workhouse children, but had somehow assumed that little ones living in a family would be better off. How could their father be so unfeeling? 'Well, come with me now and I'll see you get a hot meal.'

Charlie was already halfway out the door, but Alice hesitated. 'Will Pa be angry?'

Annie recalled the bruises they were always covered in, and kicked herself again. 'It'll be fine. Like I said, I've already spoken to him, and I'll have you back here before he gets home from the pub.'

'Well, if you say so . . .'

'I do. Now come on.'

They were almost home when Annie recalled that she'd told Mrs Otway that she might be able to get Paul to pay for their meal. She assumed that the children wouldn't have any money on them, so she would find a couple of pennies out of her own box.

She sighed. There were so many things that needed money spending on them – her rent, Clara's rent, food for the children, the shillings effectively stolen from her every time she took Hannah out on a Sunday, not to mention the amount she'd need to buy out the apprenticeship – how was she to keep up with it all? She'd been saving as carefully as she could, but that wouldn't last forever, and as it dwindled, how would she decide what to prioritise and what to give up?

She sat silently all through tea, watching Alice and Charlie eat what was no doubt their first proper meal in a good while. Of course, for her personally, there was a very simple escape from all this. Tomorrow morning she could get up, walk out and go home. However hard she'd been reminding herself to call it merely 'the shop' or 'Dale Street', or 'back in Liverpool', that's what it was: home. She could arrange to pay for a ride with a carrier heading into Liverpool, of which there were always many, or she could walk the twelve miles in a day. By this time tomorrow, she could be safe in the snug little back room with her family about her.

But she couldn't do it. Of course she couldn't. That would be running away from everything she needed to do here, and what on earth would happen to Hannah, Alice and Charlie if she just upped and left, leaving them to their fates after she'd convinced them she was their friend? What about Mrs Otway, who been so kind to her since she arrived? And Clara, who was her sister in everything except blood? And what about . . .

She shook her head, aware that she hadn't been listening to a word anyone was saying. She watched as the children finished their stew and wiped up every last drop with their slices of bread. Once they'd finished she allowed them a few moments to sit back, in the warmth of the dwindling fire and with full bellies, and then she got to her feet. 'Let's get you back, then, before your Pa gets home from the pub.'

As they made their way through the streets, Alice and Charlie hopping and skipping as their bare feet met the frozen cobbles, Annie wondered if she could possibly remonstrate with Paul. But that would be very difficult, and moreover she would have no right to do so – a father owned his children and could do what he liked with them. But she would find a way if she could.

She saw them safely into their cold, dark room and then went back to go to bed.

The following morning Annie got up on her own. Maisie, of course, didn't have to get up at half past five, and now Clara didn't either. So, once the knocker-upper had moved on, she broke the ice on the washstand and splashed as little water on her face and hands as she thought she could get away with before hurrying down alone.

The crowd walking up to the mill was thin, as it would be every day from now on, she supposed. It was also very subdued, with none of the regular chat or greetings called out.

The main gates were open today, which Annie took as a sign that the Carringtons weren't expecting whatever sort of 'unrest' they had feared, but there were still rather more watchmen than usual standing about the place. She went through, but paused upon seeing Alice and Charlie already in the yard and both in tears.

She hurried over. 'What's the matter?' She scanned their faces but couldn't see any more bruises than the ones they'd had already.

That was soon explained. 'Pa didn't come home at all last night,' sobbed Alice. 'We don't know where he is.'

Drunk in a gutter somewhere, was Annie's first thought as she recalled Paul stinking of gin in the pub. But she didn't say that. 'Are you sure he didn't just get up earlier than you, and go out?'

They both looked at her in disbelief.

'Well, all right, maybe not. But perhaps he just met with a friend and they stayed up so late that it wasn't worth coming home. I'm sure you'll see him later.' *Not that that will do them any good, the way he's been behaving*. She tried to sound cheerful. 'Anyway, you've done very well to get yourselves up and come to work without him. You get to it now, before you're late, and I'll see you when it's break time. All right?'

Alice ran her sleeve across her face and then did her best to wipe Charlie's. 'Come on then. We don't want to have our wages docked, do we?' She took his hand.

Annie watched them go, and worried about them all through the first part of her shift.

Neither she nor they ever bought breakfast at the mill, but they always went out for the break the same as everyone else, so Annie was surprised not to see them in their usual corner when she entered the yard. She stood for a while, peering round – it wasn't as if there was a great crowd they could hide in – until nudged by Grace. 'If you're looking for those kiddies, they're over there.'

She pointed, and Annie followed the direction to see Alice and Charlie over by the porter's lodge, standing with a couple of mill men – one of the overlookers from the spinning room, and another who was a clerk, judging by his collar and tie.

Annie's heart lurched as she saw that standing with them was a police constable.

'Annie!' both the children cried out and threw themselves at her as soon as she approached, clutching at her as though they were drowning.

'What is it?' she asked. 'What's wrong?' But an all-too-predictable fear was growing in her.

The constable addressed her. 'Are you a relative of these children, miss?'

'I . . . I help look after them, yes.'

'Well, I'm afraid to have to say that their father's dead.'

Four small, desperate hands clutched at Annie's apron even more tightly, and she put her arms around two thin little pairs of shoulders. 'How did it happen?'

'An accident, no question, and there were several witnesses. He was dead drunk, couldn't keep to his feet, and he was with a group larking about in the small hours when he fell in the river. They tried to pull him out but they weren't exactly sober themselves, and he was carried off. The body was found about an hour ago.'

Annie made no reply, concentrating on the children. Orphaned children. But not, if she had anything to do with it, friendless.

'So,' said the clerk, 'the question is what will happen to these two now.'

'They're good workers, I'll give 'em that,' said the overlooker. 'There's plenty more where they came from, o'course, but it'd be a shame to lose 'em.'

'Very well.' The clerk nodded. 'We can keep them on, but if they're orphans I'll see about moving them to the dormitory, and have apprentice papers drawn up for them.'

'No!' The word was out of Annie's mouth before she could stop it, and all the men looked at her in surprise.

'You wish to say something?' enquired the clerk, his expression as frosty as the ground.

'They can come and live with me,' she said. 'I'm not their sister, more of a . . . distant relative, but they'll be better off living with me.' He looked sceptical, and she suddenly recalled what Mrs Otway had once said to her: *Persuade them that it's the best thing for them.* 'That will cause you the least trouble. Sir,' she added. 'There'll be no need for you to take time drawing up papers, or to make any arrangements about the dormitory. Alice and Charlie will simply be here on time for work every day exactly as they are now.'

The clerk and the overlooker exchanged a glance, and both nodded. Annie heaved a sigh of relief.

'Well then,' said the constable, 'that sounds like it's settled, and no more for me to do.' He turned to Annie. 'I'm thinking there's probably no money saved up for a burial? He wasn't in one of those clubs?'

'I don't think so.'

'Right. I'll tell them to arrange a pauper's burial, and you don't need to worry about it.' He looked down at the children with some sympathy. 'It's hard for them, I know. You look after them, miss.'

'I will.'

The constable departed, as did the clerk, and the overlooker tapped Alice on the shoulder just as the whistle blew. 'Come on now, back to work. Keep your mind off it, that's the best thing.'

'Yes, yes it is,' said Annie, gently starting to disentangle herself. 'I'll see you here at dinnertime, and then when work finishes today we'll all go home together, all right?' She watched Alice take her brother's hand as they crossed the yard.

By the time she got back to the weaving shed, she was half a minute behind the others, and Amos shouted at her. She didn't care, letting it slide off her as she thought about the enormous responsibility she'd just taken on, about how they were all going to manage. This made Amos even more bad-tempered, and he cuffed the ear of an unsuspecting boy whose sweeping brought him within reach.

She, Annie Shaw, had two children. A younger brother and sister, as they now were, and it was going to be up to her to make sure they were housed, clothed and fed.

It was terrifying. But she would do it, and nobody was going to stop her.

* * *

'So, I had no other choice, did I?'

It was half past six and Annie, Alice and Charlie were all in the little kitchen parlour while Annie explained the day's events to Mrs Otway. The children were gripping each other's hands in wide-eyed fear while they waited to hear their fate, and even Annie was nervous. Would Mrs Otway want them in the house, for all that they could help pay their way? If not, what would she do? She could never condemn them to the horrors of the mill apprenticeship system, but would she be able to find somewhere else to live? Who would let them all lodge, given that even she herself was under age?

Annie needn't have worried. 'Cut two more slices of bread, then, and show them where the pump is,' was Mrs Otway's reply, before she spoke to the children directly. 'I'll expect you to keep clean and be careful with everything in the house, mind, but in return I'll make sure you're properly fed morning and evening.' She paused, peering at their pale faces. 'And nobody here will ever hit you.'

And that was that.

Later that evening they all sat down to talk about money. Clara, in an attempt to make herself useful, had spent the evening helping out at the pub, clearing up and sweeping, but it hadn't resulted in a job offer – the publican had good intentions, but he needed to look after his own business, so all she'd gained was sixpence and a few drinks.

Alice and Charlie earned four shillings a week each. Annie, feeling guilty, explained to them that she hadn't taken them in so that she could pilfer their wages, but that they would need to contribute towards rent and food. They looked so bewildered by the idea that she'd even *thought* of them retaining their own money that it made her sad. Paul, it transpired, had taken the entire amount off them each Saturday before they'd even made it out of the mill yard – and, to compound matters, had carried it straight to the pub instead of the baker's or the grocer's.

It was agreed that Maisie and Clara would share the house's middle room while Annie and the children had the attic. Charlie had only just turned seven, so there was no harm in his sleeping in there even though he was a boy; and, as Mrs Otway said, who knew where they'd all be by the time he was old enough for them to worry about that?

They also agreed that they would split the rent cost as a household working together, rather than as occupants of separate rooms. The overall rent for the house was fifteen shillings a week, which would have to be met in its entirety by those earning, as Mrs Otway had no income at all. With Annie, Maisie, Alice and Charlie all working, they could just about manage, although the budget for food and coals was going to have to be cut, and Annie was determined she'd find a way for the children to keep at least a penny or two for themselves even if it meant more coming out of her share. It looked as though every last farthing of her own would be allocated, which was a severe blow to her savings and to her plans for Hannah, but she'd just have to see how things went on before she decided her next move. For now, they all had a roof over their heads and they would be able to eat. Just.

Over the next few weeks of a bitterly cold January they tried out their new arrangements and found that they worked well enough, even though the situation was precarious and they couldn't afford a single misstep. However, Annie now had yet another worry to fill her mind: Mrs Otway's health. She'd always had some difficulty with her breathing, the result of so many years in the mill, but it was getting worse in the winter weather and she seemed to grow more bent and tired with each passing week. Annie and Clara took as much of the heavy load off her as possible, doing the laundry and filling the coal scuttle, but she still needed to do the shopping and the cooking and the housework during the day while Annie was at work and Clara out looking for it.

It was one Tuesday in the weaving shed, as Annie counted in her head the days and weeks since Christmas, that she realised it was the fifth of February: her birthday. She was fifteen today, another step on the road towards proper adulthood, although goodness knows she'd taken a fair few steps on that road already. It would make no difference to her income, unfortunately, as she wouldn't qualify for adult wages until she was sixteen, but it was a little cheering thought at an otherwise dark time. She couldn't really afford it, but she would call at the baker's on the way home and see if they had any end-of-the-day currant buns that she might be able to get cheap, to give Alice and Charlie a treat.

There had been nasty rumours swirling round the mill that the situation was about to get even worse, and that there might be yet more layoffs. However, Annie tried not to pay too much attention to gossip, and for now Alice and Charlie were still working hard up in the spinning room, the overlooker there realising quite quickly that their change of living circumstances hadn't made any material difference to their ability to tie threads and clean under machines – indeed, that they were actually improved in energy.

Annie was successful in her quest for cheap buns, and that evening they were all crammed in the little kitchen parlour after tea when there was a rumbling noise from the street outside. It was unmistakeably the sound of heavy wagons jolting over the cobbles, but it was half past nine at night, a very unusual time.

Annie wondered if it might be good news – perhaps a large delivery of raw cotton was coming in, after having made it through all the trouble in America to arrive in Liverpool?

The rumbling faded as the vehicles passed, and they all forgot about it.

Half an hour later there was a knocking on the door. Or, hardly a knock at all, really – more of a sort of scratching.

They all looked at each other in puzzlement. Annie got up to answer it, foot and chair at the ready, just in case, just like Sam had always taught her.

As she opened the door, she gasped in surprise. Standing on the frozen doorstep, shivering uncontrollably in her bare feet and thin garment, was Hannah.

Chapter Twelve

Annie caught the girl as she fell, swinging her off her feet to carry her inside. She weighed almost nothing.

'Bring her over to the fire,' said Mrs Otway, motioning for the others to move. 'Alice, fetch the blanket off my bed there. Clara, see if that tea's still hot.'

Between them they wrapped Hannah up and forced some warm liquid between her chattering teeth. Annie sat with the girl on her knee, her arms wrapped round her as she sought to transfer some of her own body warmth.

It took some while, but eventually Hannah's shivering lessened and then stopped, and some life came back into her features.

'Can you tell us what happened?' asked Annie. 'How did you get out of the dormitory? Will they be out looking for you?'

Hannah shook her head. 'I wasn't in the dormitory. They said there wasn't enough work for all of us any more, and they weren't going to spend money feeding and housing us to be idle. So they put half of us back in the carts and said we were going back to the workhouse.' Her face screwed up and tears began to fall. 'I didn't want to go back there, I really didn't, and as we were coming through the village I saw your door and I thought . . . so when we got out on to the main road and away from all the lights, I jumped out and ran back.' She clutched at Annie in stark, white-faced terror. 'Are you going to send me back?'

Through all this, Alice and Charlie had been whispering to each other, and they now stepped forward. 'Please,' said Alice, 'please let her stay. If there's not enough food then she can share ours – we get plenty.' Charlie nodded vigorously.

Annie felt her eyes stinging at their kindness. 'I'll do everything I can, I promise. There must be a way you can stay.'

'She's welcome to, as far as I'm concerned,' said Mrs Otway. 'She's been such a good, polite little thing every time you've brought her here, and that workhouse is no place for any child. We'll manage the food, somehow. But will they be looking for her, that's the question? Are we going to get in trouble with the law?'

Annie considered, still holding Hannah close on her lap. 'Will they really be bothered about one missing child? When they've got so many to look after?'

Clara snorted. 'Of course they won't. They won't care a fig about one orphan, except as it affects their paperwork. They'll just mark her down on their list as dead, and that'll be the end of it.'

Annie clutched at Hannah, afraid that such pitiless words would cut her deeply, but Hannah only looked at Clara with rising hope. 'So – they won't come looking for me? They won't try to take me back?'

'Why would they want to take you back and pay for your food, when they can get you off their hands to someone else?' asked Clara, again with an almost brutal directness. 'There's nippers smaller than you left to fend for themselves all over Liverpool.' She thought for a moment. 'Still, maybe don't try getting another job at the mill any time soon, in case they recognise you – not that they're taking anyone on in any case.'

Annie was doing some arithmetic in her head. Hannah would have no earnings, but if she slept in the room that they were already sharing . . . it *would* mean a bit extra on the food bill, of course, but then again she would now be able to use the money she'd been saving towards buying out the apprenticeship . . .

Everyone in the room was nodding. 'Just change your name,' said Maisie, 'to be sure. Your last name, I mean – you can still be Hannah.'

'That's a good idea,' said Annie. 'Do you mind?'

'Course not,' said Hannah, more life coming back into her expression now that the worst was over. 'Like I told you before, I never had a last name of my own, 'cos nobody asked my Ma what hers was before she died. But they had to have one for their list, so they just put Smith, like they did for some of the others.'

'Well, then,' said Annie, more brightly, 'you've got a chance that hardly anyone else gets: you can choose your own last name. What do you fancy? Anything you like.'

Hannah looked up at her. 'Can I be called Shaw? Like you?'

And that, finally, was what made Annie cry.

* * *

They settled it that Hannah would stay in the house with Mrs Otway during the day while Annie and the others were at work, at least until they were sure there was going to be no pursuit. They needn't have worried, though. It was just as Clara had predicted: nobody cared enough to chase up the case of one missing workhouse orphan. That would have been tragic under any other circumstances, but in this case it suited Annie very well.

And so Hannah swept and shopped and cooked, keeping Mrs Otway company, and Annie was glad for both of them. She was also pleased to find, one day not long after this, that Alice and Charlie were both being moved into the weaving shed. Some of the other children had left, their out-of-work parents packing up and moving their families elsewhere in search of employment, so Charlie was now to clean under and around the machines in here, rather than in the spinning room, while Alice was to be a 'chit', the term for a small girl who helped to keep looms free of fluff and loose fibres, tied up ends and ran back and forth fetching and carrying shuttles and bobbins.

Annie's pleasure at being able to keep a closer watch on Alice and Charlie during working hours was soon, however, dampened by realising that they now came under Amos's eye – and under his heavy hand and his wooden clogs, too. The overlooker had never exactly been a well-tempered man, but his mood seemed to be permanently foul these days; Annie had seen him reduce more than one weaver to tears with his bullying ways, as well as his usual habit of cuffing and kicking any children who came within his reach, whether they were working properly or not.

One Saturday morning, Annie watched as another luckless girl was shouted at, her piece of calico examined, criticised and finally rejected. She appeared to be pleading, and Annie knew what she was saying even though she couldn't hear it: the quality of the cotton they were getting in at the moment was different, inferior, and it broke all too easily, meaning that there were many more joins and knots in the threads than usual. Nobody could help it, but Amos seemed to take it all as a personal insult, and to believe that the girls were all bringing him lesser-quality cloth to inspect on purpose.

Her pleading seemed to annoy him even more and he lost his temper completely; nobody needed to be able to hear him to be aware of the sort of profanity that was coming out of his mouth. The girl cowered, and Annie started to feel annoyed herself. Why couldn't Amos see that they were all working as best they could under difficult circumstances?

It was just then that Annie caught sight of Charlie. He was on his hands and knees under the loom that was nearest to where Amos was standing, sweeping with his brush and working his way out backwards as the machinery crashed back and forth over his head.

As he shuffled bottom-first towards the edge of the machine, one of his feet emerged from under it and came into contact with Amos's leg.

It was the barest touch of a bare foot, and Amos can hardly have felt it at all, never mind been hurt by it, but he stopped dead in the middle of his tirade against the girl and looked down. Then he lifted his clogged foot and stamped hard on Charlie's ankle, following up with a vicious kick to his backside as that too emerged. Charlie cried out in pain and was propelled forward, only just managing to duck under the machinery rather than being thrown into it face first.

Annie dropped what she was doing and stormed over to shove herself in front of Amos. 'You leave him alone!' she bellowed, furiously.

He was so taken aback by her anger that for a moment he was speechless. Then he took in a deep breath, and Annie braced herself.

To her great surprise, the outburst never came. Instead, Amos was looking in consternation over her shoulder.

She turned to see that Mr Frederick was approaching. 'Is there a problem, Potter?' he asked. It wasn't as loud in here as it used to be, with fewer than half the looms in operation, so he only had to raise his voice rather than shout.

'It's this girl,' the overlooker managed to splutter. 'And that idiot boy.'

Mr Frederick was shaking his head. 'I saw what happened.' He pointed to where Charlie was sitting on the floor, crying and clutching at his swollen ankle. 'And while I have no objection to children being punished if they're misbehaving, this boy was merely doing the job that my father pays him for. And you've now rendered him unfit for at least the next few hours.'

Amos attempted to frame a reply, but Mr Frederick held up a hand to forestall him, and spoke directly to Charlie. 'Go outside, and find where the fire buckets are lined up, filled with water. You know where that is?'

Charlie nodded.

'Put your foot in the cold water and stay like that until you've counted to a hun— until you've counted to twenty, five times over, if you can do that. If anyone asks you what you're doing, tell them I sent you and that they can argue with me about it. Understand?'

Charlie nodded again and began to make his way out. Annie was relieved to see that although he was limping heavily, he could at least put some weight on his bad foot, so she hoped the injury would be temporary.

'Your brother, I take it?' Mr Frederick was speaking to her now.

'I . . . yes, sir.' It was easier than trying to explain.

'Well, he should be glad to have you on his side, at least.' Despite the volume, both of his voice and of the background noise, she could detect a tinge of amusement. 'Let him sit out for a couple of hours, or even the rest of the shift if he needs it.' He cast a glance at Amos. 'It won't be the boy's wages that get deducted for it.'

Mr Frederick walked off. Annie's gaze followed him, thinking that perhaps not all members of rich families were necessarily awful people. And, when you came to think about it, he was really quite handsome, wasn't he?

She turned back to Amos and tried to keep the smile off her face, but he saw enough to enrage him again anyway.

'You think you can make me look stupid in front of Mr Frederick, do you? You and the boy? Well, we'll see about that.' He leaned towards her. 'He won't be here next time.'

Charlie was still limping when noon came round, but his ankle looked no worse, so Annie breathed a sigh of relief. They collected their wages, and then she and Alice walked slowly with him out of the mill. 'Are you still all right to go to the square? We said we would. But if you like we can take you home, and then Alice and I can go by ourselves.'

'I'm fine,' said Charlie, through gritted teeth.

'Sure?'

'Yes.'

'All right then.'

The reason they were heading for the open space in the middle of the village – 'square' was over-egging it a bit, but that was what everyone called it – was that there was to be a public talk. Jack had organised it, bringing in a speaker from Liverpool who was going to tell them all about events in America, and also about what was happening across Lancashire, where there were hundreds of mills and thousands of workers in similar circumstances to themselves.

The square was quite crowded when they got there, with all those who were out of work jammed together with the remaining employed hands who'd come straight down from the mill. There was a chilly spring wind whipping through the space, but the warmth of so many bodies kept the worst of it away. Jack saw them as they arrived, and waved, though he didn't come over – he was talking to a man who was presumably their speaker. The stranger looked vaguely familiar to Annie, though she couldn't work out why.

Jack had been extremely busy in the weeks since he was laid off. He'd tried again to get all the unemployed workers together, and, knowing that the Carringtons wouldn't talk to him, attempted to find one among them to speak on behalf of all. However, this hadn't worked because all those who volunteered were men with grudges, or who were so angry that they couldn't be trusted to negotiate calmly, while anyone inoffensive enough to the Carringtons to have any chance of success refused to put themselves forward. Jack had tried to persuade Luke, Grace's father, to take on the task, as he was highly regarded by everyone for his honesty, and he'd never put a foot wrong in all the years he'd worked at the mill. If the Carringtons would listen to anyone, it would be him, and the initial subjects of discussion were rational rather than radical: an idea, for example, that more workers could be taken back and that they could all work shorter hours. Surely there could be no objection to that? The work would still be done, the thread and cloth produced, the same amount paid out in wages, but the losses of earnings would be better spread out. But Luke refused flat-out to take part, saying that he wanted none of it and it was better for everyone to keep their heads down.

Annie couldn't really see that this policy had done him a lot of good so far: he, with his impeccable record and loyalty to the firm and its owners, was just as much out of work as Jack was. She'd tried to get this across to Grace once or twice, worried at her friend's increasingly pinched face, but to no avail. The only job Luke had been able to find was one breaking rocks for road-building, a strenuous occupation at the best of times, and verging on torture for a man with his cough and all that damage to his chest from years in the mill. But he did it anyway: he set off in the early hours to walk five miles, spent his day swinging a pickaxe with navvies and Irishmen twice his size and half his age, then staggered and wheezed five miles home so he could collapse for a few hours before it all started again. And for this he earned less than half what he'd been paid in the mill. Nora and her elder daughter hadn't managed to find work at all, because women weren't employed for that kind of thing and there was little else.

Jack had also tried to interest the authorities in the plight of the laid-off workers, pressing them to set up additional relief, but the various boards and churches seemed indifferent, taking the view that the unemployed and poor were somehow in a situation of their own making. Annie's anger and frustration, when she heard this, were great, and she wondered how Jack could possibly have either the patience or the energy to keep going in the face of such opposition. But somehow he did. His latest venture was that the people here shouldn't see themselves in isolation, but rather as part of a much bigger picture that spread not only across the county but also over the sea, which is why he had invited someone to come and give them a talk.

A silence fell over the square as their guest stood forward to speak. Some of what he said about *Secession* and *Confederates* and *Union* went over Annie's head, but when he began to talk about the plight of American slaves she was drawn wholly into his narrative. However bad anything was here, it bore no comparison to the existence endured by those poor souls. Annie thought of their family friend Abraham, and how he might still be suffering it if he hadn't escaped, and of all the men, women and children who were still trapped and literally *owned* by their masters.

The whole crowd was spellbound, but slowly there came the realisation that it was the fight over freeing the slaves that was stopping the cotton being picked, which meant it wasn't being sent to Liverpool, which meant they had none to spin and weave. To put it bluntly, if the slaves remained slaves, the mills would go back to full capacity and the workers here would be better off.

There were one or two murmurs when this became clear, but Annie was pleased to see that they were immediately shushed and shouted down. The overwhelming feeling among the crowd was that they should stand in solidarity with the abolitionists and the slaves, and that the principle of freedom for all must be upheld no matter what. Annie's heart swelled with pride as she saw hungry people declaring their defiance and support at the top of their voices.

Next came the information of what was happening elsewhere in the county. Some other mill owners, apparently, were doing all they could to mitigate the situation: taking on extra workers on their country estates, distributing food, setting up schools and training opportunities . . . all things that were conspicuously absent here.

This time the angry murmurs weren't shouted down quite so quickly.

Annie sensed the change in the mood of the crowd, and wondered if she should start retreating before any of the more hot-headed men got too angry. She took hold of the children's hands.

Before she could move, there was some shouting and shoving, and then Mr Theodore appeared in the space where the speaker was standing. He was accompanied by some of the mill watchmen, all carrying cudgels, and also by three police constables.

There was some low-level muttering and whistling, and a few jeers, but his innate sense of superiority allowed him to ignore them effortlessly.

'This meeting has gone on long enough,' he declared. 'You can all disperse now and go back to your homes.'

'What if we don't want to?' called a belligerent voice.

Mr Theodore sighed, deliberately and performatively. 'Then it will be with great sadness that I ask one of the constables here to read the Riot Act.'

Annie didn't quite understand what he meant, but others in the crowd certainly did, and the murmur became an angry buzz. She gripped Alice and Charlie's hands more tightly.

Jack and the man who had delivered the speech were now talking to each other in low voices. This went on for a few moments, then they nodded at each other and the speaker stepped forward. 'Friends,' he said, loudly, 'let us remain calm. I had already finished what I was going to say, so there is no interruption. Please, disperse in peace to consider all that you've heard, and God bless you all.'

His tone, which contained not the least hint of alarm, went some way towards soothing the general mood, and some of those around the edges of the crowd began to drift away. To add to the general air of finality, the speaker publicly shook hands with Jack, and then the two of them walked away from their position, neither of them bothering to speak or even to look at Mr Theodore on the way past.

The two men parted, the speaker mounting a horse, and then Jack spotted Annie and made his way through the thinning crowd towards them. 'I saw you earlier. I'm glad you were able to come.'

'I wouldn't have missed it. All of what he said about slaves . . . it breaks my heart. There are people much worse off than ourselves, and we need to stand up for them.'

Jack smiled, which was such a rare occurrence that it made Annie's heart give a little flutter.

'Now,' he added, 'shall I walk you back? There's not going to be any trouble, and it's too early in the day for anyone to be drunk, but I'd like to be certain you're all home safe.'

They turned to go, but as soon as they were on the move, Jack noticed how badly Charlie was limping. 'What's this, then?'

Between them they told the tale, and his face darkened. 'That Amos Potter is a bully. He shouldn't be left in charge of women or children. This is why we need to fight for better conditions!' Then, to Charlie, 'Well, you're a brave lad, that's all I can say. Come on and I'll carry you home.'

He crouched so that Charlie could clamber on to his shoulders, and, with Annie and Alice hand-in-hand beside them, they all made their way back to the house.

Mrs Otway must have seen them coming through the window, for she was already opening the door as they reached it. 'Annie? Are you all right? I heard there was a gathering, and I was worried about you all. Come in, children, come in out of this wind, before it goes to your chest.' She looked Jack up and down, and her lined faced creased even further into a grin. 'I haven't seen you properly in years, boy – you come in too, and warm yourself.'

Jack hesitated, but Annie stood aside to usher him in. 'It's fine. Besides, what damage can it do? They've already sacked you once; they can't do it again.'

Jack looked up and down the street, but nobody was paying them any particular attention. 'All right, if you're sure.'

They all went inside. Only Mrs Otway and Hannah were there; Maisie would be at work, of course, Saturday afternoon still being relatively busy at the pub, and Annie didn't know where Clara was. Had she seen her at the meeting? She couldn't recall.

Annie and Jack both looked at Charlie's ankle and agreed that it wasn't broken, and that hopefully the swelling would go down enough for him to be able to work on Monday. He winced at their probing but declared that there was nothing wrong with him, and even tried to walk up and down to prove it, until Alice told him to stop being silly and sit down.

They weren't able to have a drink of tea, because they only had enough coals each day to light the fire in the evening, but they sat round the table together and it was warm enough with the door shut.

Jack spotted Hannah, who hadn't joined them straight away but who was hovering shyly over in the far corner. 'Hello. Sorry, am I in your chair? I can stand up . . .'

Hannah came forward. 'I know you. You're the one who helped me pick everything up when I dropped the shopping basket in the street last week.'

He looked at her more closely. 'Ah, so that was you? Of course it was, I see it now. Glad to help. If I'd known you lived here, I could have carried the basket home for you.'

'And,' she added, 'you used to come and talk to us through the fence at the mill, and pass us food, like Annie did.'

Annie looked at Jack in shock. He didn't, or couldn't, meet her gaze, and she was almost sure that he was blushing. But then something struck him and he looked more keenly at Hannah. 'So, wait, you were in the yard with the workh—' Realisation dawned. 'Is your name Hannah, by any chance?'

'Yes, that's right,' said Hannah, in a more confident tone. 'Hannah Shaw.'

Jack cast a glance at Annie, and started. 'But how . . .?' Then he stopped. 'None of my business.' He nodded at Hannah. 'But I'm glad for you.'

There was a silence, which lasted long enough to start being awkward.

More to change the subject than anything else, Annie asked, 'What's the Riot Act?'

Jack opened his mouth to reply, but was forestalled by a gasp from Mrs Otway. 'The Riot Act? Don't tell me they were threatening that today! Lord have mercy on us.'

She sounded so agitated that everyone looked at her in surprise.

'I've heard it before,' she said, grimly. 'A long time before any of you were born – why, it would be forty years ago, or thereabouts. In Manchester.'

'Yes, but what is it?'

'If they read out the right words, it means they can tell any group of people – no matter how peaceful – that they have to disperse, and if they're not gone within an hour, they can call in the troops.' She shook her head. 'I don't ever want to see that again. Innocent people dead, women and children . . .'

Annie thought that the old woman's mind might be wandering – the army? Here in England? Called out against their own people? Attacking women and children? Surely not . . . but Jack was nodding and saying he'd heard tell of it from his grandfather. Annie swallowed.

'Anyway,' said Mrs Otway, coming back to herself and looking at the three frightened children, 'enough of that now. I'm sure it won't happen here, my dears. This trouble can surely not last much longer, and then we'll all get back to normal.'

Annie would like to think so, even if only to cheer the children up, but she could see that Jack was now silently shaking his head.

Chapter Thirteen

January 1862

Annie was counting down the days until her sixteenth birthday. It would mean working longer hours, of course, because she'd be classed as an adult, but it would also mean a pay rise. And, goodness, how they needed it.

The 'trouble', as everyone still kept calling it, in America had turned out to be a full-blown war, and there was no sign of it stopping. Virtually no cotton was arriving from there at all, and they were making do with stuff of a vastly inferior quality from other parts of the world. It had short fibres and snapped far too easily, meaning that all the weavers were having pay deducted for producing substandard work, no matter how hard they tried, and that Amos was in a constant state of fury. More than one child in the weaving shed was guaranteed to end each day with bruises, and Annie was continually torn between needing to keep her job and the overwhelming desire to give him a taste of his own medicine.

Mrs Otway had passed away just as autumn turned to winter, as quietly and lightly as a falling leaf. Annie had come down one morning to find her apparently fast asleep in her bed, but it was a sleep from which she would never wake. So there was another pauper's funeral, though among the tears there was, this time, at least a sense of a life well lived and peacefully ended. She was back with her husband and children now, and Annie hoped they were all warm and happy in heaven.

They had been fortunate in being allowed to stay in the house following Mrs Otway's passing. The rent man had noted that he wouldn't normally let to a group of single young women and children, and at first he'd seemed inclined to stick to that rule. But so many properties were now standing empty, their residents either leaving of their own accord or being evicted, that he was persuaded; as long as they paid up in full every week, he said, grudgingly, they could stay. He had, in fact, made an attempt to increase the rent, but Annie had told him in no uncertain terms that there were plenty of other places they could move into whose owners would be glad to have them, and that he was lucky to have tenants who kept the place clean and neat, so he had soon backed down.

Hannah, bless her, had already been doing quite a large share of the housework since Mrs Otway had been in decline, and now she took on the rest of it too. Annie felt guilty that a child of that age should be left in charge, and on her own most of the day, but Hannah earnestly said that she preferred it to any alternative – not that there were many alternatives – and she certainly did seem to have a knack for cooking. So Annie reminded herself that there were many worse places Hannah could be, and that the girl was actually several years older than Clara had been when she'd been left in charge of Annie every day, back in the court.

What was more of a worry, and what they didn't tell the rent man, when it happened just after Christmas, was that Maisie had finally been laid off from the pub and had left the village to seek work back in Liverpool. The wages that Annie, Alice and Jack brought in were barely sufficient to cover the rent, and the only reason they had anything for bread and coals was that Clara sporadically brought home random sums. She didn't have a regular job, and Annie often asked her where she got the money from, but she only ever received an evasive reply in return. However, given that it was only this contribution from Clara that was standing between them and starvation, Annie didn't feel that she had the right to enquire too closely.

Jack had been continuing with his multi-pronged campaign of informing, offering practical help and trying to get more aid from the authorities, and he had finally made some headway. The powers-that-be had eventually realised the scale of the disaster engulfing the region, and that they couldn't send everyone to the workhouse, so they had instituted a system of relief. It wasn't given in the form of money, however; the unemployed received only tickets, which could be presented against the purchase of a strictly controlled range of items. Nobody was happy about this, and several meetings in the village had become restless.

Some of the ideas that Jack, Annie and the others had come up with were working better. A soup kitchen was set up every Sunday so that everyone, employed or not, could get something hot into them at least one day a week. Annie was able to use the schooling she'd received to set up some basic classes for children in reading, writing and arithmetic, which she did on Saturday afternoons and Sunday mornings. They had no books to read and no slates to write on, of course, but they used sticks or their fingers to make marks in the ground, or found some old wooden boards that could be scratched with stones.

In another small victory, between them, Annie and Jack had made gains for the unemployed women and girls of the village. Anyone who wanted to claim parish relief had to work for it – that was the rule – and many of the men had been set to breaking stones or even sent away to mines. However, as there wasn't any work suitable for women, they were also not allowed to claim relief, putting them in a vicious circle from which there seemed no escape. However, Annie had come up with the idea that sewing classes might count as work for this purpose, and Jack had somehow made it happen. So the women sat in the church hall and sewed, under the instruction of someone who had once been a tailor before moving into mill work; the resulting garments were sent off to be used in workhouses and charities, and the women and girls were able to claim enough parish relief to keep starvation at bay for now.

It was Sunday today, another bitterly cold frost still riming the ground in the shadows where the sun didn't warm it, and activities were in full swing. Annie was at one side of the square with a dozen children, all wrapped up in as many layers as they owned, while opposite them Jack and his volunteers set up the tables to distribute soup and bread. To Annie's surprise, Nora appeared and silently began to help, standing behind one of the tables and slicing bread into individual portions.

Annie told her pupils to continue with their alphabets and slid over the icy cobbles. 'Nora! I haven't seen you for a long time. You don't normally help here, do you?'

As she drew nearer she could see that Nora's eyes were swollen with weeping. 'No,' she said, 'I didn't use to. Luke said we should just keep ourselves to ourselves, and not risk getting involved in anything in case it led to trouble.' Suddenly, she banged her knife down on the table, making Annie jump. 'And what good did that do him? God rest his soul. He kept his head down and stayed out of trouble all his life, and now he's cold in his grave just the same.'

'Oh, Nora, I'm so sorry.' Annie hadn't known; Grace had also been laid off from the mill a couple of months earlier, leaving the son as the only member of the family still in work, and she didn't see him often or know him well enough to engage in chat.

'Anyway,' continued Nora, making a huge effort to contain herself, 'I'm going to do whatever I can now, for everyone, no matter what happens. They can't hurt me any more.'

'Well, you and Grace are welcome to join the sewing, or Grace can come to my classes and help me out. Your older daughter left, didn't she?'

'Yes, thank God, she's married now to a boy from Ormskirk who's got a farm job. So she's safe – people will always need crops growing and harvesting, so he's not likely to get laid off like we were.'

Annie squeezed Nora's hand, smiled over at Jack as he carried one side of a huge steaming cauldron, and went back to her class. As she reached it, she noticed another new arrival at the soup kitchen: Mr Frederick. She'd seen him round the place a few times, helping out and chatting with people. She'd always had him marked down as the only one of the Carringtons who cared one farthing for the workers, and he'd been proving it by his actions. They certainly didn't ever see any of the rest of his family anywhere except the occasional glance as they went in and out of the offices at the mill. The only other evidence of their presence was the occasional girl who'd been unlucky enough to encounter Mr Theodore in a situation she couldn't make a quick escape from.

Annie gazed at Mr Frederick as he began to speak with those now forming a ragged queue, unaware that Jack was looking at her just as intently.

* * *

The fifth of February was a Wednesday. Annie wasn't sure whether she could start claiming adult wages straight away, or whether she had to see out the week at her current rate, but there was only one way to find out.

She blew on her hands as she walked up to the mill with Alice and Charlie in the darkness of the early morning. Once they were all in the yard she watched them head into the weaving shed before she turned to enter the office.

The first clerk who met her eye was, by coincidence, the elderly man with spectacles who had registered her when she'd first arrived at the mill, the one who'd spoken to her nicely. She placed herself in his eyeline and stood there until he looked up and noticed her.

When he saw who it was, he smiled. 'Yes?'

'I've come to tell you that I'm sixteen today,' she began, adding 'sir,' to be on the safe side. 'So I'd like to be moved from a young person's work and wages to an adult.'

He looked pained, then cast a quick glance around him to check that nobody else was listening. 'Sixteen today? You're sure?'

'Yes, sir. I was born on the fifth of February in eighteen forty-six.'

He shook his head, before asking, more urgently, 'You're sure you haven't made a mistake about the year? It's not your *fifteenth* birthday?'

What was he playing at? Trying to keep her at lower wages for another year, no doubt. She was disappointed, having thought him pleasant before. 'No, sir, I'm definitely sixteen today,' she said, firmly and at a greater volume.

The elderly clerk looked agonised, but he didn't get the chance to reply because Robinson, the senior, had overheard. 'Well then,' he interrupted, 'if that's the case then there's nothing else for it, I'm afraid. We'll be letting you go.'

Annie wasn't sure she'd heard that correctly. 'I beg your pardon?'

'I'm under instructions to keep the wage bill down. My standing orders at the moment are to pay nobody adult wages if we can employ a young person for the same job at a lower cost.'

Annie was in such shock that her voice nearly failed her. 'You're right,' she managed to croak. 'I made a mistake about the year. I'm only fifteen today.'

The relieved elderly clerk nodded and opened his mouth to reply, but he was forestalled. 'It's too late for that now,' said Robinson. 'My colleagues and I all heard you being definite about your date of birth, so off you go.'

Annie gaped.

The older man gave her a sympathetic look. 'We can pay you for the days you've already worked this week, of course.' He fumbled in a drawer for some coins, and then pressed them into Annie's outstretched hand, which she noticed with some surprise was shaking violently.

'Now get off the premises,' said Robinson, dismissively.

Annie stood staring at the money, unable to take a single step.

The senior clerk tapped his foot. 'I have other business to attend to, miss.' He threw a nervous glance at the inner door, the one that led to the Carringtons' office. 'Please don't oblige me to summon a watchman.'

Annie's legs felt numb, but she forced herself to take a step, and then another. Soon she was outside the office. And then there was nothing for it but to walk out of the gate, perhaps for the last time.

Her head was spinning so much as she slipped and slithered her way down the hill that it was a miracle she managed to stay upright. The horror of what had just happened – the immediate loss of her wages – the difficulty of finding something else – the rent – the food – the children – she just couldn't think straight.

She felt sick and dizzy as she entered the house.

The sound of the door opening caused Hannah, who was scrubbing the table, to jump in surprise. 'Annie? What's—' Then she looked more closely and pulled out a chair. 'Sit down.'

Annie collapsed into it. She just didn't know what to do, what to say, what to think. How could they possibly manage now? What were they to do?

Hannah was wringing her hands, a worried expression on her face.

Annie needed to pull herself together. 'Is Clara in?' It would be better to talk with the only other adult in the house before breaking the news to any of the children.

'Yes, she's upstairs,' replied Hannah. She hesitated. 'I think she's crying.'

Annie didn't take that in at first, so near to tears as she was herself. Of course Clara was upset – this was a disaster. But then her mind came back to itself a little. How could Clara possibly know already? There was no way she could be aware of what had just happened up at the mill.

With an even greater feeling of foreboding, Annie mounted the stairs.

Clara was lying face down on the bed in the middle room, sobbing into a crumpled-up blanket.

Annie sat down next to her. 'Clara? What's the matter?'

A tear-ravaged gaze met her own. 'It was bound to happen one day, I suppose.'

'What was? What's happened?'

Clara scrubbed at her eyes. 'No point trying to hide it, not from you.' She took a deep breath. 'Annie, I'm going to have a baby.'

Chapter Fourteen

Annie stared blankly at the wall, watching her breath cloud in front of her in the freezing room. There was just too much to take in; she couldn't do it.

Clara was crying into the blanket again, her shoulders shaking.

That helped to rouse Annie. First things first: her own problem could wait. After all, a couple more hours wasn't going to change anything, was it?

Annie stroked her friend's hair. 'It's all right, we'll find a way through all of this, I promise.' She paused, wondering how to phrase the question. 'Is . . . is there any chance that the baby's father might marry you?'

The weeping intensified, which Annie took to mean 'No'. A man out of work with no money to support a wife? Or, God forbid, a man who was already married?

She continued trying to comfort Clara while listening to the various incoherent words being sobbed out, and then she went completely cold as she caught one with unmistakable clarity: *Carrington*.

'Clara?' Annie patted her urgently. 'Clara? Is that why you're crying? Did . . . did Mr Theodore attack you?'

Clara sat up. 'Ha!'

Annie was confused. 'I don't understand.'

'Be glad you don't.'

'I . . .'

Clara rubbed her eyes again. 'Him, I can understand. He's so obvious about it. All you have to do with him is stay out of his way.' She gave a bitter laugh. 'At least he's honest about what he's after. But the other one . . . oh, helping out, being so charming, and then making you feel like you owe him something, making you think it's *you* that's being unreasonable for not wanting to . . .'

There seemed to be only one interpretation possible, but it was so unbelievable that Annie had to ask, just to be sure. 'Clara . . . are you saying that Mr *Frederick* is your baby's father?'

'Oh yes. And I don't think I'm the only one, either. Creeping around, wanting to "help out" all those families with daughters . . . I could see right through it, but somehow I got caught out just like all the others.

Owed it to him, he said, or what's those fancy words he used? "Under an obligation" to him for everything he'd done. Pah!' she spat. 'And he said he'd do even more to help everyone out because he could see that we were all so *grateful*.'

She fell silent.

Annie's shock was profound, but as she sat with Clara, trying to comfort her, that shock slowly turned to anger, and then to seething, furious rage.

Well, there was nothing to lose, was there? Not any more.

Within moments she was outside and on her way back to the mill.

It was still early; none of the Carringtons would be here yet. But that wasn't a problem, as Annie had nothing else to do with her time. She waited outside the gates while the breakfast break came and went, hoping that Alice and Charlie wouldn't be too worried when they didn't see her in the yard, and then waited some more, stamping her feet and blowing on her hands to keep a bit of life in them.

It was late morning, by her estimation, when she saw the carriage approaching, the horses struggling with the slippery cobbles on the hill. It would have to stop in order for the main double gates to be opened, and that would be her chance.

The carriage was being driven by some kind of servant, with another sitting beside him. As soon as the vehicle came to a halt and the second man jumped down, Annie ran over and banged on the door. 'Mr Frederick? Are you in there? I need to talk to you!'

Two surprised faces appeared: both of the Carrington sons were within.

Mr Theodore took in the situation at a glance and laughed. 'Oh, dear, Fred, been a bit careless, have we?' He gave Annie an apprising look. 'No, I don't think I've had that one, so it's definitely not my problem.'

Mr Frederick was staring at her in confusion. *Trying to remember which girls he's coerced into lying with him and which he hasn't*, thought Annie. *Are there so many that he can't even remember?*

Mr Theodore guffawed again, enjoying his brother's discomfort. 'If you're too scared to talk to her, Freddie, we can always drive straight on.'

There was a tone of ridicule in his voice that seemed to needle Mr Frederick. 'I can take care of it, Theo, thanks all the same.' He waved off the servant, who had opened the gate, belatedly realised what was going on and was now putting a hand on Annie's arm to pull her away.

A pair of highly polished boots emerged from the carriage as Mr Frederick alighted, telling the driver to go on. He was wearing a heavy coat over his suit, along with a hat, scarf and a pair of fine leather gloves. He certainly wouldn't be shivering, no matter how long he had to stand outside. 'Well?'

Annie ignored her wooden clogs and increasingly threadbare shawl, her anger keeping her warm. 'I want to talk to you about my friend Clara.'

His face took on an expression of blank innocence. 'I'm not sure I know anyone of that name.'

'You do. You somehow persuaded her to lie with you, and now she's going to have a baby.'

He snorted. 'Oh, please. Some girl's got herself pregnant out of wedlock, and she wants to pin the blame on me?'

Annie stood her ground. 'She told me it was you, and I believe her.'

He made a dismissive gesture. 'Yes, but that's the point, isn't it? You might believe her, but nobody else will. It's just not my problem, I'm afraid.'

Annie was so incensed by his utter disdain that she had to concentrate hard on keeping her hands down by her sides. If she were to hit or even touch him she had no doubt that she would be straight off to gaol, and that wouldn't help anyone.

Before she could frame a suitable reply, they were interrupted by the arrival of the chief clerk, who had come puffing across the yard.

Again he exhibited the extreme deference that Annie had previously noted in his dealings with the Carringtons. 'Mr Frederick, sir,' he gasped, almost bowing to the ground, 'I'm sorry you've been . . . girl, I told you this morning you had to leave the premises – it's no good trying to beg the owners for your job back. Get away with you now, and leave him alone!'

Mr Frederick's superior smile widened even further. 'Oh dear,' he said, in a mocking tone. 'Lost your job, did you? What a shame.'

'Because of her age, Mr Frederick,' interrupted Robinson, anxiously. My orders are to—'

He was waved away. 'Yes, yes. I'm sure you've been carrying out your duties admirably. Go back to them now.'

That gloating smile was turned on Annie again. 'Short of money, are you? Thought you'd try to screw some out of me on behalf of your friend?' He laughed. 'Or maybe you'd like to find a new way to earn a bit, would you?'

'How dare—'

She hadn't even got the word out before he interrupted her, leaning forward and speaking in a sudden, unexpectedly vicious tone. 'Oh, I can very much dare. As you'll find out, if you try to cross me or talk to me again.' He lifted his head and called out to Robinson's departing back. 'You there!'

The clerk turned and scuttled back towards them. 'Yes, Mr Frederick?'

'This girl has a young brother working in the mill.' He looked consideringly at Annie. 'The one Amos Potter stamped on. Fine man, that Potter, just doing his job. And, wait . . . a sister as well, wasn't it? The girl who got caught in the machinery that time? I knew I remembered you from somewhere.'

He addressed Robinson again. 'Find them both and tell them their services are no longer required. If it will cause an issue in the weaving shed today, they can work out the rest of the day, but after that I want them gone, do you hear? Our business is too finely balanced to risk having trouble-making families working here.'

The clerk gave a servile nod and hurried back across to the office.

'Had enough for today, have you?' asked Mr Frederick, once he was sure the man was out of earshot. 'Or did you want to try my patience some more?' He examined one of his beautiful gloves. 'Might buy myself another pair with the wages we'll save from those children. Or we'll just find others to do the work, and for less. People are so *desperate* these days that they'll do anything.' He leaned in towards her. 'And, just between you and me, that includes your friend Clara. Though don't try saying that out loud, will you? I wouldn't want you to suffer any more misfortune than you already have.'

He walked through the gate, a spring in his step and his derisive laughter ringing in Annie's ears.

* * *

It was a silent room that evening.

Annie sat with Clara, Alice, Charlie and Hannah as they tried to come to terms with the enormity of what had happened to them. As of now, they had not one penny coming into the house between them. There was just enough money in the tin to pay the rent on Sunday, and then that was it. Nothing for food, for coals or for any more rent after that. Or, if they did what a lot of other people in the village had taken to doing, and hid themselves away, pretending to be out, when the rent man called, they would be able to buy enough food for another week, but at the end of it they'd be evicted.

There was certainly no other work going in the village, so the next day they all traipsed the three miles to Ormskirk and spent the day knocking on doors and asking, but there was nothing. Annie wasn't surprised, but she wasn't quite ready to give up yet, and they had a few more days in which they could look before the situation got completely desperate.

Of course, even if Clara got something then it wouldn't last long, as she'd be sacked as soon as her condition became clear in another month or two. But Annie was strong and the children were all willing, so perhaps they might just be able to manage?

By Saturday, most of her hopes had disappeared. As many had discovered before her, there was no work anywhere except breaking stones, and none of them would be taken on for that.

Annie rubbed her eyes as she stood by the table, calculating how many slices she might be able to get out of the remains of the bread, or whether she might be able to pawn the cooking pot. She'd spent half the night awake comforting Hannah, who was having continual nightmares about the prospect of going back to the workhouse, and she could see no practical solution to their problems.

Except the one she didn't really want to contemplate.

Over the last year, she'd kept up with writing her letters to Delilah, but somehow her family – her blood family – had faded a little into the distance, as she'd become increasingly caught up in the 'family' she now had here. Which made her wonder – would Delilah still welcome her back after all this time? Moreover, Annie absolutely couldn't and wouldn't leave Clara, Alice, Charlie and Hannah to their fates here, and how could she possibly expect her family to take in all of them as well?

At noon there was to be another talk in the square about the regional and international situation. Clara was tired after all the walking of the last few days and decided to stay at home and sleep, but all the children wanted to come, so Annie wrapped them up as well as she could and followed the crowds.

It was the same speaker as before: a Mr Hughes, as Annie had heard him called. He still looked naggingly familiar. Once more he was being greeted by Jack, and once more he stood forward to deliver his address.

The mood was, if anything, even darker than it had been last time. The circumstances in America seemed to be no different, but the people of Liverpool and Lancashire were suffering ever more deeply. And it was the ordinary working people, as Mr Hughes stressed, who were suffering, not the mill owners. Indeed, he continued, the owners were actually getting richer.

There was a murmur of real anger at this, and Annie struggled to listen over the noise to understand how this could possibly be. She was aghast to hear that many of the mill owners, the Carringtons included, had been hoarding the stores of raw cotton that they'd accumulated before the war broke out, because as it grew more scarce, its value increased. They had laid off workers and docked the wages of those who remained to spin and weave the inferior imports, while they *actually had enough proper American cotton to keep them all in work*. Instead of employing and paying the hard-working mill hands, they were letting them starve and die while they sat on the contents of their warehouses and got richer and richer without lifting a finger.

Annie wasn't the only one who was angered when the extent of this became fully understood. The murmur among the crowd became a full-throated roar, and there were even some cries that they should march on the mill.

The underlying mood was getting worse by the minute, and Annie had the children to think of. It was time to go.

But before she could move, both the Carrington brothers appeared along with even more watchmen and constables than last time. The speaker was bundled away and back to his horse, one of the policemen seeing him through the crowd and a good way along the road out of the village before he returned to stand with his fellows.

Mr Theodore was speaking. 'This assembly has been gathered for unlawful and riotous purposes.'

'No it hasn't!' Annie would recognise that voice anywhere, and she peered through the crowd to see Jack standing forward to confront the Carringtons. 'It's lawful to gather to listen to a speaker.'

'Not any more, it isn't,' continued Mr Theodore. 'And certainly not when you're whipping up sedition and violence against my father's property.' He nodded to one of the constables. 'Officer, arrest that man.'

Annie saw one of the uniformed constables step forward and reach out a hand towards Jack, but then he was lost to view as the crowd surged forward and there was a scuffle.

This was dangerous. Much as she wanted to try to fight her way through the crowd to reach Jack, to see that he was all right and offer what help she could, her first priority had to be keeping the children safe. 'All of you, join hands and hold on to me,' she instructed. 'Don't get separated.' But the press was thickening and she couldn't get them out of it.

One person she could still see was Mr Theodore, because he was standing up on something so his head was above the crowd. He looked almost amused, and now nodded with satisfaction at the trouble he'd caused. He spoke to someone lower down, standing by his elbow: Annie was too far away to hear the words, but she could see his lips quite clearly. 'Definitely a riotous assembly now,' he said. 'So you can read it out.'

Read it out. Read what? This surely meant that they were about to hear the Riot Act, the thought of which had so terrified Mrs Otway when she remembered it being used so many years before.

Mr Theodore jumped down, and a constable replaced him, so as to be visible to the whole crowd. He took a piece of paper from his pocket, unfolded it and called out in a booming voice that carried across the whole square and made the crowd fall silent.

'Our sovereign lady the Queen chargeth and commandeth all persons,' he thundered, the formal language frightening Annie even more than his tone, 'being assembled, immediately to disperse themselves, and peaceably to depart to their habitations, or to their lawful business, upon the pains contained in the act made in the first year of King George, for preventing tumults and riotous assemblies. God save the Queen!'

There was a moment of silent shock, and then something of a panic.

The crowd swirled and shouted and pressed in, and Annie had difficulty in making sure she was holding on to all three children at once. Charlie was being squeezed between two men, his hand slipping out of hers as he was almost carried away, but Alice managed to grab a fistful of his jacket and pull him back, pushing him closer to Annie and putting her own body between him and the strangers.

Suddenly, Jack was there.

He was pale, bleeding from a small cut over one eye, and his left arm was hanging at such a terrible angle that it must be broken.

Annie couldn't help giving a little shriek, but he shook his head. 'Never mind me. They've read the Riot Act, which means they know they can get troops here within the hour, and anyone still in the square by that time is liable to be attacked. We have to get you out of here.'

'We *all* have to get out. You included.'

'Never mind me,' he said, again. 'I'm a marked man and they'll find me somehow. But they've got nothing on you or the children, so if we can get you home you should be all right. I'll take you, and then you get inside and bar the door, and I'll come back—' he stopped with a cry of pain as he was jostled.

'We need to tie up that arm,' said Annie.

She had no idea how this was to be achieved, but fortunately a man who was being pressed against them overheard and unwound the scarf from his neck. 'Here. I saw what happened – they hit him with no provocation. You take that and good luck to you.'

Annie, still fighting against being carried away in the churning crowd, and still making sure that three sets of hands were gripping tightly to her skirt and apron, managed to tie the scarf around Jack's neck so that it supported his injured arm.

He scrutinised the square. 'Let's try to get to the edge, over there, then we can slip away.' He looked down at Charlie and the girls. 'I don't think I can carry anyone just at the moment, but you all get in between me and Annie, and lock your arms together.'

Annie wanted him to stand on her right, so his left side would be sheltered, but instead he went to her left, exposing the injury to even more harm so that he could use his good arm to protect the children.

With a huge amount of effort they managed to push their way through the crowd, but as they neared the edge of the square, Jack slowed and then stopped. Annie thought she heard him swear under his breath.

'What is it?'

'They've blocked all the ways out.'

'What?'

Jack pointed. There were several streets that led off the square, but there were mill watchmen, armed with their cudgels, standing at all entrances. A few brave souls were attempting to remonstrate or plead with them, but all they got for their trouble was a shove back into the press and the threat of worse.

Annie looked at the terrified children, and then at Jack. 'They've trapped us so we can't escape before the soldiers get here. And they've done it on purpose.'

* * *

An hour passed. A few men had tried to break out, but most of them were now lying groaning and bleeding on the ground. The rest of the crowd was subdued, frightened, penned in a tight knot in the centre of the square.

Some women were trying to plead with the Carringtons to let them, or at least their children, leave. They were addressing themselves mainly to Mr Frederick, still seeing him as the more sympathetic of the two, because they didn't know the truth about him like Annie did, but they were getting nowhere.

As she gathered the children to her and gazed across the space, Annie's eye met Mr Frederick's. He smirked at her, but she simply glared at him without blinking until he looked away. She could take no satisfaction in her small victory, though, because she was under no illusions that it was the people trapped in the square who were going to have the worst of it before the day was ended. Mr Frederick and his brother, meanwhile, would swan off unscathed and unmoved, returning to their warm home to count their day's gains.

It was Charlie who heard it first. 'What's that noise?'

Even as he spoke, more of the trapped workers were lifting their heads to listen. And it wasn't long before the sound became unmistakable: it was the tramp of many boots, all marching in step.

Not far away from Annie, a child vomited on to the cobbles of the square.

Annie felt her heart beginning to race. How could she get Alice, Charlie and Hannah out of here? Once the violence began – for there was sure to be violence now – would there be enough chaos for them to be able to slip away unnoticed? Perhaps some of the mill watchmen would leave their positions at the street entrances? Or could they maybe even climb up on to anything, to avoid being caught in the mass of grown men and trampled under all those boots and clogs?

Jack, who had been sitting down, now lurched to his feet. His face was the colour of whey, but he gritted his teeth and stayed upright.

He gave Annie a serious look. 'I'm truly sorry I couldn't get you out of here – sorry that I involved you in any of this in the first place.'

She shook her head. 'It was my own doing. And anyway, you were right. Whatever happens, we're all in the right of this, and *they*—' she threw the Carrington brothers a look of searing rage '—are in the wrong.'

'But still . . .' He glanced down at the children.

Annie looked him squarely in the eye. 'Trust me, I will defend these children until my last breath.'

He did something he'd never done before: he touched the side of her face, very gently, and then rested his hand on her shoulder for a moment. 'I know you will. But I'm here to make sure you don't have to.'

He managed to crouch to address the children. 'Now. It's scary, I know, and there's no shame in being afraid. You stay behind me, and whenever you get the chance, you get away and run. Do you hear me? Run. Run away home and hide, and don't open the door to anyone except me or Annie.'

'I'm not scared,' said Charlie, stoutly.

'Neither am I,' declared Alice, taking her little brother's hand.

'Nor me.' Hannah looked near to tears, but she raised her head defiantly. 'We'll look after each other.'

Jack swayed upright again, and he and Annie stood side by side with the children behind them as the first troops marched into the square. All around them, families and groups were doing the same.

Annie remembered Mrs Otway's tale of women and children being injured and killed at that long-ago event in Manchester, and tried hard to swallow her sobs and her guilt. It was she who had brought the children here today, and she would get them out of it somehow. No matter what the cost. She began to brace herself, clenching the fists that would be useless against bayonets and guns.

There were now at least sixty uniformed soldiers lined up on the other side of the square.

'It's the Liverpool Rifles,' she heard someone say. 'I've seen them before.'

The words hit Annie like a slap. Then she looked more closely at the line of men, examining each one in turn. It had been years since she'd seen him, but she would still—

All the breath went out of her so suddenly that she nearly fell.

There he was.

One of the soldiers on the opposite side of the square, concentrating on fixing a bayonet to his rifle, was her brother Sam.

Chapter Fifteen

Jack, standing close enough to touch Annie, had felt her momentary weakness. 'Courage, now,' he said, misunderstanding the reason for it.

But once the initial shock had worn off, Annie was emboldened rather than cowed. Sam was here. *Sam*. How could she attract his attention? How could she let him know that she was here?

Her thoughts and feelings were so strong, the stare she levelled at Sam so piercing, that somehow he seemed to become aware of it all. His bayonet now fixed, he stood in a rigid line with all his fellows as they stared straight ahead of them across the square and waited for their orders.

Annie saw the exact moment that he spotted her. Everything seemed to stand still as their eyes locked, and she knew that he had recognised her. She had never doubted that he would, even though it was more than two years since they had last met and she had changed more than he had in that time.

She couldn't look away, not for a moment, but at the same time her heightened senses kept her aware of what else was going on. Many of the riflemen were uneasy, as was their captain, at the prospect of being ordered to attack a group of unarmed men, women and children who were doing nothing more than standing quietly in the village square.

Beside her, Jack shifted. 'If everyone remains calm,' he murmured, 'there's just a chance we might be able to end all this in peace.'

But, of course, it was not to be. Someone – one of the Carringtons, or one of the watchmen, Annie didn't turn to look – somehow goaded a number of the more volatile men in the square, who made another doomed attempt to charge through and escape, and that was enough.

The officer in charge shouted something, and a line of his men – including Sam – raised their rifles. Annie heard screams from all around her as the crowd made a violent but useless surge backwards. Fortunately, she still had just enough of her wits to see that the soldiers were all aiming high in the air, well above the heads of the people in the square. It was a warning, for now.

The noise, when it came, was stupendous; the crash of dozens of rifles firing simultaneously was louder than anything she'd ever heard, even at the mill. Although nobody had been injured, the panic started in earnest now, trapped people screaming, pushing and trying to escape, while a few more roared at the soldiers and charged, in an attempt to overwhelm them while they were reloading.

But only half of them had fired. The soldiers had formed up in two ranks, and a second now stepped through the first, rifles at the ready, allowing Sam and the others to attend to their weapons.

Annie lost sight of her brother, and then of everything else, as the order to fire was given and the people in the square stampeded.

For what seemed like an eternity, but was probably no more than a few minutes, there was nothing to be done except to try to stay on her feet, hold on to the children as best she could in the tumult, and try to stop them all from being crushed or knocked over and trampled. Falling to the ground would be fatal. The whole world contracted to the few screaming, crowded yards around them – people – bodies – noise – gripping hands—

Alice shrieked as Charlie was pulled away, and then she let go of Annie in order to plunge into the crowd after her brother.

Annie had lost them both – where were they? She pushed Hannah's hand into Jack's and then threw herself into the whirl of bodies, shouting for them.

There they were! She stretched out a hand . . .

The soldiers were now in among them. They must have made a charge. Terrifying bayonets appeared, though thankfully not all that many; some of the men seemed to be using their rifles backwards, striking people with the wooden butt instead of the blade.

Annie saw Alice push Charlie to the ground as a rifleman came towards them, kicking him to relative safety under the wheels of a stationary cart. Then she screamed as the soldier raised his weapon, but a press of mill men ran into them both. The soldier laid about him, and Alice was thrown hard against the cart, her stomach striking painfully against the end of one of its long shafts, and then she too was on the ground and underneath it.

That was probably the safest place to be at the moment. Rather than dragging them out, Annie looked about her to find the others so she could pull them over, too. She saw them, Jack using his body to shield Hannah from the blows that were falling even as he was struck himself.

The two of them made it over to her just as Sam appeared.

'What in blazes are you doing here?' he bellowed.

There was no time to explain. 'I have to get the children out to safety!' She pointed.

Sam took in the situation at a glance. 'Right.' He slung his rifle on to his back, reached under the cart and pulled out Alice and Charlie. At first they screamed, but Annie was able to shout that Sam was her brother, here to help, and they understood.

Alice was crying and clutching at her stomach. Sam swept her up in one arm, using the other to fell with a single punch a man who came too close. 'Take him,' he said, pushing Charlie at Annie. Then he pointed to Jack and Hannah. 'They with you?'

'Yes!'

'All of you, follow me.'

Annie stayed as close as she could to Sam's broad back as he pushed his way forward, shoving out of his way riflemen and mill hands indiscriminately. They reached the entrance to one of the streets, which was still guarded by a watchman, but he took one look at Sam and fled.

Sam put Alice down and turned to Annie. 'I have to go back. Get away from here. And I mean right away – take them all home. I'll try to contact you there as soon as I can.'

She had only time to nod before he disappeared back into the press.

Annie took stock. Jack was still on his feet, but only just. Alice was in a bad way, but hopefully that would wear off. She herself was unharmed, as Hannah and Charlie appeared to be. Give thanks for small mercies.

She crouched and pulled Alice up on to her back. 'Hold on round my neck. You two will have to walk, and help Jack. All right?'

'Are we going home?' Hannah asked.

'Yes,' said Annie, 'but only to fetch Clara. Then we've got a much longer walk ahead of us, I'm afraid. But we're going to a place where we'll be safe.'

* * *

Clara wasn't in the house. That was clear within the first few minutes of their arrival, and it wasn't as though the place was big enough for her to have concealed herself anywhere. She also wasn't in the wash house, the privy or the yard. Annie could only assume that she'd gone out and was now caught up somewhere in the trouble.

Her heart told her that she should go back, should look for her oldest friend, but her head told her that she had three small children and an injured man who needed to be taken to shelter. They would have to go on without Clara.

There was no point attempting to leave a note, thought Annie, as she swapped her wooden clogs back for her own boots, which she had kept carefully under the bed all this time, as Clara couldn't read. All Annie could do was to hope that Clara would guess where they'd gone, and that she would follow them as and when she could.

Distressing sounds from the square were still audible as they left the house and made their way out of the village. It was already mid-afternoon, and they had twelve cold miles to walk, most of which would be in the dark. However, the road was a main one, so as long as they didn't stray off it, they shouldn't lose their way. The most important thing was to keep everyone moving – stopping anywhere out in the open overnight, in this cold and in their condition, might prove to be fatal. She encouraged and then begged them all to put one foot in front of the other, over and over again.

Annie had no idea how they managed it, but late that evening the exhausted party saw the lights of Liverpool's streets twinkling ahead of them. They were all almost dead on their feet, and she wasn't sure who out of Jack, Hannah and Charlie was helping or needing help the most as they staggered along, but she was able to use the welcome sight to cajole one more effort out of them. Annie had already been carrying Alice for the last mile or so, because the poor child was still suffering from the blow to her stomach and could hardly stand, let alone walk. 'There now,' she said, hitching Alice up a little higher on her back, 'not long to go now, and then you can have a lie down.'

There was no reply except for a quiet whimper, although Annie did feel the little hands tightening their grip around her neck. She was so shattered herself that she'd been wondering how much longer she could go on, but the sight of Liverpool spread out before her gave her one last shred of energy.

As they entered the city, it struck her that they were walking defencelessly through the Scotland Road ward, renowned for its crime rate and bordering some of the even tougher areas where notorious underworld gangs reigned supreme. Had they made it all the way here only to be set upon within a mile of home? She felt various eyes upon them as they stumbled through the streets, but evidently nobody thought they were worth robbing, and somehow they made it through unscathed.

Now they were approaching Dale Street. And now they were in it, passing the familiar frontages. Exhausted and burdened as she was, Annie almost broke into a run as they neared the shop, tears streaming openly down her cheeks. But what if nobody was there? It was so long since she'd left; anything could have happened. She had written to them, of course, but her stupid selfishness hadn't allowed them to reply, so how could she know? They could have shut the shop, they could have moved away—

The shop was still there. Empty windows, of course, on a Saturday night, but still standing, still with the name over the entrance, and the hint of light, warmth and comfort spilling out from the almost-closed door of the back room.

Annie sobbed as she put Alice down and used the very last of her remaining strength to bang on the door.

The inside of the shop suddenly lit up, and she could see the blessed sight of Frank emerging from the back room. He was suspicious at first, peering out the window into the dark street, but then as his eyes adjusted he jumped almost out of his skin, swore and ran to the door. As he fumbled with the locks he called out. 'Delilah! Get out here, quickly! Now!'

By the time Frank had wrenched the door open, Delilah had arrived at a run, and Annie fell over the threshold into her sister's arms.

Chapter Sixteen

The first few hours passed in a blur. There were exclamations and embraces, a bustle of activity and rather a lot of crying all round, but most of all there was *love*.

Delilah was . . . well, she was Delilah, and that was all Annie could say. She took four strangers into her home without question, and had not a single word of reproach for the sister who'd run away from her so callously.

Immediately after their arrival she'd sent Frank out to fetch the others, regardless of the time of night, and it wasn't long before William, Bridget, Meg and Tommy all arrived. 'Sally wanted to come too,' Annie heard Meg say, 'but I've left her at William's to mind the girls because they were asleep in bed.'

'And I knocked on Jem's door,' added Frank, 'but it didn't rouse them. I'll try again first thing in the morning.'

Of course, thought Annie, blearily. Time hadn't stood still. She'd been away so long that Jem had got married and moved out, hadn't he? And Delilah's children were . . . she couldn't think straight just now, but Daisy, who had been woken by the commotion and was crouching wide-eyed on the stairs, certainly looked older than she had done.

Annie allowed herself to be wrapped in a blanket and given hot tea, but was conscious enough to insist that Jack and Alice should be everyone's priority, and to make sure that Charlie and Hannah were safe and warm next to her.

It was such a relief to be able to lay down her responsibility, just for a little while, and let someone else be in charge. Bridget was saying something about a bone-setter, Meg was asking Tommy to carry Alice upstairs, and there was such a general whirl of things being taken care of without her input that Annie allowed her eyes to close.

She was roused, suddenly, some time later, by the piercing cry of a baby. What . . .? In her confused, half-awake state she couldn't work out where she was or what was going on. Clara was going to have a baby, wasn't she? But not yet, and anyway Clara hadn't been at home when they'd looked for her earlier . . . no, wait. *Home.* She wasn't in the house in the mill village, she was really at home. And there was no baby here, because the children had got older, and anyway it had gone quiet again now, so maybe she was just dreaming . . .

'Are you awake enough to meet your latest nephew?' came Delilah's voice, softly. 'I almost forgot that you didn't know about him.'

Annie opened her eyes to find that the room was quiet, the fire in the range now dying down and fewer people rushing about.

Delilah moved a chair and came to sit next to her, a swaddled bundle in her arms. 'Here he is.'

Annie peered into the little face, contented now he had his mother. 'He's lovely. What's his name?'

Delilah smiled. 'If he'd been a girl I was going to call her Annie, so when he turned out to be a boy we decided to go with Andrew.' She touched the baby's cheek. 'Andrew, meet your darling Auntie Annie. Having her back with us is the best thing that could have happened.'

Annie's face crumpled. 'Oh, Delilah! I've been so . . .' she couldn't go on.

She felt arms round her. Delilah had passed the baby to someone and was now embracing her, stroking her hair and making soothing noises. 'Hush, now! Everything's going to be all right. You can tell me all about it tomorrow, or whenever you feel up to it, and introduce us to everyone, but for now you just need to know that you're safe.'

And there was that word: *safe*. The word Annie had rejected and despised because she thought it was trapping her, the word used by the sister who'd cared for her like a mother all her life, who'd made a promise to their dying Ma. The sister she'd run away from.

Once her weeping had become a little less violent, Annie allowed herself to be helped upstairs by her sisters. Her old bed was still there, but Alice was now lying in it.

Annie cried out when she saw the little sleeping figure. 'Is she all right? It was earlier today, there was terrible trouble and she fell on to—'

'Shhh!' whispered Meg. 'She's sleeping just now. Her whole stomach is one big bruise, but we hope she'll be better after a good rest.'

'She can stay here as long as she needs,' added Delilah. 'Now, the other little girl is down there – we didn't have another mattress but I've laid some blankets and she said she'd be fine and didn't want to disturb the other one. Is it her sister?' She cut herself off. 'Never mind. Explanations can wait. The young man and the little boy are up in the attic, and we'll see about getting someone to look at that arm in the morning. For now, let's get you to bed too.'

Annie elected to share the floor with Hannah, so that Alice could lie in more comfort, and she hadn't been laid down more than half a minute before she was fast asleep.

She awoke the next morning to pale sunlight streaming in; she must have slept late. The room was empty as she stared at the familiar ceiling, or so she thought. The sound of breathing made her sit up and see that Alice was still lying in bed.

Jolted into full wakefulness, Annie knelt by the bed. 'Alice,' she said, quietly. 'Alice, my love, can you hear me?'

There was a murmur, a slight shifting, a whimper. 'Annie? My tummy hurts.'

'It's all right,' said Annie, relieved that Alice was at least coherent. 'You hurt it when you fell over yesterday, do you remember? When you were being such a brave girl looking out for Charlie. You'll have a big bruise for a while, but then you'll be fine.'

Alice nodded and licked her cracked lips. 'Is Charlie all right? I promised Ma . . .'

'He's fine, and you don't need to worry about him. Now, are you hungry? I'm sure I could get you something to eat.'

'No . . . thirsty, though.'

'All right. You stay there and I'll go and get you something. We have nice water here, from our own pump in the yard, or I'll see if there's tea.'

Alice nodded sleepily and Annie left the room.

Downstairs it was so crowded that the shop was full, as well as the back room. Everyone was here – the whole extended family – and Annie immediately found herself engulfed in Jem's embrace as he pushed past the others to reach her first.

Once his arms had finally loosened, he stood back a little and examined her. *You've grown.*

If she'd thought about it, Annie would have been worried that she'd lost her ability to sign, but the movements came back to her naturally. *And you're married.*

His smile widened. *We're happy. And soon, a baby.*

Annie flung her arms around him again and kissed his cheek.

He assumed a more sober expression. *Delilah cried for weeks. I should be angry, but if she's not, I'm not.*

I'm sorry. Annie repeated it, her gestures more emphatic. *SORRY.*

By now Delilah had seen her and was calling. 'Annie! I'm glad you were able to sleep. We've kept some porridge for you, or there's bread and jam, and there's tea in the pot.'

'Can I take some up to Alice first?'

'Oh, is she still bad? Poor thing. Yes, of course.'

'I'll take it, shall I?' came Bridget's quiet voice. 'And you can have something to eat and talk to everyone. The children—' she pointed at Charlie, who was playing something in the corner with Joe and Billy, and Hannah, who was sitting quietly in between Meg and Sally '—have told us a little bit, but your sisters will want to hear it from you.'

Annie nodded, then looked around. Someone was missing. 'Is William here too?'

'He's gone to fetch Mr Hughes, because from what the children said it sounded like it was the exact same place where he was yesterday, and he was worried there was going to be trouble after he left.'

Of course! If Annie hadn't been so busy with all of her mill concerns, she would have recognised him properly. The man who had spoken twice to the mill hands, who had seemed vaguely familiar, was William's employer, the printer and bookbinder Mr Hughes. Annie had never met him properly, but she'd seen him at a distance once or twice when she was younger, when she'd taken messages or William's dinner up to the shop.

Hannah left her place and came over to take Annie's hand as she sat down. 'They said I don't have to go back to the workhouse,' she whispered.

Annie cast a glance over at Meg and Sally, who certainly knew what workhouse life was like. Meg in particular seemed quite emotional about it all, and she looked at Hannah, then at Annie, and gave a firm nod.

'Food first,' said Delilah, putting a bowl of porridge and a cup of tea down on the table. 'And then you can tell us as much as you'd like.'

Annie paused before picking up the spoon. 'Is Jack all right?'

The glance that passed between Delilah and Meg wasn't *quite* as sly as some of the ones Clara and Maisie had shared when they used to tease Annie, but it was close. 'He's in pain, but he doesn't seem to have a fever, and he's had some breakfast. William thought the dispensary on Church Street might be open on a Sunday, to get him something.' Delilah paused, and then came a flash of her old motherly self. 'Now eat that all up, before it gets cold!'

The bowl was clean and the teacup nearly empty when the shop door rang and William entered, accompanied by Mr Hughes and another man Annie didn't recognise.

Mr Hughes removed his bowler hat and gave Delilah a polite bow. 'Mrs Malling. This is Doctor James.' He held up a hand to forestall any possible argument. 'He's here at my expense, I insist. Jack Howard is here injured, I know, and I gather there is also a little girl . . .?'

One of Delilah's strengths had always been knowing when not to argue. 'Thank you, sir, that's kind.'

'I'll show you the way up to the attic, sir,' said Frank to the doctor. Then he signed to Jem: *Come with us.* 'With so many brothers getting in fights when we were children, I've seen a bone or two set in my time, and you might need the help.'

The doctor agreed, hefting the large bag he carried and following them up.

Once they were gone, Delilah chivvied all the children except Hannah out of the room. 'Go and play in the yard. You'll be plenty warm enough if you run around.' Then she turned to Annie. 'Now, tell us everything that we don't already know.'

* * *

It took quite some time to go over everything – Clara, the mill, the work, the layoffs, the trouble, the children, Jack, Sam – and to answer everyone's interjected questions and exclamations. Mr Hughes was sitting at the table making notes, writing more quickly than anyone Annie had ever seen.

Just as Annie was finishing, Dr James, Frank and Jem came back down the stairs, followed shortly by Bridget.

'Brave lad,' said Frank. 'It needed some setting, that arm, and not a peep out of him.'

'He *is* brave,' replied Annie. 'He was determined to keep us all safe yesterday.'

'He's a clever and determined young man, too,' added Mr Hughes, pausing his scribbling for a moment. 'It's mainly thanks to his efforts that the situation up there isn't far, far worse.'

Annie couldn't help noticing that Delilah and Meg exchanged another glance. 'And what about Alice?'

The doctor opened his mouth, but it was Bridget's voice that was heard first. 'She's sleeping now, the little darling. We'll see how she gets on.'

Dr James, wrongly assuming William to be the figure of authority in the family, took him to one side and murmured to him. Then he took two vials from his bag and placed them on the table. 'For both of them, for the pain. A strong mixture for the young man and a weaker decoction for the little girl. I shouldn't need to call again, but do contact me if necessary.'

'Should they both stay in bed?' That was Meg.

'Avoid too much movement for the next few days, but yes, warmth and company will do them good, so if they want to come down here then that's fine.' He nodded to them all, and Frank showed him out through the shop.

'Well,' said Meg. 'It's going to be too late to have Sunday dinner on the table at the normal time, but if I get off now and make a start, we could have it this evening?'

Annie had all but forgotten the family tradition, and now her mouth watered. 'You're in for a treat,' she said to Hannah, who was still by her side. 'Meg's the best cook in Liverpool.'

Meg and Tommy exchanged one of those glances by which they were able to communicate without the need for words. 'Hannah,' said Meg, 'there's going to be so many people to cook for that I wonder if you might come and help? Sally and I could do with a hand.'

Hannah looked uncertain. 'But won't I just be in the way?'

'Not at all. Annie just told us, didn't she, that you did the cooking at your old house? I'm sure you'll be a great help. And we've got a much bigger kitchen, with all *sorts* of ingredients.'

'Oh yes, do!' chimed in Sally. 'We have such a good time while we're working. We laugh and sing.'

Annie felt Hannah's grip on her hand slacken. 'Well, if it's all right with Annie . . .'

If Annie wasn't mistaken, there was a flicker of anticipation and enjoyment in Hannah's expression – the first she'd seen for a long time. 'Of course it is! You'll enjoy it, and don't worry, you're as safe with any of my sisters as you'd ever be with me. You go, and I'll see you there later.'

Sally took Hannah's hand, and they followed Meg and Tommy out.

Mr Hughes looked up from his work. 'If Jack really is feeling up to joining us, I would very much like to hear from him, as well. I suspect that tomorrow's papers will be full of the story from the Carringtons' point of view, and I'd like to be ready with some pamphlets that can help with the real truth.'

Frank and Jem went to help Jack down, and soon he was seated by the range, in the room's most comfortable chair. It was the first time Annie had seen him since their arrival, and she was shocked by his pale face. However, he was clean and tidy, wearing what she thought was one of Frank's shirts, and his arm was neatly splinted, bound and supported.

He gave Annie a tired smile and then turned, wincing, to Delilah. 'Ma'am, I can't thank you enough—'

She waved away his gratitude. 'Any friend of my sister's is always welcome here. And especially one who broke his arm looking after her.'

Annie shook her head. 'He was even braver than that. It was already broken before he found us in the crowd, and he *still* stood between us and the danger, even though it hurt him more.'

Jem, who had been watching her, silently moved over to Jack and shook his good hand.

Mr Hughes had his pen poised again. 'Already? You were injured *before* the altercation with the troops? How?'

Jack had, it transpired, been hit by the cudgel of one of the mill's watchmen. After Mr Theodore had ordered his arrest, there had been something of a brawl as various mill men tried to prevent the constables from getting near him, and blows had been struck. Mr Hughes wrote it all down.

'So,' said Delilah, 'and I'm sorry if I'm not keeping up, this is all tied to the war in America?' As she spoke she looked over to the corner of the room, where Abraham was sitting so quietly that Annie had hardly noticed him. He was, rather incongruously for an elderly man, cuddling baby Andrew in his arms.

Jack followed her gaze. 'Sir, I don't know you or your history, but you and everyone in this room should know that we mill workers stand firmly behind the abolition of slavery, no matter what the cost to us. It's the only response a decent man could have.' He paused and cast a glance at Annie. 'Or any woman, either – and Annie's stood up in public to say that more than once herself.'

Abraham smiled. 'Young man,' he said, 'you'll go far. And if you want support for that cause, well, you're in the right place.'

It was the middle of the afternoon when Mr Hughes finally finished, saying he now had enough information to be able to set and print something tomorrow. 'I'll see you at the shop, early,' he said to William, as he stood to depart. Then he turned to Annie. 'Jack will need his rest, but perhaps you'd come too, just to correct me on any final issues before we print?'

'Of course.'

Mr Hughes left, and Annie went back upstairs to sit with Alice for a while. She looked less comfortable than she had done earlier, tossing and turning, but with each movement seeming to cause her much more pain. At one point she vomited.

Delilah helped Annie to clean everything up. 'She's certainly not well enough to go out,' she said, stroking

Alice's brow. 'But everyone will want to see you, and your other little friend will certainly want to show you what she's cooked. Why don't you let me stay here and look after Alice? I can sit in here and nurse Andrew while I watch over her.'

Annie was reluctant to leave Alice, but Delilah was first persuasive and then insistent, so Annie found herself walking over to Williamson Square with the others. Charlie skipped excitedly beside her, and Annie watched as Frank and Jem walked carefully on either side of Jack. Jack had tried to demur and say that he would have no place at the gathering, but he was defenceless against the combined might of the Shaw and Malling family affection, and his objections had been overcome.

Oh, what a delight it was to be eating Meg's cooking! Annie looked around the room with satisfaction and with very different emotions to the last time she'd been here – feeling at home, feeling loved, feeling as though she *belonged*. And she was so pleased to see that Hannah and Charlie were also content, the terrible recent events already fading. Hannah sat next to Annie and told her animatedly all about how she'd helped to prepare the vegetables, while Charlie – after wolfing down a huge dinner – was overjoyed to meet Higgins the dog. They were rolling together on the floor now,

Charlie patting him and tickling his tummy, while Higgins frolicked around and lost any pretensions he might have had to being a serious guard dog.

Annie still had plenty to worry about, of course, including Alice and Clara. But Alice would soon be well, wouldn't she, once that bruising was gone? And Clara wasn't stupid – she would work out where Annie and the others had got to, and would follow on.

As her gaze swept round in contentment, Annie realised that there was one person present who wasn't happy. Daisy, who had hardly spoken a word to her since she got back, was giving her a ferocious glare from across the room.

Annie went over to sit next to her. 'I haven't had much chance to talk to you yet, have I?'

Daisy looked away, her mouth set in a line.

'I expect you've been busy since I last saw you.'

Silence.

Then a tight, strained voice. 'You said you were just going downstairs to blow out the candle.'

Annie looked at Daisy's back and felt yet another pang of guilt. 'I did. And it was very wrong of me. I'm sorry.'

'And you were gone such a long time. And now you're back and you've brought all them with you.' Daisy made an angry gesture towards Hannah and Charlie.

Annie understood. 'Yes, I did.' What was the best way to approach this? 'We've got so much love in our family that I thought we had some to spare for children who haven't ever known it.'

Daisy made a slight turn of the head. 'It's true, then? They're all orphans, with no mummies or daddies?'

'I'm afraid it is. And . . .' Annie tried to think of the best way of putting it. Inspiration came when she looked at the tea shop's counter. 'You know Auntie Meg's lovely cakes?'

In some surprise at the apparent change of subject, Daisy now turned back to face Annie. 'What's that got to do with anything?'

'Well, imagine that my love for you, or your mummy's love for you, is a cake.'

'All right.' Daisy sounded unsure.

'So, when you were born, you had the whole cake. And then Joe came along, and then the others.'

'Yes.'

'You might have been worried that you were going to get a smaller and smaller slice of the cake, that you'd have to share Mummy's love with everyone else.'

There was a fleeting expression of unhappiness, and Daisy shrugged.

'But that's not how it works. What happened was that every time another baby was born, there was another cake to go with it. Everyone gets a whole cake each, and nobody gets any less. Do you see?'

Slowly, Daisy nodded.

'So, I've now got Hannah and Alice and Charlie to look after, and I'm going to do that as best I can. But it doesn't mean that I love you any the less.'

Daisy stared across the room. After a pause, she said, 'They do need looking after, don't they? If they've got nobody of their own?'

'They have got somebody,' said Annie, firmly. 'They've got me.'

Daisy nodded, making a decision. 'And me too. I'll help you.'

Annie hugged her niece tightly. 'You're a beautiful person, Daisy Malling.'

Jack had been watching this conversation from a distance, and he waited until Daisy had left to play with the other children before approaching Annie and carefully lowering himself into the vacant chair. 'I can't get over how busy it is.'

Annie smiled. 'That's my family for you!'

'And you've had all this waiting for you, all this time? You could have come back to this whenever you wanted? Why didn't you?'

'Because . . . it's complicated, but I didn't want to. I wanted to make my own way. And besides, I had responsibilities. What would the children have done if I'd just upped and left? Or Clara?'

'Or me.'

There was a silence, which Annie eventually broke by asking, 'So, have you worked out who's who yet?'

'I think so? There's so many of them. I never had anything like this – just me and my Ma, until she passed away.'

Annie was about to express sympathy, but he moved on briskly. 'It's not difficult to sort out which children are whose, at least, with that hair colour.' He pointed at Rosie and Maggie's flaming heads, and then at Bridget.

Annie sighed. 'I used to wish my hair colour was more interesting.'

He smiled. 'Red hair is red hair, but personally I prefer a girl who'll face down a whole troop of riflemen, armed with nothing but her own determination.' His eyes met hers.

Their conversation was interrupted by Charlie, who wanted to tell them excitedly all about the dog; and it was just as well, because Annie was completely tongue-tied.

As soon as they were home again, Annie took over Delilah's vigil next to Alice's bed. Alice spent much of the night groaning and whimpering, and Annie was frequently obliged to go down and check the clock to see if she was yet allowed to administer more of the pain-killing medicine.

The other girls all got up early on Monday morning, leaving Annie and Alice alone until Delilah appeared with a drink of tea for them both. Between them they got a little of it between Alice's lips, and then she fell asleep again.

'You need to go to William's work,' said Delilah. 'I've sent Hannah and Charlie to school with Daisy, Joe and Billy, to give them something to do so they don't sit around and fret. Charlie was quite excited about it, much to Joe's disgust, asking if there'd be arithmetic. And Daisy said she'd look after them both.'

Annie remembered yesterday's conversation. 'I'm sure she will.' Then she sighed as she looked at Alice. 'I shouldn't leave her. And you should be in the shop.'

'I know. But Bridget has come to help, and your friend Jack says Alice knows him and he'll sit with her.' She paused. 'You wouldn't find many men saying that. He seems very nice.'

There was just the hint of a question in her statement, which Annie chose to ignore. 'I'll go now, and then once Mr Hughes has finished asking me whatever questions he wants, I'll come straight back.'

Mr Hughes's premises were in Duke Street, a brisk walk of a quarter of an hour or so. The business consisted of a shop at the front, the window filled with books and pamphlets, and then a workshop behind. Annie had peeked in there once or twice in the past, awed by the huge presses and wrinkling her nose at the smell of the ink.

There was already plenty of activity going on when Annie arrived, and the shop door was unlocked.

The sound of the bell brought a young lad through from the back. 'Yes, miss? Oh, wait, are you Miss Shaw? Come through, please, you're expected.'

The workshop was a hive of activity, with men and boys scurrying around and the machines already in motion, some for binding books and the others for printing. It struck Annie that she found the presses much less daunting now that she'd worked with the huge looms at the mill.

Mr Hughes was in conversation with William at a desk at one side of the room. The boy hurried over to them and pointed her out, and they came over. William had a newspaper in his hand, and both of them had grim expressions on their faces.

'It's just as we feared,' said Mr Hughes. 'A very biased account.' He pushed the paper towards Annie and pointed with an inky finger at one column, near the bottom of the page.

She read:

A riotous assembly took place yesterday by workers and former workers at the mill of Mr C.T. Carrington. This disgraceful episode occurred after an unruly crowd was whipped into a frenzy by the words of the radical pamphleteer and speaker Mr Stephen Hughes, of Duke Street, Liverpool. At the conclusion of his speech, the assembled men, all hardened ne'er-do-wells and many of them the worse for drink, made an unprovoked attack on the family of the mill owner and on the attending constables. Fortunately, the quick thinking of Mr Carrington's two sons averted what could have been a tragic episode: they called in the Liverpool Rifles, who succeeded in quelling the uprising without unnecessary violence.

Annie gaped. She'd always been used to thinking of newspapers as the prime source of information throughout the city, written by educated men who knew the truth. But here were lies upon lies, all in front of her in black and white. 'But . . . this is all wrong! How can people believe this? What can we do?'

Mr Hughes exchanged a glance with William. 'We can produce a counter-narrative and get it out on the streets by this afternoon, to be sure.' He paused. 'But I don't think you've seen the worst part.'

With a shaking finger, William pointed to the top of the following column; Annie hadn't noticed that the article continued. 'However,' she read:

> One member of the Rifles failed abysmally in his duty, and was rightly reported for it by Mr F.W. Carrington, the younger son of the mill owner. Samuel Shaw, a man of 23 years of age and without any excuse of callow youth, declined to follow his lawful orders and was seen to break ranks and flee the scene. He was afterwards apprehended and now faces a well-deserved court martial. It is to be hoped that justice will prevail, in order to set an example to any other member of Her Majesty's forces who may consider exhibiting similar cowardice.

Annie was so shocked that she was completely winded, hardly able to breathe, let alone speak. She waved her hand and looked at William, and it was several moments before she was able to burst out. '*Lies*! Lies, all of it! Sam rescued us, and I don't know what would have happened to me or the children if he hadn't been there! And he didn't run away – all he did was get us out and then go back with the other soldiers.' She jabbed a finger at the paper. 'Why would they lie like this?'

'Because,' sighed William, 'the men who own the newspapers are the same ones – or the same sort, at least – as the mill owners. So of course they take their part.'

Annie's outrage increased as she read the false account through again. 'And—' she brought herself up short before mentioning Frederick Carrington, a loathing for him spreading through her to such an extent that she couldn't even bear to have his name in her mouth. To change the subject, she asked, 'And anyway, what's a court martial?'

'I'll tell her,' said William to Mr Hughes. He put a hand on Annie's arm. 'It's like a trial, only specifically for soldiers.' He paused, and then continued in a voice that wasn't quite steady. 'You're old enough and strong enough to hear this, so I won't lie to you. It also means that if he's found guilty, they'll shoot him.'

Chapter Seventeen

Everything began to spin.

William caught Annie as she stumbled, and Mr Hughes produced a chair from somewhere that they lowered her into. She heard him call out to someone, and soon a cup of water was being pressed to her lips.

It was the anger surging through her that brought her back to herself. She was going to right this wrong that had been done to Sam. And to all of the peaceful people who had gathered only to hear news and support each other, of course, but mainly Sam. Frederick Carrington was going to be made to pay for the error of his ways. She had no idea how to do that yet, but she would work out a way. Nobody was going to treat her brother like that.

But first, she was going to talk to Sam himself. 'Where are they holding him? It doesn't say here.'

'I would imagine that it will be in their barracks,' said Mr Hughes. 'On Upper Warwick Street, up near Prince's Park. Though I'm not sure if they'll let anyone see him.'

'I'll find a way.' Annie stood up. 'No, really, I'm fine. I'm sorry I was overcome just for a minute. I have to go and tell Delilah and check on Alice, and then I have to see Sam. To tell him that he's not alone, and that he's got his family fighting for him, like he's always done for us.'

She swept out, though not before she heard Mr Hughes say to William, 'Your brothers and sisters are quite something, aren't they?' And then, as she passed through the door. 'Now, let's get to work. I've got yesterday's notes . . .'

* * *

The flower shop was busy when Annie got back to it, so she postponed giving Delilah the news and went straight up to see Alice.

Jack was sitting by the bed, a chair having been brought up, and he turned as Annie entered.

He was worried. 'She's really not well. She's been awake and asleep, tossing and turning, and she keeps asking me what will happen to Charlie.' He reached out his good arm and stroked Alice's sweaty hair.

It had grown back after her father's cruel shaving of it – oh, so long ago now, it seemed – but it was still shorter than it had once been.

'Has she been sick again?' Annie squeezed down the narrow gap on the other side of the bed and knelt down.

'Yes. I just about managed to catch it all in that pot and get it downstairs to wash without spilling it everywhere.' He nodded at his bound-up arm. 'This is going to be awkward for a while yet.'

'But it will heal in time, and that's the main thing.'

Alice moaned, and they both leaned over her. For a moment their heads almost touched, and Annie could feel Jack's hair brushing against her own, but then he sat back abruptly and groped on the floor. 'That's the noise she made earlier. Better get the—'

They just about managed to position the pot before poor Alice was sick again. Annie was nearly ill herself when she saw what was coming up – it was horrible, a kind of dark slurry that looked like wet earth or soil.

At last Alice stopped heaving and collapsed back into Annie's arms. She looked absolutely exhausted, as well she might, and lay perfectly still.

Annie tried to comfort her. 'No wonder you felt poorly, with all that in you. Now you've got it all up you'll start to feel better, I'm sure. You have a little rest while I clear up, and then I'll go and see about something for you to drink. Some water, or maybe even a little bit of broth. I'll—'

'Annie.' It was Jack's voice, not Alice's, and it was a peculiar, gentle tone that she'd never heard him use before.

Annie kept talking, saying she knew not what, because she didn't want to hear what she knew he was going to say.

But he put a warm hand on her cold one. 'Annie,' he said, softly, 'stop, please. I . . . I don't think you're going to need to get her anything.'

Annie stared resolutely out of the window, still unable and unwilling to face it, and it was some moments before she could she force herself to look down at the little girl cradled in her arms. Alice's eyes were wide open and staring, but they would never see Annie's face again.

* * *

Annie had no idea how long she sat there. How long she wept, how long she rocked Alice in her arms, how long she held the cooling little hand.

She had failed. She'd promised to look after all the children, and now Alice was dead and it was all her fault. If only she hadn't taken them to the square that day! If only she'd realised how seriously Alice had been injured when she'd been thrown against the cart. If only—

'We need to get her downstairs,' came Delilah's voice, from a great distance. 'Where it's warmer. Can you manage to support her on one side, even with your bad arm, if I take the other?'

Annie felt herself being guided to her feet, and then there were stairs, and the back room. It was warm in there, but still she was shivering. An arm was round her – Jack's. He held her upright while Delilah put a cup to her lips. 'Hot tea, with plenty of sugar.'

Did Annie drink? She wasn't sure. Yes, she must have done; she could feel the warmth sliding down her throat.

'Can you write?' Delilah was asking Jack. 'I'll put a sign up in the shop window saying we're closed for the afternoon, but I don't know how to spell "bereavement".'

Briefly, the arm slipped away from Annie, but its comforting presence soon returned. She rested her head on Jack's shoulder and cried her heart out.

The afternoon passed in a blur. There were people coming and going, family, children, strange men ascending the stairs and then coming down again carrying a covered stretcher, words being spoken that Annie couldn't hear or understand.

The only thing that broke through into her stupor was Charlie's howls, and she roused herself enough to gather him on her knee and hold him while his body shook with the sobbing.

She thought that she might have eaten something, and then before she knew it she was being put into bed by Delilah and Bridget. Into *bed*. She and Hannah no longer needed to sleep on the floor, because Alice didn't need the bed any more. That thought gave her such a jolt that her tears started flowing again, and she cried herself to sleep.

Annie awoke very early the next morning, and stared at the ceiling as it gradually became visible. Hannah was still asleep, curled up next to her, so she didn't move, but her mind was active. She would never get over the guilt of having taken Alice to the square, but Alice's death had not been entirely due to that: it had been caused by the violence that had been unnecessarily provoked.

Caused, in other words, by the Carringtons.

And she was damned if she was going to let the Carringtons take her beloved brother away as well.

Much to everyone's surprise, Annie got up at the same time as everyone else, ate a good breakfast to fortify herself, and then stood up as soon as the older children had left for school.

'Are you feeling well enough to go?' asked Delilah, anxiously. 'We all want to come with you, but I'm absolutely sure that they won't let the whole family in. It is better if only one person tries, and as you're the youngest, and a girl, they might just be more sympathetic.'

Annie wrapped her shawl firmly about her. 'I'm sure. I'm going to see Sam, and no one's going to stop me.'

* * *

Unfortunately, they did stop her. She reached the barracks after a walk of about half an hour and gave her name and business, but she was not allowed in.

The same thing happened the next day, and the next, but she did not give up, walking to Upper Warwick Street and standing as near to the imposing brick building as she could without being moved on. There she would call out to anyone who passed that she was there because Sam Shaw, a hero who had saved women and children from danger, was being wrongly accused of cowardice. She carried a basket of food from Meg, in case she was able to pass it on to Sam, but each day she returned with it untouched.

On Friday morning they buried Alice. Annie had been terrified of another pauper's funeral, of her dear little girl being unceremoniously interred in a mass, unmarked grave, but the family had scraped together enough for a proper service. It was the barest minimum, but it was enough: Alice had her own name, and she would lie not far from Annie's own dear Ma. After the service Annie stood for a while by Ma's grave, trying and failing to remember what she looked like. But that didn't matter: the important things were love and family, and they were never forgotten, no matter how much time passed. As she gazed at the simple wooden cross, Annie made a promise, both to Ma and to herself, that from now on she would do her best for *all* the members of her family.

On Friday evening, Jack declared that he was well enough to return to the mill village, and that he had a duty to do so and would set off early the next morning.

'I have to see what happened to everyone else, and I have to keep helping out however I can,' he said, firmly, as dawn broke on Saturday.

Annie knew that she would miss him – was shocked at just how much the thought of his departure stabbed at her – but she knew it was the right thing to do. 'I'll come back too, as soon as I can, but I have to be here for Sam just at the moment.'

'Of course you do.'

They were standing alone in the shop, Delilah having tactfully ushered everyone else into the back room and shut the door.

'Look out for Clara for me, won't you? If you see her, tell her where I am?' As the week had passed, Annie had grown ever more worried about the fact that Clara had not appeared. Was she still in the otherwise empty house, with no job and no money for food or rent?

'I will. And I'll write to you as soon as I know anything. I asked your sister and wrote down this address, so my letters will come straight here.'

'Thank you.'

There was silence.

'Well,' he said, at last, 'the sun's nearly up.'

Annie found herself lost for words.

Slowly, Jack reached out to take her hand, and then squeezed it. 'We'll talk more once we know where we are with everything. But your family has to come first with you.'

She still said nothing as he walked out of the door, setting the shop bell ringing.

* * *

It was another fruitless afternoon outside the barracks, although Annie did receive the welcome news that the pamphlets Mr Hughes had printed, giving a more accurate account of what had happened the previous week, were now circulating through Liverpool. She felt pride in the truth being known, and satisfaction in the thought that the Carrington name might not yet be tarnished, but it soon would be if she had anything to do with it.

Jack didn't waste any time in writing to Annie once he got back to the mill village, and a letter arrived for her on Tuesday.

She read through it in a welter of confused emotions. He had written to her! There was her name, in his own handwriting, and there was his own at the end. And there was a small piece of good news: Grace had found a live-in position in domestic service, so she was being housed and fed, and even planned on sending some of her wages to her mother. Nora and her son – who still had his job – had taken rooms and were looking for a lodger to help with the costs, so Annie was welcome to stay safely with them whenever she was ready to come back to the village. That is, '(if you want to)', as Jack had added in afterwards by scribbling in the margin.

Unfortunately, Annie's rising mood was thoroughly dampened when she read what Jack had to say about Clara. Knowing that Annie was desperate for news of her friend, Jack had made it his business to find out as soon as he could, and he was able to tell her that she was still in the mill village, and that she had accepted a proposal of marriage from Amos Potter. They weren't married yet, but she was already living with him.

Annie had to read that twice to make sure she'd understood properly. *Amos*? Clara was going to marry Amos, the renowned bully? The man who couldn't keep his fists to himself, even at work? Annie, of course, had never seen him outside of the mill, but she had no doubt whatsoever that he would be just as horrible in his home life, and that a wife and a child – particularly a child that he would know wasn't his – would suffer the brunt of it.

Delilah, who was nursing baby Andrew at the other side of the shop's back room, sensed her agitation. 'Is everything all right with Jack?'

'I hardly know,' said Annie. 'He's said so little about himself. I assume he hasn't got any more work, because he mentions the soup kitchen. But he'll run out of his savings soon, and then what will he do?'

'He seems like a very clever, hard-working young man,' replied Delilah. 'And he knows how to use and fix all those big machines? There must be something out there for him, even if it's not in a mill. You hear about "engineers" being needed all the time these days.'

Annie nodded almost absent-mindedly, her agitation about Clara pushing even Jack's concerns temporarily to the back of her mind. 'I have to go back and talk to her.'

'Her? Who?' Delilah was confused, still obviously thinking about Jack.

'Clara.' Annie poured out the story, watching Delilah's lips form into a straighter and straighter line as she heard it.

She made no objection to Annie's suggestion; rather the opposite. 'We have to look after Clara. She's part of the family. Do you think you'll be able to persuade her to come here?'

'I honestly don't know. But I have to try.'

Delilah nodded. 'You can't walk all that way on your own. I'll ask Frank if he can think of anything, or maybe Tommy might know someone who delivers goods to the shops up there.'

Annie's next concern, of course, was how Hannah and Charlie could be cared for while she was away, but her mind was put to rest as soon as Meg and Tommy arrived; they had already decided to ask the children to stay with them for a few days.

It was obvious that Hannah found this an attractive offer, and that she had no desire to return to the mill village, but she looked torn. Despite her white face and her shaking hands, she bravely declared that if

Annie wanted or needed her, she would go too. 'After all,' she concluded in a tone that was wavering and yet full of determination, 'I'm your sister, aren't I?'

If Annie didn't know her tough-minded second sister so well, she could have sworn that Meg was wiping away a tear. 'But you can still stay with us,' she said, gently, to Hannah. 'And if you're Annie's sister then you're mine too, aren't you?'

'I never thought of that,' replied Hannah, her eyes widening.

'Well then,' said Tommy, 'you come and help Meg out for a couple of days, and I wonder if we can persuade Charlie to come too.' He turned to where Charlie and the boys were warming themselves by the range. 'Plenty of arithmetic to help with in the shop, and I'm sure Higgins would like the company?'

Charlie's face was eager, but he, too, looked at Annie first. 'It depends if Annie needs me,' was his stout reply. 'I have to look out for her.'

'It's all right,' said Annie, greatly touched. 'I can go by myself, and besides, Nora might not have room for all of us. I'll give your love to Clara, shall I? And I'll see you in a couple of days.'

They both hugged her, and that was that.

* * *

Early the following morning Annie found herself sitting alongside the driver of a grocer's cart, enjoying the sights of the spring countryside as they moved through it. By noon they were drawing near to the village, and she could see the mill looming over it ever more ominously. The carter dropped her off outside the grocer's, promising to pick her up from the same spot two days later, and went in to make his delivery. Hungry people clutching tickets were already queuing outside.

It didn't take long to ask around and find where Amos lived; he was well known. Annie set off straight away, because she knew he would be at work at this time on a weekday, and she thought she might have better success if she caught Clara alone. She reached the house – it was another of the same back-to-back ones that filled the village, but Amos rented it all to himself – and knocked.

Clara opened the door just a crack at first, but burst into a smile when she saw who it was, and flung it wide. 'Annie! Oh, it does me good to see you. I spoke to Jack the other day and he told me all about how you'd gone back to Liverpool. I didn't think I'd see you again!'

Annie listened to this outpouring of joy while looking at Clara's swollen black eye and split lip. 'Can I come in?'

Clara ushered her in. 'Look at this! A whole house.'

'Amos lives here alone? Or, he did until now? How did he do all his housework?'

'Oh, he had a girl come in, who cleaned and washed during the day, then cooked his tea and left it ready for him. But he's got rid of her now – says there's no point paying anyone if he's got a wife to do it all for free.'

'Wife?' Annie was instantly on the alert.

Clara waved dismissively. 'Oh, that. We'll get round to making it official soon.'

Annie wasn't here to beat about the bush. 'Clara, you can't do this.'

'Can't do what?

'You can't marry Amos. You know what he's like! And I bet you didn't get that by accident.' She pointed at Clara's eye.

She was answered with another airy wave. 'That's just what men are. They're all the same. He's got a wage and a roof, which is better than a lot of others.' Her face darkened for a moment. 'And it's not like Mr Frederick was going to do anything for his child, was it?'

'But you could do so much better!'

'Yeah? How?'

Annie paused. 'Well, for a start, you could come back to Liverpool. Delilah told me to ask you if you'd consider living and working at the shop for a while.'

'She's kind, I know,' said Clara, her voice softening. 'She always was. But I'm not a nipper any more, to be helping out round the place and running errands. You should know that better than anyone – you want me to go and do exactly the thing you were desperate to get away from? I'll be twenty-one in the summer!'

She had a point, Annie had to admit. But she wasn't going to give up so easily. 'Amos isn't good enough for you.'

Clara snorted. 'Look around you, girl! A house. A whole house, with three rooms, just for the two of us, and the baby, when it comes. I never had such luxury, and I'm not giving it up, even if it means a few bruises.'

'It won't be just a few bruises, though, will it? Not as time goes by. You know how this goes – it'll get worse and worse. And what if he turns against the baby, or if he's violent to it?'

That did seem to affect Clara, and she put a protective hand over her stomach. 'I'll look after it.'

Annie shook her head. 'Like your Ma did? Or like all my brothers and sisters used to try to stand up to our Pa?'

Clara shook her head stubbornly. 'I tell you, this is the best it's ever going to get, for me, so you might as well stop trying to talk me out of it.'

Annie gazed steadily at her friend, wondering how such a wonderful person could think so little of herself.

Clara said nothing, but eventually she looked away and down at the floor.

Annie got up to go. 'I'm not finished with you yet, Clara Tate. I'm going to be back here trying to get you away as soon as ever I can. You might think you don't deserve any better than a life with Amos, but I do. Do you hear me? I know you, and I know you're worth more than this.'

She embraced Clara and left, wondering if she'd made at least a tiny crack in those defences.

She would try again, but now it was time to put into action the second part of her plan, the part she hadn't told Delilah about. She had come back here to talk to Clara, that was true; but now she bent her steps towards the mill.

It was time to confront Frederick Carrington.

Chapter Eighteen

If she stopped to think, she probably wouldn't go through with it.

The best thing, then, was not to think about it at all, but rather to take a deep breath, march up the hill, through the gate and into the mill offices without pausing.

'Here! Stop!' called out one of the clerks, as she passed him and reached the door to the Carringtons' private office. 'You can't go in there!'

'You try and stop me,' said Annie, under her breath, as she pushed it open.

Both of the Carrington brothers were inside, and both looked up in surprise at being disturbed without the usual deferential knock.

'I've business with Frederick,' said Annie, finally coming to a halt. She wouldn't dignify him with the

'Mr', not any more. That was for honest, upright men like Mr Hughes.

'Oh, really?' Theodore Carrington looked amused, raising his eyebrows at his brother. 'Tsk, tsk. Another one? This is getting tiresome, Freddie. I'll have her removed.'

He began to signal to the several clerks who were hovering outside the door – *still* too afraid to come in without an invitation, Annie thought, scornfully, even given the circumstances – but Frederick, recognising Annie, stopped him. 'No, I'll hear what she has to say.'

Theodore's eyebrows nearly disappeared into his hair. 'In the middle of the afternoon? Well, if you need to step through, feel free.' He nodded at a door Annie had never noticed before, in the far corner of the room and disguised as part of the wooden panelling.

Frederick cleared his throat. 'Not just now, Theo – I'll talk to her in here, if you'd be so good as to go for a walk somewhere.'

Smirking, Theodore walked out.

Frederick moved to shut the door. Then he stood in front of it and folded his arms. 'Well, well, if it isn't Annie Shaw, sister to a coward and walking out with a criminal agitator.'

Annie refused to be drawn. 'And don't forget "friend to a wronged girl".'

He rolled his eyes. 'Don't tell me you're back here about that again.'

'No, I'm not. She's better off without you, baby or no baby. I'm here about my brother.'

'Ah, the fellow destined to face a court martial for his spinelessness. I wonder if they'll hang him or put him in front of a firing squad?'

Annie just about avoided the temptation to slap his arrogant face. 'You need to take it back. What you said about him.'

He laughed. 'And why in the world would I do that?'

She glared at him in cold fury. 'It's too much to expect, I know, that you might do it because your accusation is a lie. We've already established that you're no gentleman. But how widely do you want that known?'

'Why? Who are you going to tell?'

'It's not just me. Mr Hughes has been printing pamphlets about what really happened here that day.'

Frederick snorted. 'Pamphlets! As if anybody pays attention to those. You know, don't you, that the men who own the newspapers – the *real* way people get their information – are all friends of my father? They'll all continue to print whatever we want them to, and your puny little bits of paper will lie in the gutter where you and all your family belong.'

'You don't know—'

'Oh, yes I do. I know exactly that. I'm the sort of man who will always be believed. Your brother? Not so much. What is he – some urchin who managed to get swept up by a recruiter so he could get a square meal?' His cruel laughter sounded again.

Annie was trying to marshal her thoughts in order to come back at him, when he held up a hand. 'Oh, now, wait. I've just had the most splendid idea.'

'What, that you're going to tell the truth for a change?'

'Tsk, what would be the fun in that? No, I've thought of a way you can convince me to drop the charges against your brother.'

Annie looked uneasily at the door, which he was still blocking. But there were at least half a dozen clerks out there – surely even cowed little men like them wouldn't stand by if they heard her screaming that she was being assaulted?

He knew what she was thinking. 'No need to worry about that, dear girl. Theo might not be averse to using a bit of physical force, but that's not my style. I prefer my girls to be willing, however unwillingly.'

Annie didn't understand.

'I'll explain carefully,' he said, with exaggerated slowness, as though he was talking to a halfwit. 'Girls agree to come to me "willingly", for many reasons. They're hungry, or their families are. Or someone needs a job, or a favour. Or they feel that they owe it to me for my *many* kindnesses.'

'You trick them and bully them, you mean.'

'"Bully" is such a bitter word, don't you think? I prefer "persuade". Anyway, I expect you think that you'd do anything to save your brother's life, don't you? Lay down your own, et cetera?'

'Of course.'

'Well then.' He spread his arms wide.

The full realisation of what he was suggesting hit Annie like a train, and she felt sick. 'Never!'

'Really? You wouldn't do this one little thing, putting aside your own pride, to save your brother? How disappointed he would be in you.'

Annie opened her mouth again, but it felt dry and no words came out.

'Let us be clear,' said Frederick, 'and lay out the details of the bargain. That's how good business is done, after all.' He took a couple of paces and began to speak as though he was dictating to a clerk. 'I'm not suggesting that this encounter takes place now, today. I'm too busy, for one thing, and besides, I want you to have plenty of time to think about it. No. What I'm proposing is that you come to me at any point between now and your brother's court martial – which isn't going to be for several weeks, I understand, the wheels of army justice moving slowly at present – and *beg* me for my attentions.'

He cast a sly glance at her, to see what effect his words were having, before he continued. 'When my father was building up this business he worked so hard that he often had to sleep here, so there are private apartments that are still furnished.' He nodded at the hidden door. 'We will retire there, and . . . well, I'm sure you're aware of what we'll be doing, innocent as you may seem. If I'm satisfied with your suitably obedient and submissive behaviour, I will write immediately to the regiment – you can watch me do it – and say that I was mistaken about what I previously reported, and that I have no charges to make.'

Annie felt dizzy.

'It's not that I'll particularly enjoy the act itself, of course,' he continued, in a fake sorrowful tone. 'Not with you, when there are so many better opportunities around. No, my enjoyment will derive solely from the knowledge that you will be hating every moment, and that the humiliation will stay with you for the rest of your life. *That* will teach you to know your place.' He paused. 'So, do we have a bargain?'

'Never.' Her tone was defiant.

'Is it that you don't believe me? We can address that.' He sat at the desk, took up paper and pen, and sat writing for several minutes. 'There.'

He held up a letter so that she could read it. The text was a retraction of all his accusations against Sam, and Annie thought it would certainly be enough to have the court martial dropped. She reached out for it.

He snatched it back. 'Ah-ah! Not yet. You get this when you come back to me, as per our bargain.' He folded it and put it in his coat pocket.

'I told you, there is no bargain,' Annie spat the words out at him.

He only smirked. 'You say that now, but as the court martial draws nearer, you'll change your mind. Your dear brother, whom nobody will believe when he disputes my account. Tell me, how much do you love him?'

'More than anyone will ever love you,' she retorted. 'To be honest, I pity you. We might not have much money, but I've had more love in a day from my family than you've ever had in your whole life.' His pacing had taken him away from the door to the outer office, and she now put a hand towards it. 'You'll see me here again, but it won't be to agree to your bargain.'

His only reply was a mocking bow, and he actually pulled open the door and held it for her. 'You'll change your mind, little miss. I'll see you again, Annie Shaw, and soon.'

She ignored him and swept out past the clerks with her head held high.

Chapter Nineteen

Annie didn't tell anyone what had happened at the mill. Not Nora, when she arrived to spend the night at the rented rooms; not Clara, when she saw her again the following day during another futile attempt to talk her away from Amos and his fists; and certainly not Jack.

It preyed on her mind during the silent journey back to Liverpool, and in the bustle of family life at the shop, and as she went back to her daily vigil in front of the barracks. She had it within her power to have the charges against Sam dropped; all she had to do was get hold of that letter. But the thought of what she'd have to do to gain possession of it was just so hideous, so sickening, that she could hardly bear to think about it. Such humiliation for her, and such a triumph for Frederick Carrington and all he stood for. But what other choice was there, if Sam's life was on the line? Oh, if only she could talk to him! That might help her to make more sense of it all, and they could plan a way forward together.

Miracles did sometimes happen, especially when they were helped along by determination like Annie's, and on the following Sunday afternoon the duty officer at the barracks finally got fed up and ordered that she be admitted. Her basket was searched and found to contain nothing that might help Sam escape, and then she was ushered through a number of passages and stairwells until she found herself outside a sturdy locked door.

The soldier accompanying her sorted through a number of keys on a large ring, using the jangling noise as cover to mutter under his breath. 'We all know your brother's not a coward, miss, and this ain't right, but we're under orders not to talk. Now, I'm supposed to stay here outside the door, but I'll take a few steps down the hallway so you can say what you like to him without me hearing. When you're ready to come out, you bang on that door and I'll come and unlock it.'

Annie thanked him, and within moments she was inside the cell and face to face with Sam.

He was already on his feet, having heard the noise from the passageway, and she dropped the basket and threw herself at him.

'Oh!' he said as he hugged her tightly. 'I'm so glad to see you! What happened? Did you get away? They wouldn't tell me anything. I've been sitting here all this time without knowing—'

Annie wasn't very coherent, but, still in his tight embrace, she managed to get across that she'd escaped and was now back home with Delilah, and that she'd seen all the family.

'Let me look at you,' he said, eventually, pulling back from her and holding her by the shoulders. 'You've grown since I last you, I thought that when I saw you at the village – you're a proper grown-up now, like Delilah and Meg.'

'Not quite,' said Annie, reminded of all the juvenile mistakes she'd made in the last couple of years. 'But I'm working on it.' She wiped her eyes. 'Now, first things first. I've brought you some food, in case you're not getting enough.'

'From Meg?' Sam picked the basket up and sat down on the cell's narrow and very uncomfortable-looking bed. He began to rifle through the contents, exclaiming with joy at everything he found. 'Ah, you all look after me, my sisters, for all I don't deserve it.'

'Of course you deserve it!'

He shook his head but said nothing, either because he was unwilling or because he'd just taken a huge mouthful of pound cake.

'Sam, you saved me from all that danger, and Jack and the chil—' She brought herself up short with stinging eyes. But what had happened to Alice certainly wasn't Sam's fault, and they could all have been dead or badly injured if it hadn't been for him.

He looked at her thoughtfully as he chewed and swallowed. 'If I have, then that's the first useful thing I've ever done for any of you.'

This conversation hadn't started off the way Annie had intended. But perhaps everything was preying on his mind – it certainly would on hers if she were to be locked in a tiny confined space like this, with nothing to do except brood on past mistakes. 'All three of your sisters love you,' she said, firmly, 'and you mustn't forget that.'

He put the remains of the cake down. 'Five.'

'What?'

'I've got five sisters, or I did have.'

Annie stared for a moment, and then recalled the conversation she'd had with Delilah all that time ago. 'Rosie and Jemima.'

He nodded. 'I'm your brother, and I'm supposed to protect you all.'

'But—'

He waved away her interruption, 'Yes, I know I'm not the oldest, but Jonny was such a bully he'd do you more harm than good, and William – well, he's a good man, but he'd never win a fight, would he? And our Jem . . . anyway, it was always up to me to look after you girls, and I failed you all one after the other.'

This wasn't what Annie had come to talk about, but she couldn't help herself. Her lifelong curiosity about her family history was so strong it was the only thing that could have distracted her. 'Who's Jonny?'

Sam stared. 'I forget, sometimes, how much younger you are than the rest of us. You really don't know much about everything that happened, do you?'

'Only because nobody will tell me!' Annie felt some of her old agitation returning. 'I don't even know how many brothers and sisters I have, or did have.' *Or will have, if I don't take Frederick Carrington up on his offer.* 'I've heard the names Rosie and Jemima, once, but never Jonny. How many more are there that I don't know about?'

Sam frowned as he ran a list through his head. 'That's it.' He shrugged. 'Well, I haven't got anything else to do while I'm stuck in here, so if you're not in a hurry then I'll tell you all of it. Better coming from me than Delilah anyway, because she gets so upset about it.'

He patted the bed beside him, and she sat down as he began. 'Ma had twelve babies altogether, though three died when they were born.'

'Leaving nine.' This was already news to Annie, and mentally she began to count.

Sam was doing the same on his fingers. 'Delilah, then Jonny – he was the eldest of us boys. He was killed in an accident at the docks when he was fifteen, the same one that crippled Pa. You would only have been a baby back then, so you wouldn't remember him.'

'I remember Pa.'

Sam scowled and shook his head. 'Well, he's best forgotten. He was a bully, and Jonny was turning out just like him. After Ma died, Delilah and William worked so hard to keep us housed and fed, and Pa would steal it all for his drink, and get violent. He used to hit all of us, and he even tried to break your arm once, to get Delilah to hand over money, even though you were only a tot.'

Annie was hit by a sudden, vivid memory of the stink of gin on Pa's breath and the shooting pain in her arm. So *that* was why . . .

Sam was continuing. 'I wasn't there,' he said, moodily, 'Or I'd have tried to stop him. William told me about it after, and I swore I'd look after you from that day on.' He gave a hollow laugh. 'Maybe to do a better job than I did with the others!'

Annie tried to put her memories to one side, and resumed her mental arithmetic. 'So, Delilah and Jonny. And then William?'

Sam nodded. 'Yes. And then Meg, me and Jem, and then Rosie and you, and lastly Jemima – that was after the accident, and Ma died having her.'

Annie was thunderstruck. 'You mean – I'm not the youngest?'

'No. But hang on, let's go in order. I was no use to Delilah, and we had to leave our house in Brick Street and move to that court. Then we got so poor that Meg and Rosie had to go to the workhouse.' He got up and started pacing. 'I'll always be here for you, I said to Meg, the night before she went, and I wasn't. We scraped and we saved, and I tried to add a bit of money to the pot – did some things I wasn't too proud of – but it was so long before Delilah could go to pick them up again that she was told they'd both died.'

Annie gasped. 'But . . .'

'We found out Meg was alive about a year later, and it was the happiest moment I can ever remember.

But Rosie really did die, and it was because I couldn't help, I didn't earn enough, I didn't do enough. I let her down.' His voice was starting to break, and he fell silent, though he continued to stride up and down.

'But you can't have been more than about ten or eleven yourself at the time! How could you possibly do any more than you did?'

The cell was only wide enough to allow Sam three paces in either direction, and his constant marching and turning was starting to make Annie dizzy. 'I should have found a way. I should have—' He stopped and stood with his back to her.

'And . . . what happened to Jemima? Did she die along with Ma? Or later?'

Sam was still facing the wall. 'Jemima's not dead.'

'*What*?'

'Or, at least, she wasn't last we heard, but that was a long time ago. We couldn't keep her, could we, after Ma died? We couldn't feed her, and she would have starved. So some neighbours took her in. They brought her to Delilah's wedding, I remember that; she would have been about three. But then we lost touch – I think her new Ma died, and she and the father moved away somewhere.'

He sat down, heavily. 'So that's another sister lost. And if that wasn't bad enough, I had to watch

Delilah torture herself every day with not knowing what'd happened to Jemima, and whether she's still out there somewhere. It's been more than ten years, and I swear, every single time that shop door rings she expects her baby sister to walk in, and every time she's disappointed.' He paused. '*Now* do you see how much I've failed?'

Annie's head was spinning, and she realised that it wasn't from Sam's twisting and turning, it was from the shock. She had another sister . . .

And then a greater jolt hit her. Delilah was already tormented by the thought of the sister she'd lost contact with. And then she, Annie, had run away and not told Delilah where she was going. The distress and agony she must have caused her eldest sister – the sister who'd been a mother to her – was beyond belief. Never mind what Sam had or hadn't done: Annie had let everyone down just as badly, or worse.

They both sat in silence for a while.

It was Sam who broke it. 'Do you want any of this?' He pointed to the basket.

'No, I'm well fed enough, thank you. You keep it, or share it out with your friends. That man who let me in seemed sympathetic.'

Sam started on a pork pie. 'The lads know I wouldn't ever run away.'

'They know you're brave.'

He gave a hollow laugh. 'Oh, yes. Got a medal for it, didn't I?'

'You did, didn't you? Though you never said exactly what it was for.'

He dug in his pocket. 'Here. They let me keep it, God knows why. I don't want it, because it just reminds me of . . .' he opened her hand and slapped a medal and ribbon down into it, the metal warm to the touch. 'You have it. Something to remember me by when I'm gone.'

His words bit into her again. 'But what can be done? What can we all do to help you?' She knew the answer to that question all too well, but surely there must be another way out?

Sam shrugged. 'Nothing. Thing is, nobody from the regiment saw what happened either way, 'cos they were busy trying to follow their orders without actually killing anyone. So it's just my word against that rich fella's, and we all know how that ends.'

Annie's fury rose along with the gorge in her throat, at this recognition of exactly what Frederick Carrington had said himself. But how could Sam be so nonchalant about it? Did he even know? Surely he must. 'Sam, William says if you're found guilty they'll . . .' she tailed off, unable to finish.

He looked at her, put the pie down, and took both her hands in his. 'I know. And I ought to be scared. But I was in danger of death all the time I was in the Crimea, so why should I be frightened of it now? No,' he continued, 'if this is the one thing I've ever done to protect one of my sisters, then I'm proud of it, and I'll take the consequences. This Carrington, or whatever his name is, can have his way.'

'Not if I have anything to do with it!' burst out Annie, furiously.

Sam eyed her. 'You know him?'

She snorted. 'And some.'

Annie poured out the story of almost everything he'd done. She missed out their most recent encounter, of course, but still had plenty to say about his pretence and duplicity, what he'd done to Clara and what she'd subsequently heard him say about her.

Sam's scowl deepened through all of it, and by the time she'd finished his face was thunderous. 'Said that to you, did he? And Clara – I remember her. Feisty girl, she was.'

Annie sighed. 'She still is. But she's another one who needs looking after. I do try, but . . .'

'She wasn't there, was she, that day? Or I didn't see her. But who were those others? The fella and the littl'uns? Friends of yours?'

Another long monologue followed, it now being Annie's turn to pace up and down the tiny cell.

When she got to Alice's death, she burst into tears, and Sam stood to put his arms around her. 'Oh, you poor lass,' he said. 'What a thing for you to suffer, and after all I just told you, as well.' Then he cursed. 'If only I'd got to you five minutes earlier!'

'Oh, Sam, will you stop making everything your fault?'

He said nothing.

'And this,' she said, 'is why I don't want to lose you too!' She attempted to shake his shoulders, but it was like trying a move a rock. 'There must be something – something else – that I can do to help!'

He looked at her shrewdly. 'Something *else*? Why, have you already tried something?'

She made no reply.

Sam shook his head. 'No. No! Whatever it was, if you've got any regard for me as a brother, you'll stay out of all this and not put yourself into any more danger or trouble. If I really did save you, then it's the one thing in my life I can feel proud of, and I'll stand for it now, or in court, or in front of a firing squad.'

Tears ran down Annie's face. 'No! I won't let that happen. And – and – think what it would do to

Delilah if she lost you, too. And Meg, and William, and poor Jem!' She would have to do it, wouldn't she? To save them all from the agony. She could force herself to go through with it and then never speak of it to anyone, if it would spare those she loved from any further pain.

The mention of Jem seemed to catch Sam with greater force than anything she'd said so far. He collapsed back on the bed and rubbed his face. 'I tell you, you're not to put yourself in any danger.' But he sounded less sure of himself, less belligerent. 'Nor any of the others, neither. This is my problem.'

'What's your problem is my problem too,' said Annie, firmly, wiping her eyes. 'And that goes for all of us. You've got friends and family, Sam, and we're going to get you through this, whatever it takes. You'll be eating your Sunday dinner with us again soon, just you wait and see.'

There was a knocking at the door. 'Miss? I know I said you was to call me when you wanted to come out, but you've already been much longer than I was supposed to let you have, and it's getting dark outside.'

'All right,' called Sam. He stood up again, and he and Annie held each other in a long embrace. She felt the warmth of his body and the strength of his arms –

the strength he'd used to look out for his family all his life, since he was a little boy.

She stepped back and began to unpack the remaining provisions. 'I'll take the basket back, and bring more next time I come.'

There had been some delicacies in among the plainer food, and Sam picked up a packet of macaroons wrapped in paper. When the door opened, he held them out to the soldier outside. 'You make sure my sister gets safely out of here, will you, Walt? And as far up the street as you're allowed to see her.'

'I've been off duty the last half hour, officially,' said Walt, waving the package away. 'So I can walk her properly home if that's all right with you, Sam. At least then I feel like I'm doing something for you.'

Sam nodded and gave Annie one more swift, fierce hug, and then she was outside and the door was clanging shut.

'We're all on his side,' said Walt, as they made their way back through the maze of passageways. 'And if people knew the truth, they would be too. But how to get it out there?'

As it happened, he didn't need to take Annie all the way home, because when they emerged from the barracks building into the evening gloom, she found Frank was waiting for her. He questioned her eagerly, knowing that she'd been inside for so long that she must have seen Sam, but she gave him only short answers as they walked, distracted by her own thoughts, and he soon lapsed into silence.

His word against mine, that's what they'd both said, Sam and Frederick. Nobody would believe Sam or Annie when they told the truth, and the newspapers would print whatever the Carringtons wanted. But how to get the truth out there? Walt had asked. And what would happen if the real truth *did* become known, and it was believed by a large number of people? The rich might run Liverpool, but they were vastly outnumbered by the people lower down the social scale, whose opinions must count for something.

Annie thought of poor Luke, keeping his head down and causing no trouble all his life, and dying because of it. Leaving Nora a grieving widow and the rest of their family scattered to the four winds. *It's just the way of things*, he used to say. Well, if this really was the way of things, then things needed to change. And we'll be stronger if we all work together, thought Annie, reminded of Jack and his tireless efforts to help the laid-off mill workers – not because they were all his family and friends, but because they were good people who deserved better, and because they were more effective when they pulled together. There was strength in numbers.

By the time they reached the shop, Annie had a plan.

* * *

Early the following morning, Annie went to Mr Hughes's premises and asked to see him.

He welcomed her and they stepped into his office, a cramped space containing a desk so piled high with papers that it could barely be seen.

'I was thinking,' began Annie, without preamble, 'about those pamphlets you printed. About the trouble at the mill and how you were able to get people to see a bit more of the truth.'

'Yes. Going straight to the public themselves is often the best idea.'

'Well, I was wondering if we could do something the same about Sam.'

His brow wrinkled. 'In what respect?'

'When I was at the barracks, one of the other soldiers said they all knew Sam wasn't a coward, but he didn't know how they would get the truth out. Why can't we make more pamphlets that say that?'

'Hmm. And would any of these fellow soldiers be prepared to say so, publicly? We'd need some kind of evidence.'

'I don't think so,' she said, regretfully. 'He said they weren't allowed to say anything. But Sam did win a medal while he was in the Crimea, so he must have been brave. Would that do? Could we write about that? Here, he gave it to me to look after.'

Annie took it from her pocket and put it on Mr Hughes's desk. It was a funny shape for a medal, now she came to think of it – weren't they normally round? This one was cross-shaped, hanging on a scarlet ribbon.

Mr Hughes's eyes opened very wide. He blinked a couple of times, bent to examine it, and then strode to the door. He pulled it open and called to a passing boy. 'Would you ask Mr Shaw to step in here, please?'

William appeared within moments, surprised to see Annie. He didn't get a chance to say anything to her, though, because Mr Hughes was pointing at the medal. 'William,' he asked, his voice incredulous, 'were you aware that your brother was the holder of a Victoria Cross?'

'No, I – *What*?'

Annie was confused. 'Is it something particularly special?'

'I should say.' William was staring in amazement at the medal. 'I remember when they were first introduced a few years ago – didn't we write something about it?'

'We did,' replied Mr Hughes. 'And I can even remember the official wording we had to use; it came straight from the War Office. These are only awarded for "most conspicuous bravery, or some daring or pre-eminent act of valour or self-sacrifice, or extreme devotion to duty in the presence of the enemy" – and very, very few of them have been given out.' He turned to Annie. 'Your brother must have done something remarkable. I take it that you don't know what that was?'

'No. And I don't think he'd tell me if I asked, either.' A thought struck her. 'But . . . if it was for killing lots of enemy soldiers, he wouldn't want to boast about it, would he?' Although she was well aware that Sam was in the army, somehow she'd never really associated that with him actually killing anyone, and she didn't like the thought of it.

'Not necessarily.' Mr Hughes absent-mindedly picked up a pencil and began tapping it on his teeth. 'All awards of the Victoria Cross are listed in the *London Gazette*.'

'They have copies of that at the Union Newsroom, I think?' said William.

The pencil was pointed at him. 'Yes! Look, we can manage without you for a couple of hours. It's only down the road: get down there and see what you can find out, and we'll draw something up this afternoon and get it to print.'

William and Annie both thanked him profusely, but he only smiled. 'This is important – and besides, if our little pamphlets can get a scoop that the big newspapers haven't got hold of, it will be good for business.'

* * *

The Union Newsroom turned out to be a very impressive building indeed, on the corner of Duke Street and Slater Street, and Annie felt out of place as she passed between tall, graceful columns and high arched windows to enter the ground-floor hall. William seemed to know exactly where he was going, though, and spoke to the staff with confidence. Annie recalled that Mr Hughes, although calling him by his first name, had referred to him as 'Mr Shaw' to the boy. She looked at her eldest brother with affection. He might not, as Sam had pointed out, win many fights, but life wasn't all about fisticuffs and she was proud to have William on her side.

Before long they found themselves seated at a large table with a stack of old papers in front of them. 'The Victoria Cross was instituted in January 1856,' said

William, contemplating the pile, 'although the first actual award wasn't until the year afterwards, I think.'

Annie nodded. 'You start with 1856, then, and I'll take 1857.'

The print was small, and some of it had got smudged during the years that the papers had been stored, but Annie set to with a will. Next to her William did the same, scanning each page carefully.

It was in an issue from June 1857 that Annie found it. Under the heading 'War Office' there was a section in which 'The Queen has been graciously pleased to signify her intention to confer the Decoration of the Victoria Cross on the undermentioned . . .' and there, in black and white, was the name Samuel Shaw. Annie grabbed William's arm and they both bent their heads eagerly over the entry.

> For gallantry in the attack on the Redan, 8th September, 1855, on which occasion he saved the life of an officer and three wounded men. Jumping over the parapet, Shaw – then aged just 17 – proceeded across open ground, under murderous enemy fire, to convey the officer, whose leg was badly broken, to safety. He then repeated this act no fewer than three times, under constant fire and at risk

```
of his own life, to rescue three other
men of his own regiment. All were able to
be treated, and, thanks to Shaw's heroic
actions, all survived.
```

Annie jumped back from the paper just in time to stop a large tear falling on it, which would have blotted the print.

'That's our Sam,' said William, softly.

'Always a protector,' Annie managed to choke.

William had taken a notebook and pencil from his pocket and was copying the entry word for word, as well as making a note of the date and page of the *Gazette*.

'Will this help?' Annie asked anxiously. 'It must do, surely.'

William made a last full stop, punching the pencil down so that it made a dent in the page of his notebook. 'Oh yes. You wait until Mr Hughes has this as ammunition.'

And just you wait until this becomes public knowledge, Frederick Carrington, thought Annie. Everyone was about to see who really had the power to change the way things were.

Chapter Twenty

'And that's why we all have to do this together,' concluded Annie.

It was Monday evening, and the whole extended family was gathered in Meg's tea room, the only place big enough to seat them all while they held a council. Annie had stood up and given an impassioned speech about how they needed to get the truth out far and wide, in order to counter the power of the Carringtons and the newspapers, and that if they all put their minds to it they could spread the word and save Sam.

There were dangers, of course. Who knew whether the power of those whose interests lay in suppressing the truth might damage the family and its various businesses? Lost trade or lost jobs might result, and they could be risking everything they'd worked for over the last decade, everything that had lifted them out of the poverty-stricken life they once led.

Delilah and Meg, of course, had been nodding all along, but it was the two men who had married into the family who spoke first to offer their whole-hearted support.

'We'll take as many pamphlets as you can get us,' said Tommy, firmly, 'and they'll go on the counter in here, and in the grocer's shop, and in every box I send out for delivery.' He reached out to take Meg's hand while Sally stood behind them, looking as fierce as she knew how.

'I don't think I need to ask Delilah if she'll put some in the shop,' said Frank, 'and I'll get a pile into Lime Street, somehow.'

And to every station I call at, added Jem.

Amy, who was by now in the final stages of pregnancy, smiled at her husband before turning to the others. *It's not much, I know, but I can take some to the deaf school*. Annie hugged her.

The children were whispering. 'We can take some to school, too,' declared Daisy, while the others nodded vigorously.

'There'll be lots of men at the docks who'll want to hear this,' said Abraham.

'And lots of women round about the place who'll be glad to hear about a good man protecting women and children,' added Bridget. 'They might not all be able to read, but I can talk to as many as I can while we're all washing and cleaning, and get them to pass it on.'

'And it goes without saying,' said William, 'that Mr Hughes and I will circulate as widely as possible as well.'

Annie looked at them all, her heart swelling with pride. 'The mill villages are the other places to try,' she said. 'Jack's not here, but I'll answer for him helping, and so will Nora and everyone else who's been laid off, or been to the soup kitchens or the sewing lessons.'

Mr Hughes set his staff to working on the pamphlets, the men and boys all glad to stay behind after hours. William was a senior employee but was very popular – hardworking himself and fair with the juniors – and Annie thought that Amos Potter and others could well take some lessons.

The pile of papers grew and grew, and Annie could see on each of them the details of Sam's heroics.

`The gallant Samuel Shaw`

ran the first line, in large letters. It was followed by a paragraph of text:

```
was one of the first men to be awarded
the Victoria Cross, the realm's highest
decoration for bravery, for saving the
```

lives of wounded men in danger. Recently he again rescued from peril fellow creatures, this time not only an injured man but also a woman and children, who owe their lives to his bravery. Yet now he faces a court martial.

The next line contained a single word, in capitals:

WHY?

And then more text gave all the details, painting the Carringtons and their actions in a much less favourable light than Annie had seen elsewhere.

As fast as they were printed, the stacks were taken away and distributed. Annie's heart was screwed up with the tension, wondering if this was all going to work, and telling herself over and over again that she would save Sam's life the other way if she had to.

The first few days and weeks were disappointing, with many hundreds of pamphlets being distributed to seemingly little effect. Everything seemed to hang in the balance.

But then, slowly, a swell began to form, and it soon became a flood.

It was Jem who brought the first news of it. His workmates on the trains knew that he had a brother in the army and had put two and two together when they heard the name Shaw. They'd all expressed solidarity with Jem and the family, and with any working-class man who was being trodden down by the rich. They helped to spread the word, and soon the story was up and down the length of the railway.

And then it was all over Liverpool, too: the case of the wrongly accused Sam Shaw, hero of the Crimea and protector of women and children, was discussed in pubs and on street corners, at the docks and in the cellar kitchens where domestic servants worked. The name 'Carrington' was spoken disparagingly, and 'Shaw' with the pride of the people of his home city.

Annie glowed every time she heard of it, but Sam wasn't out of the woods yet; indeed, he was still in captivity, and he passed his birthday there in May. Annie went to visit him with a cake, and was warmly welcomed by every soldier she met, who knew the efforts she was making on her brother's behalf.

They had been keeping him informed of developments, she found, and it was a more buoyant Sam that she met this time in the little cell. She unpacked the cake – cut into slices already, as she knew they wouldn't let her bring in a knife – and they sat side by side on the hard, narrow bed to enjoy it.

She waited until they'd polished off a piece each before she spoke. 'And there's more good news,' she said. 'Amy's had her baby, a little boy, and they're all well.'

Sam's smile lit up the cell. 'She's a good lass.' He shook his head almost in disbelief. 'And our Jem, a father! So, what have they called him?'

Annie hugged herself. 'Can't you guess? His name's Sam.'

To her immense surprise, Sam – her big, tough, brother, the one who'd never backed down from anything in his life – turned away from her and wiped his eyes.

'And this is another reason why we're going to get you out of here,' she said, to his back. 'You've got so much to live for, so many people who love you.'

He nodded without speaking.

'It's not over yet, but we're in a better situation than we were before.'

He turned back. 'Thanks to you.'

'Thanks to all of us. Yes, I asked about having the pamphlets printed, but everyone has passed them about – and it was your own bravery that got you your medal, which has made all the difference in how people see you.'

Sam sighed. 'I still see the other two, you know.'

'What other two?'

'The ones I didn't save. I was young, see, and not as strong as I am now, and I could only carry them one at a time. There was an officer and five men stuck out there after the explosion, and it took me so long that the last two were hit again before I could go back for them.'

Annie took his hand. 'Sam, you have to stop this. You have to stop blaming yourself for everything. Four men survived because of you, men who would have died. And even the two that were lost died knowing that you were on your way back, that somebody cared and was coming for them.'

He nodded, slowly. 'I'll try. But it's hard.'

Annie was reminded of another conversation in another place. 'Just because you can't help everyone, it doesn't mean you shouldn't help anyone. Think, if you can, of all the people you *have* helped and saved. Why, those men are probably married and with children of their own, now, and that wouldn't have happened without you. Or maybe they had children already, and you stopped them being orphans and sent to the workhouse.'

'You're right, I know it deep down. But I just can't help it.' He gave her a frank look. 'And you could do with taking your own advice, and all.'

'Me?'

'I know how badly you felt after your little girl died – you told me all about it, remember? But she died in your arms, knowing she was loved, and you've rescued the other two from a life of God-knows-what.'

Now it was Annie's turn to look away. She nodded, and waited a few moments until she felt able to speak. 'You're right. And Hannah and Charlie are much happier now.' She managed a wan smile. 'So that's two off my list, and just another two to worry about.'

His brow wrinkled. 'Two?'

'You, and Clara.'

Sam clapped her on the shoulder, so hard that she nearly fell off the bed. 'Do you know what? I reckon you will. You're a real Shaw, you are, and when you put your mind to it, you make things happen.' He laughed. 'You're turning out just like Delilah and Meg, and Ma.'

He began to rummage for a second slice of cake, unaware that he'd just paid Annie the highest compliment imaginable.

* * *

It was about a week after this that several major breakthroughs were made. First, the officer whose life

Sam had saved in the Crimea came forward to speak on his behalf, saying that he would go before any court martial and vouch for Private Shaw's good conduct and his courage under fire. Second, some very important man or other had encountered the Carrington brothers at their club, and he had done something called 'cutting' them. This was not, as a relieved Annie found, anything to do with swords or knives: it merely meant that he had refused to shake their hands or even acknowledge their presence. This sounded like a very minor occurrence to her, but apparently it was terribly serious in their kind of society. The servants from big houses who came to the shop to collect their flowers were all full of the gossip.

The third and most important development was that the *Liverpool Mercury* changed sides. Whether this was due to a falling-out with the Carringtons, or a realisation that Mr Hughes's version of events was the truth, or even a recognition that the opinion of the ordinary people of Liverpool was worth something, Annie didn't know. But in the last week of May an editorial appeared in which the paper deplored the 'mistaken and perhaps even ungentlemanly' actions of Frederick Carrington and praised 'young Shaw, who was only trying to protect those weaker than himself, at a great personal cost'.

In the first week of June, the army decided not to proceed with the court martial.

Sam was free.

The rejoicing at the next family gathering was like nothing Annie had ever experienced. The laughter, the happiness, the shining faces, the food . . . she was in heaven. Or, at least, she would have been were it not for the nagging sense of unfinished business; but she was forming a plan for that, so she was able to put it to the back of her mind temporarily while she enjoyed the present.

Sam had met both of his newest nephews. He declined holding either of them, terrified he'd drop or break such fragile little things, but he sat for a good while with Jem and Amy, and Annie saw the soppiest grin spread across his face when his finger was firmly grasped by a tiny hand.

Charlie was romping happily with the other children and the dog, and Annie delighted in seeing how he'd weathered his storms. The poor boy had lost his entire family, but – as with anyone who came within the Shaw orbit – he had found another one. So too had Hannah. For this special occasion she had been allowed to bake a batch of small cakes entirely by herself, and she was now anxiously watching them being eaten.

Frank, who was much more perceptive than he was often given credit for, winked at Annie and began praising the cakes to the skies, loudly encouraging everyone else to do the same. 'Are these not the finest cakes you've ever tasted?' he asked some of the children. 'Saving your Auntie Meg's, of course, before she hears that and clouts me. But these are the food of the angels . . .'

Hannah looked cheered and relieved, but her main attention was focused on Annie and Meg. 'These are delicious,' said Annie, with conviction, and Hannah managed a small smile as she turned to the real expert.

Meg made a show of taking her time with the tasting. 'An excellent start,' was her verdict. 'You really took care to beat the sugar and the butter thoroughly, which is what makes them so light and airy, and you folded in the flour with an excellent technique.'

Although this wasn't quite as effusive as Frank's praise, Hannah looked even more gratified. She sat down modestly next to Annie, but allowed a quiet, private smile to play across her face.

Annie and Delilah had already spoken to Meg and Tommy, so now seemed the best time to broach the all-important subject with the children.

Charlie was called over, and Annie took both his hand and Hannah's. 'Now, what I'm going to say might sound a little unusual to you, maybe even a bit scary. But remember – it's not because I love you any less, but because I love you more and I want the best for you.'

Their faces took on worried expressions, and she hastened to continue. 'We all want you both to live and to grow up in a place where you'll be happy and safe. At the moment, I don't have a proper home of my own, and what I can offer you isn't much.'

'I don't care,' said Hannah, fiercely. 'You're the best friend and sister anyone could have – it doesn't matter about money. I'll get a job to help.'

Charlie agreed, and Annie hugged them both tightly. 'You're lovely. But what we thought was that you both might like to stay living with Meg and Tommy. Charlie, you can go to school in the mornings and help in the grocer's in the afternoon, and learn the trade. Hannah, now that you're eleven you're a bit old to be starting school, though you can if you want to, or you can just help Meg here in the tea shop and the kitchen.'

Meg and Tommy both voiced their support for the idea, repeating the invitation, and they all waited to see what Hannah and Charlie would say. It would be good for them *and* for Meg and Tommy, Annie was convinced, but it had to be the children's own decision.

Charlie looked about him, and particularly at the kind and steady Tommy, who was so different from his own Pa and whom he was already beginning to hero-worship. 'I'd like that,' he said, though with a little hesitancy. This was soon explained, as his next words to Annie were, 'If you're sure *you'll* be all right?'

Annie kissed the top of his head. 'Do you know what, Charlie Jackson? You're a wonderful boy, and you're going to grow up into a wonderful man.'

He looked from one grown-up to another. 'Can I ask something?'

'Of course,' they all said, in unison, which brought a grin to his face.

'Well . . . you know how Hannah changed her name when she came to stay with us? Can I change mine too? My last name, I mean?'

'Of course you can,' said Annie.

She knew what was coming next, though the others hadn't quite grasped it yet. They were probably expecting him to ask to change his name to Shaw, but Annie knew better.

She wasn't surprised, then, when Charlie made a firm request to be called Hopkins, and both Meg and Tommy went very red around the eyes.

Hannah had been considering carefully, and now she took Annie's hand again. 'It would be lovely to stay here, and I could be useful, I know I could. But I'd really miss you.'

'I know you would, my love, just as I'd miss you.' It was true: parting from Hannah would be a wrench. 'But this is best for you.'

Hannah still looked torn.

It was Meg who made everything right. 'We really would love to have you stay with us,' she said to Hannah. 'And, you know – it would be the best thing for Annie too. She's got to go and find herself another job, and that will be easier by herself. If you stayed with us, you'd be helping her.'

And that was what did it. Hannah might have been reluctant to take up an offer that would only provide happiness for herself, but if would help Annie then she had no hesitation, and accepted.

'But,' she added, 'I still want to be called Shaw, please, like you.'

'Of course. And Meg was a Shaw before she got married, don't forget. So we can all be sisters together.'

Annie left the new little family to talk over their excitement and their ideas for the future. She had plans, too, and this time she was going to save everyone, not just a chosen few.

Sam was over with the other men. 'So,' she heard him say as she drew near, 'I can leave if I want to – and with all my back pay in my pocket – so I think I will.' He laughed. 'I've gone off the army, for some reason!'

'What will you do?' asked William.

'Don't know yet, but I'll have enough money to let me take a few weeks to decide.'

'Well, you know you've always got a roof over your head with us,' said Frank.

And us, added Jem.

Abraham was looking thoughtful. 'A strong young man like you, with your army training? There's bound to be opportunities in labouring, or more likely in guarding – a watchman job, something like that. Let me ask around at the docks, and I'm sure one or other of the companies would bite your hand off. Proper, waged work, too – not just insecure daily labour.'

'You were always so good to us,' said Sam, and William nodded.

'I've good reason to be,' said Abraham. Then he changed the subject, briskly. 'So, you'll have a few days off, will you, while we all look round for something?'

'I'll do anything that needs doing,' said Sam. 'Any of you wants boxes moving, house repairs, anything like that, while I've got time on my hands, you just say.'

That was Annie's opportunity. 'Actually, Sam, I've got something I'd like you to help with.'

'Ah, the heroine of the hour!' cried William. He stood up and pulled another chair over so she could join their circle.

Sam leaned over and kissed Annie on the cheek. 'Anything for you, little sister, any time.'

'Could you bear to come back to the mill village with me? Even though it's where all this trouble started?'

'Of course I could. But why?'

'Because I have unfinished business.'

'All right.' He narrowed his eyes. 'And, as a matter of interest, are we going to finish this business while we're there?'

'Oh yes,' said Annie. 'We certainly are.'

Chapter Twenty-One

A couple of days later, Annie found herself preparing to do something she'd never even considered. She was going to travel on a train!

The railway, of course, was a subject of great interest in their family, but it was a source of employment, not a service to be used or enjoyed themselves. But Sam, in a fit of generosity while he had money in his pocket, was going to buy tickets for himself and Annie to travel from Liverpool to Ormskirk, and then they would walk the shorter distance to the mill village.

By now it was nearly midsummer, and the day began early. Despite everything she knew was ahead, a flutter of excitement went through Annie as they walked up to Lime Street station and inside. They were dressed in the smartest clothes they could find, and Annie didn't feel too shabby next to the other passengers queuing at the ticket office, even though she didn't have a summer hat like some of the other women.

Sam bought two third-class tickets, and they made their way on to the platform. The waiting locomotive seemed huge, but Annie reminded herself that it worked almost the same as the mill machinery, and that however modern and technological it looked, it functioned by manpower, the stokers shovelling coal into it as fast as they could. Jem wouldn't be on this one, she knew, as he was on a different line to Manchester today.

The third-class carriages were the ones immediately behind the engine. 'So we get covered in smuts rather than the rich folk dirtying their clothes,' explained Sam – following up, rather disconcertingly, with, 'and so they'll be furthest away if the engine explodes.'

Annie clutched at him, and he laughed. 'I'm only teasing. Now, you get in first.' He held her steady while she climbed up into the open carriage and found a place on one of the wooden benches.

She was reminded of her first journey to the mill, taken more than two years ago now, sitting on a similar bench in the wagon. But she soon noticed the difference once the train set off and left the station: she had never moved so fast in her life. She had to screw up her eyes against the wind.

'Forty miles an hour, on the straight bits, that's what Jem said,' shouted Sam in her ear as the wind whistled past them.

Annie was astonished – how was it even possible for the human body to withstand travelling at such speed? But she wasn't scared; she was exhilarated. She felt as though she could whoop for joy as the engine puffed, the carriage clattered, and her hair, coming loose from its pins, streamed out behind her. She didn't, of course, because she was a grown-up and a respectable passenger, but she did now understand why Jem loved his trains so much.

They were in Ormskirk within half an hour. The modern world was amazing!

Annie's feeling of exultation stayed with her as she alighted from the train and shook her hair to clear the smuts out of it, laughing with Sam. Then she saw Jack standing at the end of the platform, gazing at her in what she could only describe as open-mouthed admiration. At once she made to tie up her hair in a more respectable fashion, but secretly she was glad that he had seen her looking to advantage in that unguarded moment.

She hurried over to him. 'Jack! What are you doing here? How did you know we were coming on the train?'

'I didn't,' he replied. 'I know you said in your last letter that you were going to come back sometime soon, but I had no idea it would be today, or here. I stayed over last night and I was just about to walk back. I was in Ormskirk yesterday about an engineering job – you remember me saying they made machinery here? Well . . .' he tailed off and made an effort to collect himself. 'Anyway, sorry, I shouldn't be rambling on about myself.' He cast a glance at Sam, looming by Annie's side. 'Is this . . .?'

Annie remembered her manners. 'Oh! Of course you've never met properly, not since . . . Jack, this is my brother Sam. Sam, this is my friend Jack.'

To her immense joy and relief, they both smiled and seemed eager to take the other's hand. 'I need to thank you,' said Jack, immediately, 'for getting us all out of the trouble in the square that day. I'm afraid I wasn't at my best, and I wasn't doing very well.'

'You were doing just fine,' replied Sam, pumping Jack's arm up and down so vigorously that Annie was glad it wasn't the one that had been injured. 'I've heard all about you from Annie and the others, and you're sound.'

Jack took this as the high compliment that was intended, and they all made their way to the station exit. 'All right if I walk with you? I was on my way back, anyway, like I said.'

'Of course,' said Sam. 'Here, you walk in the middle, so you can talk to both of us.' He stepped sideways and shoved Jack into the vacant space next to Annie.

Honestly, he was as bad as Delilah and Meg – though Annie certainly didn't mind the result of his interference. 'How's your arm?'

Jack flexed it a few times. 'Going very well. Still a bit weaker than the other, but that will improve. That doctor did a wonderful job setting the bone.'

'I'm glad.' She certainly was. If Jack's injury had proved to be permanent, it would have blighted the whole of the rest of his working life, and she would hate to see someone so clever and active reduced to infirmity and unemployment, or in long-term pain.

The three miles passed quickly enough, in good company and blazing sunshine.

Annie slowed as they neared the village, considering her next steps. 'I think we'll go to Clara first, if that's all right?'

'I'm here to do whatever you need,' said Sam. 'So you tell me.'

Annie squinted at the sun. Thanks to the speed of the train, it was still not yet noon. 'Yes, we'll go there first.' She looked at Jack. 'I assume Amos is still working at the mill, so he won't be at home?'

'That's right. Look, I've got some time . . . I could come too, if you think I might be useful?'

'Yes. Yes, please do.'

Annie felt very proud indeed, as she entered the village, to be walking with two such fine men. But her confidence was not due to the strength of their fists; it came from within herself. She knew that today's result was going to be different from the last time, both when she saw Clara and when she went to the mill afterwards.

She found Amos's house and knocked. As before, Clara opened the door just a crack until she could see who it was. As before, her face was bruised – in fact this time it was worse. And her pregnancy was much further advanced, to the point where she must be due within weeks.

'Annie!' came the joyful cry, but hardly had Clara started on 'Come i—' when she saw who else was standing on the threshold. 'Sam!' she squeaked, in excitement. 'Sam Shaw! Oh, I haven't seen you in *years*, I've been asking Annie how you were—'

Sam wasn't smiling. 'Who,' he asked, pointing to the bruises on Clara's face, 'did that to you?'

'That would be Amos Potter,' said Annie. 'Clara, can we all come in?'

Clara stood aside, saying nothing but still staring at Sam. He could hardly take his eyes off her, either. *Oh, Sam*, thought Annie, *never change*. As she had correctly predicted, Sam's protective instincts were immediately engaged. It was terrible that Clara had those bruises today, but in this particular respect they were quite useful – and, if everything went according to Annie's plan, they would be the last ones she'd ever have to endure.

Annie swept in, placed a chair for Clara and helped her lower herself into it.

'And where will I find Amos Potter?' rumbled Sam, as soon as he was inside.

Annie shook her head. 'You leave him alone – you've just got out of trouble.' It really was tempting to think that Amos, who had bullied and hurt so many women and children, might get his just deserts, but Annie wasn't here for revenge – she just wanted to get Clara safely away. And so far, things were looking hopeful.

Sam shook his head. 'I'm not having anyone treating Clara like that. She deserves better.'

Annie had said that to Clara herself, on more than one occasion, but the result hadn't been Clara staring at her with shining eyes, like she was doing to Sam now. Good.

'Really?' asked Clara.

'Really,' said Sam. He looked about the house. 'Whoever he is, you're not staying with him. Pack yourself a bag, and you can come straight back to Liverpool with us.'

'I can't—'

'Yes you can, and don't argue.'

To be honest, Annie thought that was a bit much. If Sam or anyone else had tried to order her around like that, they'd have got short shrift. But in Clara's case it seemed to be just what she needed. A direct instruction, given with authority, was something she was used to, and it was actually far more effective than all Annie's attempts at gentle persuasion. 'Well, if you say so, Sam . . .'

'I do. You're not going to get any sort of job looking like that, so you need taking care of. And you'll get that better with us than here.' Sam looked at Annie. 'Well, that's that sorted. Do you want me to come with you to the mill?'

'No, you stay here with Clara. I'll be back as soon as I can.'

'I'll go with you,' said Jack, who had remained silent while Annie's sly matchmaking was going on.

'All right.' Annie gave Clara a brief hug, and then she and Jack left.

Once they were outside, Annie put one finger to her lips and her ear to the door. She wasn't really eavesdropping, she just wanted to make sure that . . . 'So, Sam,' she heard Clara say, 'are you still in the army? Or are you going to be around a bit more? Tell me all about it.'

Annie smiled and tiptoed away.

* * *

The watchman wouldn't let Jack inside the mill grounds. Annie tried to plead, but he was adamant. 'I know who you are,' he growled at Jack, 'and it'd be more than my job's worth to let you through this here gate.'

Jack looked at Annie in frustration.

But she'd come here to achieve her goal, and she wasn't going to be prevented now. She hadn't expected to have Jack here in the first place, so – although she'd much rather have him by her side as not – she hadn't lost anything.

'Fine.' She drew herself up. 'I'll come in on my own then.' She held up a hand as the watchman began to demur. 'I have business with Frederick Carrington, and I'm expected.'

He hesitated.

'It'd be more than your job's worth to make me late, if I tell him the reason for it.'

He saw the wisdom of this and stood aside.

'I'll be here,' said Jack. 'Waiting until you come out.'

'I'll see you then.'

Now that the moment had come, Annie was oddly nervous. But she wasn't going to back out now. *This time I'm going to save everyone. All those girls who work here, and who will do in the future.*

Once again she swept into the clerks' office. This time she didn't need to burst into the inner sanctum, because Frederick Carrington was already there, in the process of berating some poor junior.

'You!' He certainly knew who she was this time, and he didn't hesitate in shouting at the clerks to throw her out.

'You will not touch me,' declared Annie, in a tone of such confidence and authority that they all stopped dead in their tracks, their timidity playing into her hands.

She turned to Frederick. 'I'm not leaving until you've heard what I've got to say.'

He was so angry that he hardly seemed to notice that they were still in public. 'Say it, then, and get out.'

His humiliation at the hands of the newspapers had cut him deeply, she could see, and that was all to the good. 'You've had a lesson in what people will or won't believe,' she began, 'and it serves you right. You lied about my brother and you've been called out for it. So now you're going to do something else. You're going to stop taking advantage of vulnerable girls, do you hear? You and your brother. As of right now.'

'I *beg* your pardon?'

Annie wondered if she was the first person who'd ever dared to speak to him in such a way. In all probability, she was. 'Your name is already mud, in the newspapers and in your own set. But you'll be thinking that you might eventually recover your footing. I'll let that happen if you stop what you're doing. If you don't, then there are going to be more pamphlets and more newspaper articles exposing you for what you are. See how your high society likes you then!'

Frederick was so outraged that he couldn't get a word out.

The only sound came from a shuffle by one of the clerks behind Annie, and she whipped round to face them. 'And as for you lot! Cowards, all of you. How long have you worked here, and how many girls have you seen going in and out of that office? You must have been aware of what was going on, and not one of you said a word. Call yourselves men? Proud of your white collars and ties, are you? Well, there's honest working men out there that are worth ten of you – and honest women, too.'

Robinson, the chief clerk, began to frame a reply, but he was forestalled by the very elderly man with spectacles, the one whose intentions Annie had misunderstood as he'd tried to save her job.

He cleared his throat. 'This young lady is right. I've worked here for forty years, Mr Frederick, and I've seen the hard work of your father pay off, meaning that you and your brother never had to struggle in the same way. Instead you've allowed yourselves to exhibit corrupt morals and even criminal behaviour.' He drew himself up. 'I'm well aware that I will lose my position for speaking to you in this manner, so I hereby resign it. I don't expect that my younger colleagues will be in a position to follow suit, but I have to stand up for my conscience, and I will not stand by in shame while a chit of a girl shows more honesty and courage than the rest of us put together.'

He bowed to Annie. 'Miss, I salute you. And I will go further. Should any of the young women who have been mistreated by Mr Frederick – or Mr Theodore – choose to press charges, I will be happy to act as a witness on her behalf.' Then he addressed Frederick again, his old voice whip-sharp. 'You, sir, are a disgrace to your name and profession.'

Frederick was so angry he looked like he might literally burst.

Annie was so proud of the elderly man – standing up like that after such a lifetime of servitude, and putting his livelihood on the line! That took courage.

And then came the icing on the cake. All the other clerks moved to stand behind her and her companion, leaving Frederick red-faced and gaping like a fish on the other side of the room. 'I couldn't have put it better myself,' said Robinson, 'although I'm not resigning my post. If you sack all of us then the mill simply won't run. I might only be a humble employee, but I care about this business, sir, and I'd rather see it return to honest manufacture and trade than sink into an abyss of immorality.'

Frederick's pent-up rage burst forth. Predictably it was directed neither at Robinson nor at the elderly clerk, but at Annie, and he took two swift steps towards her. 'You little bitch, coming in here, thinking you can tell me what to do. Me! I'll teach you . . .' he raised a hand to strike her.

Several of the men cried out and made as if to step forward and protect her, but they didn't need to. Annie wasn't Sam's sister for nothing, and she lashed out with a perfectly timed and balanced fist, all the weight of her arm and shoulder behind it. She had never intended to cause violence here today, of course she hadn't, but self-defence was another matter entirely. And she *did* have to admit that the smacking sound of her knuckles connecting with Frederick Carrington's eye-socket was satisfying.

He staggered back, ran into a desk, tripped and fell to the floor.

'You harpy!' he blustered, one hand to his eye. 'I'll see you in court for assault for this!'

'Oh, really?' Annie stepped forward and leaned over him. 'You really want to tell the world that you've just been sent flying by a sixteen-year-old girl?' She remembered all his previous boasts. 'Who would believe you? And, more to the point, would you want them to? You're a laughing-stock already, so I suggest you don't make it any worse.' She jabbed a finger close to his face. 'Leave the mill girls alone. If you don't, I'll hear about it, and you know what will follow.'

He made one last attempt, waving an arm wildly at the clerks. 'They all saw what happened.'

The elderly man took off his spectacles to polish them, and addressed the ceiling. 'I don't think I saw anything. As Miss Shaw here has already made plain, that appears to be something we've been very good at over the years.' He replaced his spectacles, picked up a hat, bent his arm and offered the crook of his elbow to Annie. 'Might I have the pleasure of escorting you out?'

Annie took his arm and exited the office for the final time, leaving Frederick Carrington sprawled in humiliation on the floor.

'My dear,' her companion said as they crossed the mill yard, 'that was quite the best thing I've ever seen in all my years working here. You've done so much good today.'

'If it keeps his and his brother's hands off the mill girls then it was all worth it,' replied Annie, 'though I'm sorry that you lost your job.'

'It's no matter. I was near to being asked to leave due to my age anyway, and I have savings and several children in good employment.'

They reached the gate, where Annie could see that Jack was waiting. 'I've just realised, sir,' said Annie, as she slipped her arm out from under the clerk's, 'I don't even know what your name is.'

He smiled, and a gleam came into his eye in the midsummer afternoon sun. 'Ah. That's one of the reasons I took particular notice of you when you arrived, and then remembered who you were later on. We're not related, my dear, but coincidentally my name is also Shaw. As of today I shall be even more proud of it than ever.' He bowed to her and walked out of the gate, setting his hat firmly on his head and not looking back.

Jack met Annie as she stepped through. 'What happened?'

Perhaps it was because she'd just been walking thus with someone else, but without thinking Annie slipped her arm through his. 'I'll tell you all about it. But let's go and find Sam and Clara, and get her away before the end of the day.'

* * *

By the time they reached the house, Clara had already packed – it hadn't taken her long to put her few spare clothes into the one small bag now lying at her feet. She and Sam were sitting companionably, and Annie saw straight away that their hands were joined where they lay on the table. Today was just getting better and better.

Annie was now wondering how on earth they were going to get Clara all the way to Ormskirk, for she surely couldn't walk that far in her condition, but it turned out that the two of them had already sorted this out.

'Got a lift in a cart going that way,' said Sam. 'But he says he's only got room for two, so you girls go, and then wait for me at the station. I won't be far behind.'

Jack cleared his throat. 'I wonder,' he said, 'if Clara might be better off having you with her, to look after her in case there's any hold-up or if it's a bad road? I don't mind walking to Ormskirk with Annie, and then coming back. It'll be light until late.'

Sam, of course, would normally have dismissed that sort of suggestion out of hand, but he looked from Jack's face to Annie's and then at Clara, and nodded. 'See you get her there safe, then.'

'I will.'

They set out. Sam settled Clara as comfortably as possible in the seat next to the driver, and then put his arm around her as she leaned against him.

'You planned all that, didn't you?' asked Jack, nodding at the cart as it drew away.

'I hoped,' admitted Annie. 'But I know them both so well that I was fairly confident.' She sighed. 'Clara had a . . . difficult childhood, and she really does need someone to keep an eye on her. And Sam always needs someone to protect.'

'What will he think about the baby, though, when it comes? If it's not his?'

'I think . . . I think that we Shaws are good at taking the word "family" in its widest sense, and Sam will love it because it's hers.'

'Well, I don't know him like you do, of course, but from the little I've seen of him, I'd say you were right. And good luck to them both.'

They walked on for some while in a comfortable silence.

It was Jack who eventually broke it. 'So, have you given any thought to what you'll do next?'

'Nothing specific yet – I needed to get all this sorted out first. But I think Delilah won't make any objection to me finding another job, rather than staying to help in the shop.'

He smiled. 'Just tell her where you're going this time.'

'I would . . .' Annie paused as she realised the truth. 'I would like to stay closer to them all, though. And I don't think there are any other mills nearer to Liverpool – they're all further away. And they're not likely to be taking on any new hands just now, even weavers with experience.'

Jack made no reply, which Annie thought was odd, but then he said, 'About that.'

'About what?'

'You finding a new job. What I was going to tell you this morning was that I've found something. It's an engineering job in a factory just on the edge of Liverpool.'

Annie felt a warm glow of pleasure. 'So, you'll be much nearer to the city?'

'Yes. And . . . while I was seeing them yesterday, I did take the opportunity to ask if they ever employed women.'

Lots of new ideas rushed into Annie's mind. 'And do they?'

'As it happens, yes. There's one part of the works where some quite small components need to be put together, and they prefer women for that, as their hands are nimbler.' His words started to come out more quickly. 'I know it's not a mill, and you might to prefer to keep on weaving, but maybe think about it? It's good steady work, and with the way things are being mechanised in agriculture and other areas, I think there's only going to be more of it in future.'

Annie considered for a few moments. Or, at least, she pretended to, for her mind was already made up. 'Would they take working in a mill as experience, do you think?'

He blushed. 'I might already have asked them that, too.'

Annie smiled and took his arm again as they walked the rest of the way to the station.

Chapter Twenty-Two

The vicar had seen too many pregnant brides to bat an eyelid at Clara's shape as she waddled up the aisle in the middle of August; weddings held just in time to make a child legitimate were commonplace.

Clara hadn't been able to contact any of her own brothers to bring her to the church, so, of the many available offers from Sam's family, she had chosen Jem to give her away. That *did* flummox the vicar for a few moments, but he accepted Jem's signs and gestures in lieu of the accustomed words, and the ceremony proceeded as normal.

Annie watched all her married brothers and sisters sharing Sam and Clara's joy, and then turning to their own spouses with smiles and memories of their own special days. Her turn would come one day, she thought – she hoped – but certainly not for a good while yet, and she was very happy with that. She was enjoying her job at the factory, where she had made some new friends among the girls her own age, and she was able to see Jack most days during the dinner break. Then she made her way home to the flower shop, where she was now the proud paying lodger in the attic. Jack lived in a room in a respectable boarding house, and both of them were well paid enough to be saving some of their wages. They were now officially walking out, strolling through the park on Sundays and even having been to a music hall once or twice. And Jack joined the extended family during their monthly Sunday dinners, fitting in seamlessly, although he still occasionally seemed a little overwhelmed by the numbers.

Annie had been in such a reverie that she almost didn't notice that the wedding was over. The newlyweds made their joyful way out of the church, followed by all their well-wishers, and they repaired to the public house on the corner of Brick Street and Jamaica Street, nearest to their own home. Sam, as expected, had been able to take his pick from several job offers, and he was now a watchman at Queen's Dock, ensuring that ships were loaded and unloaded, and their cargoes packed, stored or transported, without any pilfering. The number of unemployed youths hanging around hoping to snatch anything unattended had decreased markedly, as had the number of fights between sailors or dockworkers that were a constant problem. Sam's employer, proud of their war hero and recognising the benefit of good publicity, insisted that he wear his medal; the mere sight of it was enough to quell all but the most rowdy quarrellers, and Sam's fists and stout cudgel did the rest.

What was most odd about the situation was that Sam and Clara had ended up living in the very road where all the Shaws had started their lives. Annie didn't remember it, of course, but Delilah, William and Meg were all quite emotional the first time they dropped in to Brick Street with housewarming presents. The house was like all the others in the area: a room downstairs that was both kitchen and parlour, and two bedrooms upstairs. But it also had a back yard of its own, and access to a pump and a clean privy, both of which were shared with only three other houses. Clara thought she was in heaven, and she kept it all scrupulously clean and tidy despite her uncomfortable size.

It was just two weeks after the wedding when Sam came flying up to the shop early on a Friday evening to tell them all – in a greater panic than Annie had ever seen him – that Clara's labour had started. Brick Street being the community it was, a couple of the women from neighbouring houses were already with her, even though they had only known her such a short time, but she was asking for the comfort of familiar faces.

Delilah sent him off to the others and immediately sprang into action, issuing instructions and collecting towels and linens. Within half an hour all was arranged, and she, Meg and Bridget were setting off. Frank was still at work, so Annie was to mind the children. If the labour went on into the following morning, Meg was to return to open the flower shop while Annie went to work, leaving Sally to manage the tea room. 'Well, leaving Hannah to manage, really,' confided Meg to Annie, in a brief moment. 'Sally can run the kitchen for a morning, but she still has problems with the till and the money, which Hannah has picked up really quickly. What a wonderful girl she is.' Then Meg pecked Annie on the cheek and followed the others out.

Thankfully, Clara proved as adept as her mother at giving birth without too many problems – though Annie sincerely hoped she wouldn't do it as many times as her mother had – and the good news arrived before she set out for the factory on Saturday morning. She hugged herself about it all morning, and then almost skipped down to Brick Street in the afternoon once work was finished.

Delilah and Bridget were still there, and Sam came home for his dinner just as Annie was arriving at the door. He gave her a hug that swept her right off her feet, and they went in and up the stairs together. Clara was sitting up in bed, cradling her little girl, and Sam went to sit by her and put his arms around both of them.

Clara smiled at Annie. 'Do you want to come and see her?'

Annie nodded and crept forward, kneeling by the edge of the bed and putting out one gentle finger to stroke the tiny, wrinkled face. 'What are you going to call her?'

Sam and Clara looked at each other. 'You tell her,' said Sam.

'Well, with all you've done for me and for Sam, and – actually, never mind that, it's just because we love you so much – we decided early on that if it was a girl, we'd call her Annie.'

Annie was speechless with joy, just shaking her head in silence while she tried to stop tears from falling.

'Ah, look at that,' said Sam, in a mock-teasing tone. 'She'll face down the mill owners, the newspapers and the whole damned army, but one little baby and she goes to pieces. You daft ha'penny, you.' He leaned away from his wife and daughter for a moment to kiss his sister. 'It's all turned out all right, just like you said it would. Neither of us – none of us, I should say,' he corrected himself, looking with infatuation at the baby, 'would be here if it wasn't for you.'

'And now you're my sister, too, as well as my friend,' added Clara, starting to sound a little sleepy, 'and the baby's got the best auntie as well as the best Pa.'

'And I *am* her Pa,' said Sam, firmly. 'Anyone who disagrees will answer for it.'

Annie sat with them a few minutes longer before tiptoeing out to leave them with their happiness, while she went downstairs to share her own all over again.

* * *

The autumn passed quickly, and before Annie could have believed it possible, it was Christmas Eve.

They were having their family meal this evening, as the weather was unusually fine for the time of year and they intended to go for a Christmas walk tomorrow, in their Sunday best, to make the most of the daylight and the winter sunshine.

Heavenly aromas wafted into the tea room from Meg's kitchen. Annie had been a little bit worried about Meg, who'd seemed off colour for a couple of weeks, but she was on fine form today and was flying about supervising a dozen different pots and pans as the Christmas dinner came together.

After an amazing main course and three cheers for all three cooks, everyone sat back for a while and broke into their little groups, so full that they were happy to wait for the pudding which had been steaming all morning.

Annie sat to one side with her two sisters.

Delilah's face shone with contentment. 'Christmas was always lucky for our family, and we've had more than one miracle.' Meg was sitting in the middle, and Delilah reached out to take her hand and kiss it. 'It was a Christmas Eve, years ago, that our darling Meg was returned to us, and that was the greatest wonder of them all.'

Meg made no reply, her eyes actually drooping a little with tiredness – unsurprising, Annie thought, after all that hard work – but she smiled.

Annie looked around at the noisy, happy room. There were so many people here! How fortunate she was to have such a family. And how lucky Hannah and Charlie were, too. Hannah was over in a corner with Daisy, their heads bent over a book. Hannah had never been confident enough to go to school with the others, having missed so much of it and feeling embarrassed about being so far behind at her age, but

Daisy sat with her a couple of times every week and was patiently teaching her to read and write. The two girls had become fast friends, just as Charlie had with Billy, Joe, Rosie and Maggie. They were all tearing about the place now, Eliza chasing and struggling to keep up, but their antics were being looked on with indulgence by all the adults.

'Eleven,' said Annie, in wonder.

Delilah peered at her. 'Eleven what?'

'Eleven children, altogether, including the babies. Can you believe it!'

Delilah reached round and poked her. 'Well, don't you be thinking about making it a round dozen any time soon. You're too young to get married yet.'

'Of course not. And maybe you should take a break from childbearing yourself,' was Annie's friendly retort. 'You're the most likely of us to have the next one.'

'Actually . . .' said Meg.

There was a moment of stupefied silence. Slowly, Annie turned to face her, seeing that the open-mouthed Delilah was doing the same from the other side.

'Surely you don't mean . . .' spluttered Delilah.

Meg had one hand on her stomach. 'Yes. And it was so unbelievable to us that I even went to see a doctor, and he confirmed it.'

Annie blinked. 'But you're . . .'

'I'm twenty-seven,' said Meg. 'And I've been married for eight years without ever falling pregnant before.' She turned shining eyes to Delilah. 'How's that for a Christmas miracle?'

Delilah was laughing and crying at the same time as she hugged her sister.

Annie could hardly believe it, but then another thought struck her. 'Will you . . . will you still want to keep Hannah and Charlie, once you've got a baby of your own?' Annie, of course, would do anything to support them herself, but they were so happy here and it would be yet another upheaval for them—

The old, less dreamy Meg reappeared for a moment. 'Annie Shaw, how can you say such a thing? Have you had so much goose that it's addled your brain? Of course they'll stay here. Tommy and I, we love them to bits, just like you do. They're part of the family, forever.'

Annie should have realised that, of course. She also hugged Meg.

Further conversation was interrupted by Frank. 'What are you girls doing over here, then?'

Delilah looked at him fondly. 'Plotting. Making plans.'

Frank shook his head. 'Terrifying. Absolutely terrifying.' He turned to Tommy and Jack, who were just behind him, the latter holding a newspaper that he'd been out to fetch. 'It's too late for us two,' he said, in mock sorrow to Jack. 'But you can always back out and run away. I'll hold them off chasing you for as long as I can.'

'Not on your life,' said Jack, who seemed filled with excitement. 'There's nowhere I'd rather be than here. And . . .' he shook the newspaper, hardly able to continue.

'What?' asked Annie. 'Has something happened?'

'Oh yes. You wait until you hear.'

His eagerness was infectious, and soon all the adults in the room were gathered around him. 'It's a miracle. Well, two miracles, in fact.'

Annie, Meg and Delilah exchanged a glance, and Delilah mouthed the word 'Christmas' at them.

'There's been a report to parliament,' said Jack. 'And to something called the privy council, though I don't know exactly what that is.'

'It's—' began William, before pulling himself up. 'It doesn't matter. Sorry, please go on.'

'And in this report,' continued Jack, 'they've said how bad conditions are in mills and factories. Not just in Liverpool, mind, but all through England. And this man who did the report, he said . . .' Jack ran his finger down a newspaper column until he found the place he wanted. 'He said that "to be able to redress that wrong is perhaps among the greatest opportunities for good which human institutions can afford".' Jack stopped and looked at Annie. 'They took notice.'

'Yes,' she said. 'But are they actually going to *do* anything, or is it just talk?'

Jack's smile lit up the room. 'They're doing it all,' he said, exultantly. 'Or, nearly everything we could ask for.' He could hardly keep still, hopping from foot to foot. 'Minimum age for working to be raised to nine years, and to be strictly enforced – and we'll get that even higher in years to come, you wait. Children and young people to work no more than ten hours a day, not twelve. Regulation of hours for women as well as children, so they all have to have half an hour for breakfast and a full hour for dinner. Minimum standards of accommodation for children, and more hours of elementary education to be provided – and, again, all to be properly enforced.' He looked about him until he spotted Hannah, who had appeared next to Annie. 'And all this applies to workhouse children and apprentices, as well as children who work with their families. And, finally, machines to have better safeguards so they're not so dangerous.'

By the time he'd finished, astonishment had given way to jubilation.

William took Jack's hand and pumped it. 'You did it.'

Jack shook his head. 'No, *we* did it. Working people up and down the country did it by pushing for this together. All sorts of people: Annie, everyone else at the mill, Mr Hughes and his speeches, the papers that finally picked up on it, the men in government, everyone.' He gave Annie a brilliant smile all to herself. 'We didn't just pick and choose – these improvements will benefit everyone.'

They all agreed it was truly a miracle. And then Abraham added, 'And you've done all this without backing down on your support for getting rid of slavery.'

'Oh!' cried Jack. 'Yes! That's the second miracle.' He rustled the newspaper and found another section. 'It does look as though the war in America is going to come to an end. And someone called Abraham Lincoln, who is a leader there, has actually sent a letter to England, addressed to the cotton workers of Lancashire. He heard what we'd all said about supporting the abolition of slavery, no matter what, and he wanted to reply to us directly. Listen.' He found his place, then began to read:

I know and deeply deplore the sufferings which the workingmen at Manchester and in all Europe are called to endure in

> this crisis. It has been often and studiously represented that the attempt to overthrow this government, which was built upon the foundation of human rights, and to substitute for it one which should rest exclusively on the basis of human slavery, was likely to obtain the favor of Europe. Through the actions of our disloyal citizens the workingmen of Europe have been subjected to a severe trial, for the purpose of forcing their sanction to that attempt. Under these circumstances, I cannot but regard your decisive utterance upon the question as an instance of sublime Christian heroism which has not been surpassed in any age or in any country. It is, indeed, an energetic and reinspiring assurance of the inherent power of truth and of the ultimate and universal triumph of justice, humanity, and freedom.

There was a deep silence.

'Sublime Christian heroism,' said Abraham, eventually, his voice catching.

'Justice, humanity and freedom,' added Annie, in wonder.

'Is it time for pudding yet?' asked Charlie.

They all laughed at that, and the spell was broken as Meg and Sally bustled off to the kitchen.

* * *

Later, when it was time to light the candles and the lamps, the family was still gathered together. The children were sleepy by now, drowsing on laps and in corners, and the adults' conversation was sporadic, but nobody was particularly inclined to leave the warm, comfortable, love-filled room and head out into the cold streets for the walk home.

Annie was sitting once more with her sisters. This time she was in the middle, and she reached out to take both their hands in her own. 'I'm sorry,' she said, with feeling, 'for all the trouble I caused you.'

Her right hand was squeezed by Delilah. 'I was upset at the time, but most of it was my own fault. I treated you like a child, when I should have seen that you were on your way to growing into the fine young woman you are now.' She sighed. 'Meg explained that she'd spoken to you not long before you left, and that you only wanted a chance to work at your own life, instead of having it handed to you on a plate.' She paused a moment before deciding to continue. 'I was going to talk to you about it, but I never got the chance before you left.'

Annie swallowed. 'I'm so ashamed. I shouldn't have . . .'

Delilah interlaced her fingers with Annie's. 'Don't be. You couldn't have known I was going to change my mind, that I was going to respect your decision. D'you hear me, Annie? I respect you, and I'm sorry I've never said that. More than that, in fact – I'm so *proud* of you, and all you've done.'

Meg now pressed Annie's left hand. 'And if you hadn't gone, where would Hannah and Charlie be now? And Sam?'

'It did all turn out right in the end,' said Annie, 'but that doesn't mean I didn't make lots of mistakes along the way. And the worst of those mistakes was causing pain to my family. I won't do it again, I promise.' She took a deep breath and looked at Delilah. 'And . . . I mean that as a daughter as well as a sister.' She had to pause to gather herself before continuing. 'I screamed at you, a few days before I left, that you weren't my mother. But I was wrong, because you *are* my mother, in all the ways that matter. And you always will be.'

She hadn't meant to make Delilah cry.

Dear Meg always knew the right thing to say. 'Ma would be proud of you both,' she murmured. 'Now, no tears, you hear me? Let's look forward, not back.'

Both Annie's hands were pressed.

'Well, we certainly *have* got plenty to look forward to,' said Delilah, smiling and wiping her eyes.

'We have,' said Meg. 'And I'm too lazy to get up and fetch us anything to drink, but let's have a little toast.' She waved a tired arm and yawned. 'Annie, you think of something to say.'

Annie thought for a moment. She looked about her in the twinkling Christmas candlelight, at the whole extended group of family and friends. 'To facing the future,' she said, 'whatever it brings.' She dropped Meg's hand to raise an imaginary glass, and the others did the same. 'To the Shaw family – its lovely brothers, but particularly its sisters.'

She glanced again at Delilah, thinking of what she'd lost, and wondering if it would make things better or worse to bring up the subject. 'The Shaw sisters, *all* of them, whoever and wherever they may be.'

Meg and Delilah both nodded, and spoke with smiling pride in unison. 'The Shaw sisters.'

'Together,' added Annie under her breath, 'we can do anything.'

Read on for 'behind the scenes'
research by Judy Summers.

Dear Readers,

I'm so glad you decided to join me in the world of the Shaw family. Some of you may already know it well, from reading *The Forgotten Sister* and *A Winter's Wish*, my earlier books focusing on Meg and Delilah when they were younger; others might be visiting for the first time. You're all equally welcome! *A Daughter's Promise* can easily be read on its own, but if you're familiar with the other books then you'll know more about the background not only of the Shaw family, but also of some of the characters who are peripheral here, such as Sally, Bridget and Abraham, who all have fascinating stories of their own. I hope you like the way the Shaws and their friends have grown and developed while we were away from them during the latter half of the 1850s.

As you will have noticed, we've moved a little outside of Liverpool for some of *A Daughter's Promise*, and this was for two reasons. The first was factual, in that there were no cotton mills within the city limits at this time – Liverpool was England's biggest centre for the *importing* of raw cotton, but it was then transported further away before being spun and woven. The second reason was related to my own plot purposes: Annie needed to have her own story, distinct from those of her older sisters. If I'd left her in Liverpool she would have been very well looked after but much less likely to experience risk or adventure. On the plus side, this slight removal has given us the opportunity to explore a little further and to find out what went on in the mills and other towns in that part of Lancashire. If you ever visit Ormskirk, by the way, you should *definitely* join Annie in eating some of the local gingerbread.

Cotton mills are so much a part of the Lancashire landscape, and so closely linked to Liverpool and its trade, that it was inevitable my characters would encounter them at some point. Indeed, I very much wanted to put them there as the mills have long been an interest of my own. This is in part due to my family history research, where I found ancestors working in mills; they were often listed in census returns not just as mill hands, but with intriguingly specific job titles such as 'tyer on of warp', which made me want to learn more. I also have vivid childhood memories of my siblings and I being taken to visit Quarry Bank Mill in Cheshire, and seeing how the mill worked and what the conditions were like, particularly in the

Apprentice House. In this grim, uninviting building, many small pauper children lived – if you can call it that – packed two to a bed and given only food and board in return for their long days of gruelling labour. All of this made a great impression on me, and I'm glad to be able to shine a little bit more light on these children and the reality of their lives. Quarry Bank Mill remains open to the public and is well worth a visit if you want to learn more about the mills and about the huge disparities in lifestyle between the owners and the workers.

Life in the cotton mills in the 1860s was more or less as I have described it here, with long hours, terrible working conditions and great job insecurity. Children really were employed from the age of eight – and many of them were even younger than that if, like Charlie, their parents and the mill officials decided to turn a blind eye. Conditions for workhouse 'apprentices' were particularly horrible, as they were effectively bought and sold with no adult family to care for them.

By coincidence, as I write this letter, a recent excavation at Fewston (near Harrogate) is being widely reported in the news. More than 150 skeletons have been found, most of them children or teenagers who were pauper apprentices at a mill and who lived very short lives of acute misery. All of the skeletons show signs of stunted growth, respiratory and other diseases, and evidence of a diet so poor that it was no better than that of the victims of the contemporary Irish famine. And this, of course, is unequivocal scientific evidence, not just hearsay or an embellished tale of hardship. I sometimes feel as though I might be over-exaggerating the tribulations faced by my fictional characters, but in the case of these poor mites the truth is even more horrifying and tragic.

The early 1860s was a time of boom and bust for the mills, as production increased and then declined very suddenly when the imports of raw cotton from America collapsed, causing what was known as the Lancashire Cotton Famine. This threw a great many people out of work and into poverty, with women and children experiencing particular suffering as they could neither find other jobs nor claim parish relief. The mill owners reacted in very different ways, with some doing everything possible to help their employees while others – like the fictional Carringtons here – were concerned with nothing but their own profits.

Throughout all of this, the working people stood together and in solidarity with those who were enslaved in America, just as Annie, Jack and the others do in *A Daughter's Promise*. There was a huge sense of camaraderie among mill workers (it is the subject most often mentioned by those who wrote memoirs of their experiences, in the twentieth century as well as the nineteenth), and this extended to sympathy for those who were even worse off than themselves.

The Lancashire mill workers collectively wrote to Abraham Lincoln to assure him of their support, despite their own circumstances, and to tell him that the progress he was making on the other side of the Atlantic 'fills us with hope that every stain on your freedom will shortly be removed' and that they hoped for the complete erasure of slavery, 'that foul blot on civilisation'. To do this while they themselves were starving, as a direct result of the war in America, took quite some courage and shows that moral fibre certainly wasn't the preserve of the rich. President Lincoln really did write back to thank them, in the exact words that Annie sees in the newspaper in our final chapter, although for my plot purposes I have brought the date of the letter forward a few weeks from mid-January 1863 to Christmas Eve 1862. It is also true that collective action and pressure during this time of hardship led to improvements in working conditions which were later built upon further.

Annie, of course, is fictional, as are all her family and friends (although Mr Hughes is partly inspired by Hugh Shimmin, a campaigning journalist, printer and bookbinder who wrote shocking exposés of the living conditions of Liverpool's poor during the 1860s, and who gained both friends and enemies as a result). But although all the characters in *A Daughter's Promise* are a figment of my imagination, they represent the very many real people who worked and struggled in these hard times, doing the best they could for their friends and families. I hope that as you read, you will join me in honouring the memories of all those men, women and children who lived and died in Liverpool and Lancashire during the Cotton Famine.

So, what next for the Shaw family? Delilah, Meg and Annie have all found their happy endings, but they're still plagued by the torment of not knowing what happened to their youngest sister when she was separated from them all those years ago. I hope, therefore, that you'll join me again soon to find out what happened to Jemima.

Yours truly,
Judy Summers

About the Author

Judy Summers is an avid reader, historian and mother of three. Her forebears – some of whom probably entered England via Liverpool in the Victorian era – were miners, labourers and domestic servants. She finds these lives far more interesting than those of the upper classes.

Judy lives in the English countryside with her family and is a keen baker and gardener.